MW00720487

The Infinite Man

THE

INFINITE MAN

Daniel F. Galouye

PHOENIX PICK

an imprint of

ARC

Rockville, Maryland

The Infinite Man Copyright © 1973 by Bantam Books. Copyright © 2001 by Carmel Galouye. All rights reserved. This book may not be copied or reproduced, in whole or in part, by any means, electronic, mechanical or otherwise without written permission from the publisher except by a reviewer who may quote brief passages in a review.

This is a work of fiction. Any resemblance to any actual persons, events or localities is purely coincidental and beyond the intent of the author and publisher.

Tarikian, TARK Classic Fiction, Arc Manor, Arc Manor Classic Reprints, Phoenix Pick, Phoenix Science Fiction Classics, Phoenix Rider, The Stellar Guild Series, Manor Thrift and logos associated with those imprints are trademarks or registered trademarks of Arc Manor, LLC, Rockville, Maryland. All other trademarks and trademarked names are properties of their respective owners.

This book is presented as is, without any warranties (implied or otherwise) as to the accuracy of the production, text or translation.

ISBN: 978-1-61242-250-3

www.PhoenixPick.com
Great Science Fiction & Fantasy
Free Ebook Every Month

Published by Phoenix Pick
an imprint of Arc Manor
P. O. Box 10339
Rockville, MD 20849-0339
www.ArcManor.com

Prelude

When the creation-wave detector sent its imperious alarm grating through Command Post, Project Genesis was mired in one of its more disconcerting days.

To begin with, Director Duncan had had to fend off persistent newsmen with the repeated denial: "No, this is *not* hocus-pocus to cover up testing of a sophisticated defense network. All objectives are exactly as outlined in our prospectus."

Each such refutation had elicited diverse responses:

Either (advanced by a newsman who obviously would have been more at home covering the Rotary Club): "But you actually expect us to believe *matter* is being created *out of nothing* all around us?"

Or (from one who had evidently had the enterprise to consult a textbook): "You're trying to *verify* the steady-state theory by looking for newly-created hydrogen atoms?"

"Neutrons. They decay into hydrogen atoms in a few minutes."

"Neutrons, then. But *here*—in a major metropolitan area?"

"Electromagnetic fields associated with a city will help determine whether continuous creation is affected by other basic forces."

A. J. Duncan, whose copious white hair dignified his doctorate in cosmology and a lesser degree in nuclear physics, let the alarm's stridor swamp his memory of that press conference which, after all, had been only the first of many distractions on this September 15, 1980.

The second distraction—Dr. Julius Montague, observer from the Research Council—refused to let Duncan off the shaft of his persistent stare. "The alarm!" he exclaimed. "Aren't we going to run down the coordinates?"

Duncan's smile begrudged indulgence as he indicated a technician feeding data into the master keyboard across the room. "It'll take a minute or so to correlate our bearings from the slave posts. Then our computer will give us a triangulation and—"

"But shouldn't we be getting ready to *move*?"

The abrupt *clop-clop* of a helicopter's rotors obviated any direct answer. Command Post personnel were, if nothing else, alert.

Duncan surveyed the brace of computer consoles, the massive Genesis wave-detector with its parabolic antennas, shelves lined with snap-in components for the main and ancillary equipment. Then he turned his appraising eyes back on Montague.

Hunched over a filing drawer with one foot poised above the floor, the latter resembled an emaciated, black crane. Suit, tie, shoes, eyes, and even the veins in his bald scalp, were dark. The severe lines of his face would require only bowed head and folded hands to suggest ministerial austerity. This casual assessment of the man was not off the mark, Duncan felt. Montague had spent three years in a seminary before deciding that his intellectual investigation of the universe would be physical rather than doctrinal. But now that he had earned minimal bureaucratic acceptance as an armchair cosmologist, he seemed reluctant to relinquish his theologic approach—as though still unable to decide whether his world required a spiritual or material perspective.

Just then the computerman announced: "Coordinates established." The technician read off additional numerical values.

"Suburban," Duncan said. "A workable fix."

He gestured toward Montague. "Let's see if we can't draw up a ringside seat for this neoneutron's first postgenesis reaction."

Montague reared to his poplarlike height. "Have you actually *detected* the beta-negative emission?"

"We have suggested on a sufficient number of occasions a direct relationship between quantum injection and subsequent beta decay." Even in offhand conversation with the pompous Research Council observer, Duncan found it difficult to avoid the syntax of an official report form.

"Chances of catching the beta emission of *this* neoneutron are pretty slim though, Julius." He paused to watch for any encouraging response to his initiation of first-name informality but saw none. "It may have already kicked out its beta particle. After all, the half-life of a free neutron is only twelve minutes."

Hand on the doorknob, he instructed the technician: "Crank up your it-went-that-a-way box so you can feed us guidance signals."

Puzzlement tugged at Montague's features. "It-went-that-a-way box?"

"One of those computers considers the magnetic field and a number of other factors that might be jostling our neutron from its point of birth. It establishes a probable vector, then plots an intercept course."

Waiting for the helicopter-to-Command Post communication hookup to be tested, Duncan closed his eyes for a moment's meditation on the profundity of Project Genesis' research. How could he feel anything less than awe over the scientific miracle he was working: forcing Nature to surrender her secrets of the structure, origin, and mechanistic processes of the universe? For many years the academic pendulum had swung between "Big Bang" and "steady state."

He had always recoiled from the Big Bang concept that *all* matter existed at one time as an ultradense, superhot sphere, smaller in circumference than the solar system. How exquisitely reasonable the steady state concept was. One needed only to concede the basic hypothesis of continuous creation. Then it was no longer necessary to postulate a beginning. Genesis, as a definite event in a specific space-time framework, became expendable. Instead: The universe *always* existed! Basic units of matter—neutrons—are continuously being created *everywhere.* As the huge galaxies fly apart, the intergalactic neutrons-turned-hydrogen atoms respond to mutual gravitational forces and form new galaxies comprised of new suns, clusters, planets, satellites. The earlier-formed galaxies, meanwhile, tend to expend themselves by transforming their stellar matter into photons that speed off and eventually lose themselves in infinity. But the continuous creation of neutrons sustains even these old galaxies by replacing that lost matter.

Hardly hearing the exchange of "loud and clear" between helicopter pilot and Command Post, Duncan nodded humbly. He had already determined that neutrons were indeed being created *everywhere.* And he had now only to establish whether the frequency of continuous creation was sufficient to account for the universe's rate of expansion.

When he led Montague outside, the latter drew back, obviously confounded by the scene before him. "What, Dr. Duncan, is *this* all about?" the Research Council observer demanded.

Between the idling helicopter and Project Genesis' Command Post was a shouting, gesticulating congregation of placard-flaunting youths.

"PROJECT GENESIS? GET SERIOUS!" read one of the signs. Another: "PROJECT PROVOCATION!" A third: "NO COVER-UP FOR ARMS ESCALATION!" And: "LET THE PEOPLE'S LIBERATION *HAVE* TURKEY OR WE'LL EAT CROW!" "NO MANHATTAN PROJECT HERE!"

Most of them gaudily costumed, some sandaled and headbanded, some dangling an abundance of hair, colorful beads, and pendants, the protesters spread out to seal off Genesis' helicopter. Many faces were transfigured with indignation and the sincerity of their convictions.

Across the Quadrangle, the new engineering hall's skeletal framework took on a squirming, slithering animation as scores of excited figures slid down upright beams and scurried along horizontal ones to reach the ground. Sun glinting off silvered helmets, the workers congregated in a wedge and charged off toward the demonstrators.

On the right, however, activity came to an abrupt halt at the site of the old Reserve Officers Training Corps Headquarters, being demolished to make room for a new Liberal Arts Building. Bulldozers ground to a halt. The ponderous skullcracker, swinging from the end of its crane, took a final swipe at the structure, sent bricks cascading down, and remained embedded in the masonry. Demolition workers poured from their machines and out of the building, outflanking the construction contingent. Opposing workmen joined the skirmish a half block away from the student demonstration.

Duncan pushed on toward his helicopter, disdainful of the collegians all around him for their refusal to appreciate the sweeping significance of his research. They just didn't understand! And he resented their intrusion as he would resent random effects in a controlled experiment. His face drawn with dignity and dedication, he thrust aside a sign that read "CONTINUOUS CREATION—OR DISCONTINUOUS DESTRUCTION?" and led Montague into the waiting helicopter.

As the aircraft rose to horizontal plane-of-position X and leveled off at 350 feet, Montague passed a wadded handkerchief across his forehead. "The council has no idea your project is running into such resentment. Are there any valid reasons for this?"

Duncan stared out the window at the distant downtown section of the city. "Reasons, yes. Valid, no. Government-subsidized research. Army surplus helicopters. Air Force personnel detailed to the project. The assumption that our Defense Department is involved in this work is understandable, I suppose."

Montague made notes on a pad. Then: "Do you consider your research really essential, in the face of all this opposition?"

"Continuous creation is a fact of nature. It's worth exhaustive study. If we can find out how, when, where neutrons pop into existence out of nothing, we may usher in a new branch of science."

"The council is interested in quantitative aspects, Dr. Duncan. Why, for instance, have we staked out a volume 500 feet high over a 300 square-mile equilateral triangle? What is the basis of your estimate that twenty-one neutrons a day will be 'created' in this space?"

Duncan was inclined to blurt out his response that the answers could all be found in Genesis' prospectus. Instead, he pinched his ruddy cheek and said:

"Hoyle postulates creation of 125,000 neutrons—correction, he believes the quantum of continuous creation is the hydrogen atom itself, rather than the neutron—125,000 quanta, then, every second in an earth-size volume. This frequency is necessary to satisfy both Hubble's constant and the observed rate of expansion of the universe."

The Research Council man's pen skittered upon his pad. His expression was that of a father confessor ferreting out the reason behind a mortal sin. "Yes?"

"It figures out to twenty-one neoneutrons every twenty-four hours in the space we have under observation."

"Why a triangular area?"

"Our master detection apparatus is located at one apex, on the university campus. The slave sensors occupy the other two apexes—each located on tracts being subdivided by Progress and Development Enterprises, thanks to the cooperative spirit of P & D's President Gerstal Hedgmore. All three stations take bearings on any wavefront resulting from quantum injection into the creation field."

The helicopter paralleled a many-laned expressway for a while and Montague sat staring off into the distance. His face was fixed in profound concentration. The pen and pad slipped from his grip and fell to the floor. He let them lie there.

"Dr. Montague." Duncan reached over to shake the man's bony shoulder. "Dr. Montague, is something wrong?"

"God," said the other, his features rigid, "is *not* dead."

"What's that?"

"God's Act of Creation was *not* a single sweep of His majestic arm." Montague's voice was deep with pulpital resonance. "The Almighty is a living force. The neutron is His instrument of generation. His universe always will be, since He is regenerating it through continuous creation."

The cabin speaker squawked, "Command Post to Dr. Duncan."

"Yes, Jenkins," Duncan called into the pickup grid, still staring askance at the Research Council observer. "What is it?"

"We've just detected another creation-quantum wavefront. But the signal strength—it was unbelievable! As though *millions* of neutrons had been generated at the same time!"

Duncan started and shrank from the prospect of unanticipated random effects. "You get a fix?"

"Just a crude one. Our sensor coils fused at all three detector stations before we could refine the locus."

"Let's have your rough coordinates. Meanwhile, replace those coils with plug-ins and get our sensors back in operation." What, Duncan wondered, could it possibly mean? At most, he had been prepared to accept the coincidence of two or three neutrons being generated in the same place at the same time. But—*nothing like this!*

X, Y, and Z values rasped from the speaker and he jotted them down. "That's at the very edge of our observation area, isn't it?"

"Right on the border," Jenkins replied. "Our chart indicates it's in that freight yard east of town. Practically ground level."

The project director gave new instructions to the pilot.

"What on earth is happening?" Montague reflected.

"If Jenkins is right, millions of neutrons materialized at one time, in a space so small that it should spawn only one every hundred million years or so."

"Millions?" Montague was once again the inquisitor.

"Very well, then, an infinite number, if we're going to face the matter squarely. Those detector coils were designed for asymptotic induction, approaching critical resistance only as the strength of the creation-field disturbance approaches infinity. But never actually *reaching* breakdown value. They *couldn't* have failed."

"But they did."

Indeed they had, the Director admitted. But he was still unable to accept the impossible fact.

Ten minutes later the aircraft eased down between two spur tracks, landing next to a warehouse. Crews that had been unloading a freight car paused to watch.

"As close as we can estimate," the pilot said, "your rough locus is somewhere in that boxcar."

Duncan uncased his radiation counter. It was a crude device for detecting beta emission, compared with their helicopter-borne instrumentation. But if an infinite number of neutrons had burst through the creation barrier, his apparatus would be equal to the challenge of tagging an unlimited total of postgenesis electron ejections. He laughed at the impossible aspects, then frowned over his failure to conceive of an alternate explanation for the sensor coils' breakdown.

With Montague in tow, he mounted the concrete steps to the warehouse platform. They were intercepted by a burly receiving clerk. "If you don't get that egg-beater off the tracks, Mac, you gonna be in trouble. Yard cops are crawling all over the place. What d'you want?"

One of his crew shouted, "Hey! That's Mr., Mr.—ah, Neuron!"

The receiving clerk recognized Duncan and laughed. "Yeah—Mr. Nootrawn! Find li'l' bugs lately, Doc?"

"I'd like permission to check this boxcar," Duncan said.

"Yeah, sure." The project director absorbed a thumping slap on his back. "Go ahead, Doc. But if you find a nootrawn, I wanna see what it looks like." More guffaws.

Duncan spent five minutes clambering over crates in the freight car. But no matter where he aimed the counter, it ticked at a negligible rate of about ten times a minute. Normal background radiation. Yet, if *millions* of neutrons had sprung into existence here, the instrument ought to be vibrating out of his hand as it registered subsequent beta emissions.

When he exited and brushed himself off, the clerk, Montague, and two yard policemen ringed him in.

"Find anything, Mr. Nootrawn?" The clerk was still snickering.

"Better get your 'copter out of there, Dr. Duncan," one of the policemen advised. "A string of cars is about to roll in."

"If you're going to be around a while," the other cop added, "keep your eye open for a 'bo. One of 'em just rode in on this car."

Approaching the helicopter, Duncan was met by his pilot, who trotted forward waving a slip of paper.

"Jenkins reported just now that the same thing happened all over again!" the airman exclaimed.

"All three coils fused?" Duncan grimaced. The foundation of his work was crumbling beneath him, in some way he couldn't understand.

"All at the same time. Just as soon as master control cut them back in." The pilot handed over his slip of paper. "Here are the coordinates. Jenkins says our chart pinpoints the locus somewhere in a slop house called the Day Lily Diner on South Ruston."

"That's in Hipurbia, just a few blocks away," Duncan observed. "You report back with the helicopter. We'll make it on our own from here. And tell Jenkins to get those detectors back in operation!"

There was a two-block walk over rails, followed by a half-mile taxi ride into an area of the city that reveled in its own disorder, flaunted time-worn façades of chock-a-block buildings, embraced the garish and bead-bedecked youths and older self-styled bohemians who loitered along its sidewalks.

"Somehow," Montague complained, alighting from the cab, "we seem to be far removed from an atmosphere of scientific investigation."

He regarded Duncan along the gun sights of his nasal ridge. "What's going on?"

The Director shied from a huge, full-bearded youth whose Indian headband barely showed through a profuse forest. "I'm at a complete loss. I didn't anticipate there'd be *this sort* of complication. Our sensors *have* to be right. But they *can't* be." Surveying the Day Lily Diner's shabby exterior, he asked the cab driver to wait.

A frail girl, whose thinness was accentuated by the paisley printed sari that enveloped her like a shroud, came forward from the midst of other costumed youths who were gathering outside the diner. She handed Duncan a bouquet of wilted daisies. "O, avatar of Brahma," she intoned, "may Vishnu speed thee on thy quest for the Blessed Secrets of His Creation. May thou escape the wiles of Siva. May …"

The project director hurried on into the restaurant, where he was rebuffed by a provoked proprietor who objected to the "commotion you're stirring up outside" and who would "be damned if I'm going to have the pigs rooting around my tail!"

"Anyway," the man huffed toward his aggrieved conclusion, "I run a up-and-up joint—no acid, no buttons, no tabs, snuff, sticks …"

Under cover of the other's longwindedness, Duncan completed his unobtrusive scanning of the place, turned off his counter and yielded. "I'll be out of here in a minute if you'll let me use your phone."

Jenkins' excited voice rattled the earpiece's diaphragm as he reported that the sensor coils had fused three more times. The first breakdown had indicated an extension of the straight line from the freight yard to the diner, yielding a fix several blocks away. The second and third failures had pinpointed loci that were identical with each other, again extending the straight line.

Referring the latter unrefined coordinates to both the master chart and an aerial photographic blowup of the area, the technician was able to narrow the latter two instances of creation-field quanta injection to a volume of but a few cubic feet It was, he reported, located within shrubbery next to a broad oak near the right-hand column of Midcity Park's southern gateway.

Fifteen minutes later Duncan, poking his counter into the shrubbery, tripped over a pair of inert, sandaled feet and went sprawling.

Montague came to his assistance and they found themselves in a small clearing beneath low-hanging branches. But Duncan, seated now, was already aiming his instrument at the pale, bearded youth who slept fitfully on the ground, trembling, tossing, thrashing occasionally—adding still more rents to his already tattered shirt and trousers. The slumberer was tall and blond, with a lean but handsome face, despite the light scar near his right temple.

"Suppose he's ill?" Montague said, concerned.

"He's obviously on a trip. Some drug. Oblivion. As they say: 'bohemian nirvana'."

Convinced that he was again encountering only normal background radiation, Duncan slung the counter over his shoulder. "Keep an eye on him while I get to that phone booth. I've a friend, Dr. Boris Powers, who runs a psychiatric clinic. I'd like him to take this kid in and look him over."

"But why?"

"We don't ignore *any* random effects in our research. And we have one here. It's obvious that our sensors fused at the moment they picked up this boy on a freight car at extreme range. Each time we replaced the burnt-out circuits, they immediately fused again while giving us another fix—somewhere along a straight line from the freight yard to this spot. God only knows *how*, but there's some sort of relationship between this hopped-up bohemian and one of the parameters measured by our sensors."

Montague's chin unhinged and his dark eyes widened, making the nasal ridge between them seem all the more bladelike. "It's—it's as though the force responsible for continuous creation exists *right here on earth*!" he exclaimed somberly. "As though all the neutrons that are being called into existence originate right here, in the vicinity of this boy, before they are dispersed in all directions through hyperdimensional space so that they can 'pop' into being in their designated places *throughout the universe*!"

The Research Council observer clasped his hands, glanced at the youth, then lifted his eyes to the sky. "It's as though God were *not* everywhere, but *just here on earth* ... with His mechanics of creation being *reflected* by this—this young man!"

Duncan turned contemptuously from the supposed scientist and his superstitious hangup. "Nonsense!" he snapped. "Ridiculous hypothesis! There's a simple explanation within the realm of physics. We'll find it. I'm going to call Dr. Powers. And Mr. Hedgmore too; he's vitally interested in our work. If his Progress and Development Enterprises can help us, over and above our formal grants, he'll be quick to cooperate—and generous also."

I

The universe, limitless though it was, offered no concealment. Nowhere could Bradford find sanctuary—not anywhere. Not in any of the dense dust clouds or great rifts of fluorescing gases. Nor in the glittering star clusters and far-flung arms of nebulous spirals. Not even in the fierce hydrogen-helium furnaces or the remote galaxies. Yet he had *to escape It. For Its power was awesome, and he* was *frightened.*

Fight It, Brad! Search everywhere! Search even yourself!

The voice boomed like a thousand novae, rippling the universal fabric, causing stars, clusters, and galaxies alike to tremble. But the voice was not Its voice. *The words had been those of an observer detached from the fury and horror of the chase.*

Bradford recoiled, protesting, No! I've got to *hide!*

Island universes fled by as desperation drove him ever onward.

No, Brad! *the demanding voice thundered.* Don't run! *Hunt It* down!

But he couldn't. The fear of encounter was overpowering. There! That huge cluster of galaxies ahead: Surely it would offer refuge!

All right, *the voice relented.* Come back. We'll try another time.

···◆···

Milton Bradford felt the needle withdraw from his arm, leaving its counteractant to neutralize the "talk-out drug's" molecules. Eventually he opened his eyes to see the mahogany-paneled richness of his inner office. He struggled for reorientation. His lack of will to move meant that this hypnotherapeutic session had not yet ended.

"Welcome back," said a pleasant voice somehow resembling the one that had pounded at him in the hollow recesses of infinity.

Cradled in the softness of a leather reclining chair, Bradford glanced at his massive oak desk.

Smiling at him over its polished surface was a spritelike face that radiated gentleness and good nature: Dr. Boris Ludwig Powers. Small, meek, sensitive—negative qualities which, together with kindly blue eyes and unprepossessing brows, hardly suggested a psychiatrist.

"How do you feel?" Powers asked.

"Like I've been tripping. I used to get turned on just like that when I was popping peyote in the border towns."

Powers rose and laughed. "Figures. Peyote. Mescale buttons. Stuff I just used is a derivative of mescaline. Bad trip, huh?"

Bradford wanted to nod his head, but couldn't—not until he was completely released from narcotherapy. "Real bad. Freakout."

"Very well, then. Forget the whole episode. You won't remember anything at all about your unpleasant happening."

Bradford parroted: "I won't remember ..."

But what was it he was trying to remember to forget?

"I suppose that wraps it up," Powers said. "Anyway, your secretary's been rapping at the door. Must be something important."

Bradford's catalepsy evaporated as he stretched to his angular height and adjusted the fall of blond hair across his forehead. Still trying to remember what had gone on during the session, he flexed his thighs within the constriction of their goldenapple leg-huggers. His many-ringed fingers came up to straighten the color-riotous four-in-hand chest protector against his shirt's orange and green pinstripes.

"Well?" he said, accepting his neo-Edwardian double-breasted jacket from the psychiatrist. "Any progress?"

"Oh, yes." The other effused confidence. "But we have some distance to go yet."

Bradford settled down at his desk and poured water from the frosted carafe. "Tell all your neurotic cats that Doc?"

"Oh, come now, Brad. Don't insist upon a neurosis."

"What else? Complexes and obsessions make neuroses." Bradford ran a hand over his lean face and fingered the slight scar near his right temple—evidence of a "demonstration" so remote in the past that he couldn't even remember the political discontent behind it.

Powers shrugged, a gesture that was difficult for shoulders drooping at ski-slope angles. "Complexes and obsessions you may have. But the circumstances behind them are sufficiently peculiar to justify classification below the neurotic level."

When Bradford didn't answer, the other continued: "Yes, indeed. Questionable circumstances. Any normal mind would seek to rationalize the improbable. Five years ago—a bum, 'bo, groover. Then suddenly—"

Bradford nodded. "Suddenly you come to my rescue, spend months getting me off the kick, straightening out my life—"

"Oh, I do that for a lot of unfortunates who find themselves hooked on narcotics."

"You snatch me off acid. Then Gerstal B. Hedgmore, a cat I never heard of, does his flip off a cliff. His will is read. And I find myself owner of Progress and Development Enterprises."

"Sole beneficiary."

"And now here I sit, at 27, on top of the biggest financial kingdom in the state. All because old Gerstal B. sired an illegitimate son—a bastard he refused to acknowledge in life because the old slob thought it would bring his empire crashing down on his head. What a hell of a Victorian hangup!"

Bradford walked to the window and looked down into the street. Powers came over. "You're struggling with a confusion of factors, son. Snatched from poverty to wealth, nonentity to prestige. Had to come down off the acid too. Or almost, anyway. Don't think I don't know you're still dropping the stuff once in a while. And you still hate the fact that Hedgmore resented your illegitimacy. So, through association, you disapprove of all this windfall—especially when you're talented enough to reap your own harvest. Still you can't justify everything. But you've got to learn to accept without question, to concede that there *are* gift horses, to assert your executive status. That's what I'm trying to help you do."

Damnit to hell! How he had learned to resent this P & D windfall! Bradford recalled his initial eager acceptance of the plum. More bread than could be turned out by all of the country's bakeries working overtime! Rags, Chicks. Why, he'd bedded more biddies than he ever thought existed! Cadillacs—fleets of them in five different cities across the nation. And fame too. He hadn't been left holding the "schort end of the schtick" when it came to singing talent. Oh, P & D's directors had given him a lot of guff at the time. But he'd shouted them down and launched "Hocker's Mock Rockers." It was his way of poking fun at the establishment, of which he'd become a part "Hocker." The assumed handle swung it with the directors; somehow they felt that an alias would let them off the hook.

Hocker's Mock Rockers. Fame. Bookings everywhere. Platters by the millions. More network offers than he could ever accept. More bread. Bread. Bread. Bread—for himself; for the P & D coffers, his chicks, for causes and crusades, for get-the-troops-out and bring-the-boys-home. (He'd never had to go. Powers had been by his side all the while, attesting to his ineligibility.)

Then, just two years ago: his drop through the clouds. More go-dawful than getting spaced out on a warehouse full of downers! He *had* to assume executive functions at P & D. There were legal pinchers his directors could apply to tie his hands or separate him from the biggest supply of bread in the state. And Powers had *agreed* with the square cats. But that was after he had started tripping *without benefit of acid*—in the middle of a restful night, or while simply walking down the sidewalk on a sunny day.

So he had split the Hocker's Mock Rockers scene, shaved, gone mod—or was it "mad"?—and tried to settle down into the establishment's nine-to-five rut, hoping that by squaring off he might end his unprovoked trips. Two years ago. And still it hadn't helped. Still he was freaking-out even without crystal.

Bradford tensed before the window. There—that cat on the corner! The same one? It was hard to tell at this distance. But he *was* casing the P & D Building entrance, wasn't he?

"Brad," Powers pleaded, looking into the street. "Forget it. No one is watching you. You've got to fight this obsession!"

"It *is* the same one! I saw him twice yesterday. He even pulled me back out of the stream of traffic when I stepped off the curb."

"And you find something suspicious in that? Wouldn't you do the same for anyone else?"

There was a knock upon the stout double doors.

"Come in, Miss Fowler," Powers called out. "We've finished."

Bradford's secretary paused in the doorway, regarding the psychiatrist from the depths of her expressive brown eyes. Tall but well-proportioned, she wore waistlength dark hair slicked back alongside her face, framing a harmony of olive complexion and attractive features. Her belted business tunic flared out like a flower's sepals around sheer skintighters that embraced the soft curves of hips and thighs.

"Your staff is waiting in the conference room, Mr. Bradford," she announced.

"'Brad'!" he snapped, "We're the only halfway hip people around here. Let us simple souls communicate. 'Brad'—'Ann.' Check?"

She glanced uncertainly at Powers. "But it wouldn't—office protocol ..."

The psychiatrist stepped between them. "Perhaps, Miss Fowler, it would be helpful if you and Brad *were* more informal, in the privacy of this inner office, of course. Outside, Mr. Bradford must learn to project—"

"Oh, hell!" Bradford strode for the door. "Quit reducing everything to psychotherapy!"

"I'll wait until you've finished your morning conference," Powers said. "There's more we ought to talk about."

The door thudded shut and Ann and Powers were left staring at each other. Finally she trembled and hid her face in her hands. "I'm afraid!" she exclaimed. "O, God! I'm afraid!"

Powers took her gently by the wrists and lowered her arms, revealing a brow now creased with concern. "Things will turn out all right," he promised. "You'll see."

"But I can't go on; I'm not an—actress!"

"We must all be actors or ..." He left the consequences hanging.

"I don't want to be around him. And yet I *do*—oh, so much! I feel so sorry for him. Sorry that he doesn't even *know*. Sorry over what all this may do to him, what it's *already* doing to him." Her voice was vibrant with compassion. "O, God! Why did *It* have to pick *him*? Why couldn't It have left him alone? Then we might have met under different circumstances. And he might even have had time to accept the love I want, oh, so much, to give him!"

Powers patted her hand. "There, there, child," he commiserated. "You do love him so much, don't you? And we *wanted* someone around him who'd feel a deep sense of personal involvement, who could relate. But, as I said, we must all be actors. No move may be made except on cue. We *all* have to put our personal feelings aside—completely."

Stiffening, she said bravely, "I—I suppose I'll be all right."

"Of course you will. But for the present we have something else to worry about: He's spotted Armstrong."

"No!" She brought a trembling hand to her lips.

"He's been certain for a couple of days now. Certain enough to recognize him down there in the street just a few minutes ago."

Anxiety widened her eyes. "What'll we do?"

"We must report it to Duncan, of course."

Impatience had pervaded the board room by the time Bradford entered. Glances were being exchanged above eyeglass rims. Fingers drummed the table. Clark was twirling his wrist-watch on the polished surface.

Bradford sank back against the head chair's tufted upholstery. But he felt no comfort, having long since despaired of being at home on a "throne" that was so patently a projection of Papa Hedgmore (a "philanderer," by the definition of his day). Bemused, he lapsed into exploration of the proposition that, if it had not been for Papa's belated "pangs of conscience," his illegitimate son might never have entered this confusing world of power financing. And all of the antediluvian squares around this table would not now be so humiliated by having to tolerate bastardy among them. But resentment of him ran deeper than that, he reflected gloatingly as he surveyed their antiquated dark suits with narrow lapels and ribbon-thin ties, comparing them with his own stylish rags. Damn consies!

Clark—Managing Director Adrian P. Clark—cleared his throat. "Hadn't we better get started, Mr. Chairman?" The stout man with bloated cheeks, who always seemed to bask in his own self-competence, demanded action with the severity of his stare.

"Could have gone on without me making the scene," Bradford gruffed. "I don't dig half of what happens here anyway."

"We understand that, Mr. Bradford," said the small man at the far end of the table—Ronald Bankston, in charge of real estate holdings. "It's commendable that you're frank enough to concede your present limitations. However, as Mr. Hedgmore's son, you *are*

P & D Enterprises. Therefore, if you'll bear with us we can promise that within a few years you'll develop your father's business acumen. We're hopeful you'll acquire some of his other traits too," he added, obviously trying not to stare at his Chairman's organdy wrist bows and suede ankleboots, one of which was propped against the edge of the table.

Papa, Bradford mused, had bequeathed more than apartment complexes, office buildings and hotels soaring into the sky, an investment arm, scattered real estate, a theater chain, newspapers, and TV stations. He had also left a self-sufficient chicken that could get along damn well without its head, thanks to the best managers the old buzzard's bread could buy.

"Sorry," he said. "I'll try to get with it and make like I can contribute something to P & D." After all, Powers believed diligence and purpose might end his unplanned freakouts. But he gagged on the thought that one day he *might* fit their concept of responsibility. Maybe he could interest them in his becoming "Hocker" once again and letting P & D capitalize on the "Mock Rockers" thing. But no: That wasn't any way out—not with Powers convinced that his pace of life as "Hocker" had brought on his tendency to flash *without* hash.

George Rawlins, in charge of theaters, riffled through the sheaf of papers stacked before him. "We've completed negotiations with that British distributor. We can have the cream of the foreign flicks flowing into our projection booths within a month."

"Has our legal staff drawn up the contract?" Bradford asked. Then he started as he noticed that Rawlins was wearing a six-inch-wide cerise chest protector instead of his usual dark two-incher.

"Everything's ready for signatures." Touching his tie, Rawlins acknowledged the partial concession to his chairman's taste in rags.

"Have the papers delivered to my office. Draft a cordial letter, too, since we'll want to look ahead to future relations." Might as well spout executive jargon once in a while, for kicks if for no other reason. "Wouldn't be a bad idea to invite the distributor and his family over as our guests for a contract-signing ceremony."

Bradford could see Bankston smiling and nodding approval over this display of self-assertion that had come from the head of the table. The real estate manager seemed to be tripping off on his heady hopes of seeing the chairman of P & D go conservative and come down off the mod kick. Stupid, hungup consy!

Apartments manager, Theodore Marshall, rose. "About our new complex in Westhills; architectural groundwork has been laid and we're ready to call for contractors' bids. Would you care to set a date?"

"First of August ought to do," Bradford suggested. "Close enough to the winter slump that we should get a break in bid levels."

This brought the managing director to his feet. "No! No!" Clark protested. "Now is *not* the time to let out construction—not with civic slum clearance and the municipal building program just starting. The only way we can go ahead with our own construction plans is to abandon Mr. Hedgmore's policy of limiting bidding to local contractors."

"All right," Marshall agreed. "I'll adjust to current circumstances in the building market, providing Mr. Bradford is willing."

"I'd suggest—" Bradford began.

"Won't do," Clark objected. "I'm not at all in favor of going ahead with Westhills anyway. Not at the moment."

"But now's the time," Marshall insisted. "There's never been a more severe housing shortage and—"

"Not now!" Clark rapped the table, his jowls puffing like an adder's.

"Perhaps," Bradford tried once more, "if we bought into an established construction firm and—"

But Clark only ignored him. "The Westhills project would mean liquidation of our portfolio D, unless we turned to underwriters. We—"

Bradford lurched erect. "Damnit! Doesn't a bastard have a chance to say anything in his own business?"

Silence cloaked the room. He repressed an amused grin: If there was one thing he could count upon, it was the shock value of any allusion to his illegitimacy—any rattling of what they regarded as the "closeted skeleton."

Pushing his advantage, he asked, "Why shouldn't we call for outside financing? Three of our properties are already underwritten."

The managing director was first to regain his aplomb. Clark explained, "We're in a potential hell of a fix financially. And please, Mr. Bradford, let's not bring unpleasantries out into the open."

Bradford decided to rattle the skeleton's bones again, just for effect. "My old man's alley-catting twenty-eight years ago may be an unpleasantry to P & D. But, to me, it's only a fact of nature. And, really, it doesn't bug me at all. Now, what's all this about 'a potential hell of a fix'?"

From the other end of the table Bankston's smile of approval shone upon him. And he accepted the expression as reflecting favorable comparison between Gerstal B., the father, and Bradford, the son, who now willfully rejected the Hedgmore name that had been denied him at birth.

"We could go under," Clark warned. "P & D has maintained a delicate balance between investments and obligations to underwriters. But now Regional Basin, our biggest institutional investor, wants to pull out. If Bradley Burroughs decides to unload Basin's P & D holdings, it'll depress hell out of the market for our securities."

"If *Burroughs* decides?"

"I'll admit none of his directors agrees with him. But everybody knows Burroughs pulls all the strings. And he's hurting for uncommitted capital. Wants to invest heavily in defense industries. Can't say I blame him, what with Turkey already cut almost in half."

Bradford traced the scar on his brow. "P & D has always been on the best of terms with Regional Basin. Burroughs, I understand, is one of your close friends, Mr. Clark. You should be able to influence him."

The other only shook his head. "Perhaps I waited too long to bring this up. But Burroughs is—well, disillusioned with us."

"Why?"

"Frankly, he wants to rid himself of his P & D portfolio because he doubts our stability. He's been influenced by the—ah, rumors."

"What rumors?"

"That besides being young, disinterested, and unreliable, you've been seeing a psychiatrist. Burroughs is also—well, sort of contemptuous toward you personally. He's a—ah, square from way back. A real—ah, consy. Doesn't even allow any of his employees to grow sideburns below midear level."

"Well, damn Burroughs! *I* don't like the way *he* stinks up the scene either! And I have been seeing a psychiatrist. Isn't everybody these days?"

"But only *we* are supposed to know that. If it became general knowledge it would play hell with our institutional image!"

Bradford rose and planted his fists on the tabletop, noticing that even Bankston had abandoned his smile of sanction. "I've laid it on the line with you cats all along. First time I climbed aboard here I said I was a tripper but was coming down off it with help. I also told you why Hedgmore left all his bread, everything to someone none of you had ever heard of. Showed you his suicide letter telling me I was his bastard—"

"Yes, yes," Clark interrupted, as though impatient over the distasteful reminders.

"The point is: I've never sat on anything. And that's how it's going to be—both inside and outside this pad!"

"What are you proposing?" Clark seemed to sense something he knew he wouldn't like.

"If Burroughs turns his directors against P & D we may get frigged financially?"

"I'm afraid that's the way it is."

"Then arrange a meeting between Burroughs and me. I think I can straighten him out."

"No! No!" Clark shouted. "We're your advisers and you've got to listen to us! Mr. Hedgmore would have wanted it that way."

Bradford stood firm. "Call on Mr. Burroughs at his Regional Basin office today. Arrange the meeting as soon as possible."

…◆…

It was midafternoon before Dr. Powers and Bradford could resume their discussion on the latter's mental health. After the morning conference, Ann relayed an excuse for the psychiatrist's absence: His normally self-sufficient clinic, it seemed, had required his diagnostic consultation. Bradford welcomed the reprieve, having often felt that Powers' curative effort bugged him as much as it helped resolve pressing dilemmas, real or imaginary.

Actually, the one prescription he could buy outright was: Escape from office routine—or, as the doctor would often put it, "Hell, you're too young to wrap yourself in the full-time executive image; take a break whenever you get a chance."

So he took a break that afternoon. First there was lunch with Ann, notwithstanding her superficial objections that she was spaced out on work. Then there was a pleasant couple of hours in the park. She, particularly, seemed to sparkle as they fed swans, canoed, and watched children at play.

Since he'd hired her recently, on Powers' recommendation, she had seemed to carry an invisible shield. Not that she wasn't warm and congenial. Rather, it was that the promise of her intimacy appeared to be held in restraint by something he couldn't jab with his finger.

Not this afternoon, however. Now she was everything lively and feminine, eager, and gentle. And she had kissed him ardently several times as he lay with his head in her lap on the cool grass. Her sincerity demanded that she be more than just another chick. And, on the spot, he resolved that if he bedded her it would be with such intensity as he had brought to no other biddie in his past.

As she kissed him one final time, clinging to his lips for more than a minute, he sensed that bedding was not far off. He'd have to be certain, though, that he'd not freak-out as he had done so many times before without even having dropped a single microgram. That would louse up the whole, sweet deal.

Disquiet clouded anticipation, however, as they strolled beneath the moss-covered oak that sentineled the park's southern entrance. It was near here, he had been told, that he was "rescued" by Powers. Since then, though, he'd been unable to decide whether it was rescue or entrapment, even considering his two years as Hocker with the Mock Rockers.

Withdrawn in concentration as they stood beside the tree's massive trunk, he turned away from Ann's curious stare.

There—within the shrubbery just ahead! Had he seen the brim of a hat and the shadowed face beneath it pulling back out of sight just as he looked? Or had it been only an illusion?

No, he decided. He wouldn't go thrashing after his phantom while Ann watched. He turned again to avoid her concern-filled eyes as they shifted from the bushes back to him.

Shortly he was pacing his inner office, telling a recently arrived Powers about the latest manifestation of his obsession. Seated at Bradford's desk, the other nodded all the while, his cheerful grin resembling that of a beardless little department-store Santa listening to the amusing patter of excited children.

His smile ebbed as the account ended. "It's encouraging that you didn't chase off after your illusory shadower. Shows healthy doubt as to the validity of your impressions."

Bradford leaned across the desk. "But—why? If it's all hallucination, why do I imagine I'm being followed? Why do I think I see the same cats watching me wherever I go? Why do I have the feeling they may be *protecting* me?"

"Look at it this way, Brad. You're the self-searching type who demands one thing—rationalism. All the pegs have to fit. You've got to know *why* for everything that happens.

"Let's postulate a man who's been an orphan practically from birth, well set in defeatist philosophy acquired through institutional life. But our subject is also above ordinary in ability and ambition. He acquires his full education, then is trapped by the lure of bohemianism. Flip, flop. And flip again. Acceptance of convention, then—"

"All right, then: I'm—unsteady." He'd considered, then rejected using the word "unstable."

"But even your unsteadiness is unsteady. And suddenly you find yourself with assets in the millions. The hand of fate has been good to you. You're basking in the benevolence of Somebody up There. Either your guardian angel is on double duty, or there are whole shifts of heavenly hosts watching over you, seeing that you escape harm."

"My unconscious reaction can't be *that* simple."

"I believe it is. And that's why I rule out a deeply embedded neurosis. If it were the latter, these shadowers would be conspiring to kill you or relieve you of your fortune."

While Bradford mulled it over, Powers went on: "I've taken the liberty of arranging—I won't call it an experiment. Let's just say it may be a means of attacking the foundations of obsession." He leaned toward the intercom. "Miss Fowler, please send Mr. Davidson in."

Powers introduced the man as "Chuck." He was tall as Bradford, though perhaps fifty pounds heavier and ten years his senior. His jacket gripped the athletic slenderness of waist and hips. Hugger slacks were molded by corded thighs and bulging calves. His face, though amiable, was blunt, terminating in a squared-off chin and thickset neck. Bradford's snap judgment, which later proved justified, was that Chuck must be hip at restraining intractable patients in the clinic.

"I've decided to allow you a bodyguard," Powers disclosed.

Bradford smiled. "Pampering my obsession?"

"No. Attacking it. Chuck'll be with you at all times, ready to verify or disprove your suspicions. I'm sure you can even find a place for him in your P & D Towers penthouse."

"Plenty of room. But how do I explain him to my staff?"

Powers shrugged. "Let's say you've got a crackpot idea. You want to assert yourself, so you're thinking about a chain of physical culture facilities. Chuck's the advisor you've dug up."

"In other words, I'm obsessed with the idea." Bradford grinned. "I like it. It's far-out enough to rattle the hell out of all of P & D's consies."

"Very well. Prepare for Chuck's appearance on the scene Monday."

Bradford accompanied them to the door and received another crushing handgrip from his physical culture adviser who said, "See you, boss."

An excited managing director followed Bradford back into his office. "Have you heard," Clark began, "that—"

"Yes. Caught the newscast on my way back here. Security Council takes no action on intervening in Turkey's civil war. U.S. decides unilaterally to grant Ankara's request for armed assistance."

"That too. But—" Clark paused to honk into his handkerchief.

"I know. Now Burroughs will be itching all the more to pull the rug out from under us and invest in defense industries."

"Burroughs," Clark rumbled, "is dead. He was killed in an auto accident. That puts us over the hump. His directors will decide that Regional Basin is to remain among our underwriters."

II

Creation: So infinitely complex in concept, design, function. When simplicity could *have been the permanent order of all things. But that would have led to ennui.*

Actually, it had been so boring when there were only a few land masses and seas nestling under the spheres of the wanderers and all enveloped by the sphere of fixed jewels. (The latter had to be provided—an inspired stroke of ornamentation—when light was separated from dark.)

A gratifying era that was. Oh, there had been the other force. But even that *was only a self-imposed diversionary challenge.*

(Proposition: Another force can be created greater than the Primary. Resolution: false.)

Oversophistication: That was the trouble. Supercomplexity, however, was but another self-imposed condition.

(Proposition: It is possible to make Nature so intricate that not even the Supreme Self-Contester can forestall its collapse. Proposition: The self-defier cannot frustrate the self-defied.

(Propositions unresolved.)

But the contest had become so heated! There was now such a perplexing array of matter and force, action and reaction, time and space! All spread along the spectrum of "reality"—from the basic act of neutron birth to regeneration of new stars; from the hurtling masses of galaxies atwirl, to the entire universe.

Yet, what a magnificent substitute for the flat, lethargic "world" that had once dozed at the center of its simple system! (A Copernicus, among others, had been inspired to "discover" abandonment of the spheres-within-spheres model.)

But now there were so many self-imposed complexities, even including those fashioned by the free-will Creatures!

Proposition: Self-challenger can confound self-challenged.
(Proof: pending.)

...◆...

His steps hastened with urgency but measured by reluctance, Dr. A. J. Duncan emerged from the rear of Powers' clinic. He trod the flagstone walkway, passing through patches of light cast by a gibbous moon and disappearing into the umbrae of scrub trees in the courtyard. On his right and left, shadowy hulks of buildings seemed to crush the downtown oasis like the jaws of a vise.

The toll of time, he felt, was beginning to crush him in similar manner. It had been only four years since Project Genesis was abandoned on his recommendation. Yet that brief span had swept away his thick shock of hair, leaving only a few white strands to overlie his mottled scalp. His face was now coarse with depression. Less than five years since that fateful September 15th, 1980. But five years encompassing an eternity.

Exiting through double gates, he crossed a service alley and entered the rear of a shabby three-story building, fronting on Addison Avenue. Its opaque windows could betray none of the brisk activity or sophisticated instrumentation within.

The foundation. His. No, not his—humanity's. Nor was that right either. It was an institution that represented the interest of *every*thing, *every*where, throughout *all* time, *all* space.

On his way to the conference room Duncan had to pass through many areas of specialized activity—all tenanted by workers and technicians, who pursued their duties in grim, determined manner.

In Security, Hawthorn was checking out the night shift, There were men, most of whom had not been fully indoctrinated in the nature of the foundation, who understood only that they were to provide surreptitious protection for an important person. Later they would learn the full truth. And from then on they would know only terror.

Several intently occupied technicians sat around an oval table in Scientific Survey. Some pored over technical journals and reports, read magazines and newspapers, listened to radios through headsets. Others examined astronomical plates, measuring celestial distances and angles with fine instruments.

In the Investments Section, Hedgmore—dear, utterly selfless Gerstal, who had not been outside of foundation headquarters since he had "committed suicide"—was presiding over a conference. Here was the institution's financial nerve center and, in a sense, one of its most important activities. Assets had to be milked dry. For there could be no more capitalizing through the "manna" route. The balance was so delicate now that further trifling with Bradford could be disastrous.

Continuing to the third floor, Duncan regretted his impetuous decision to close out Project Genesis. For that had deprived him of the opportunity to embezzle more appropriations and use the money to fund his establishment. Odd, he thought as he entered the conference room, that he had never regarded the thefts as immoral. But understandable. For, just as the entire universe had suddenly been revalued, so had the concepts of ethical behavior.

Dr. Powers was already there, slouched in a chair, hands folded over his waist, short legs thrust out at the angle of a taut lean-to. Ann Fowler sat opposite the psychiatrist. Her sensually rounded lips and alert brown eyes were barriers of exquisiteness that seemed, in their own persistence, to be holding back an impending doom. On her right and grave in his tenseness: Ronald Bankston, Progress and Development Enterprises' real estate specialist.

Duncan apologized for his tardiness, then came directly to the point: "It's been three days, Ann, since he was dissuaded from the conviction that he's being watched. As a precautionary measure, we've had to pull our security agents back into the bushes, so to speak. Is he still harping upon his—ah, obsession?"

"I don't know," the girl whispered, not looking up.

"But you've *got* to know! We placed you at the most important observation post so you could be the foundation's eyes on just such matters. Why *don't* you know?" Duncan didn't relish being rough on her. But he sensed tension that might respond to a simple dose of severity.

"I've avoided him," she said. "As much as I *want* to be with him, always, there're times when I'm frightened of what he represents. I took yesterday off. I had to—for relief."

"We know that, Ann. We're aware of not only *his* movements, but of the activities of everyone who is, or comes near him."

Dismay assailed the stoic bulwark of her piquant features. "It's like this," she complained. "I've got so many forces bugging me from so many different directions: my obligation to the foundation, the whole world, the entire universe; the nearness of It whenever I'm around Brad; his deep interest in me—I can sense it; the way I feel about him. Why, when we kissed in the park—"

"We have independent reports on that episode," Duncan interrupted. "All observations have been collated and both conclusions and predictions are now being drafted."

She rose, her hands became small, pleading fists pressed against sculpturesque breasts. "But don't you see that I'm *good* for him? It's been *three days* since that interlude in the park. And nothing's happened! If—if I gave fully, if I became the center of his interest, if it were only he and I, alone, together—then maybe his sense of fulfillment would pacify that—*that Thing!*"

Duncan couldn't understand her questioning the foundation's approach. Powers' conditioning procedure should have prevented such emotional reaction. "We must act on direction and do nothing independently," he admonished. "Some of the best scientific minds in the country are charting our course. We're lost—*everything's* lost—if we deviate from our programmed functions."

"The pressure will be relieved Monday, Ann," Powers soothed, evidently choosing to ignore her plea for total intimacy with Bradford. "That's when Chuck goes on station as P & D's physical culture consultant. In the role of constant companion he'll be in even closer contact than you."

When she had regained her composure she looked at the psychiatrist. "I think I need booster conditioning. Can you do it now?"

"The clinic's only just across the service alley. I'll bring you over and let Swanson take care of it. I'm all wrapped up in Chuck at the moment."

Duncan watched them leave, feeling an uncomfortable mixture of compassion and relief. If Powers had not imbued Ann with a completely Spartan approach to awesome responsibility, he had at least instilled in her the compulsion to request further conditioning.

The foundation director took his chair and glanced over at Bradford's real estate expert. "And how are you making out, Ronald?"

Bankston removed his eyeglasses. "I've just reported in to financial manipulation that I bilked P & D out of almost $15,000 this past month."

"Helps," Duncan acknowledged. "Helps considerably." It had been wise to enlist Bankston. Not only had the foundation acquired a second close check on Bradford, but it had also established another constant source of income.

Hawthorn strode in and straddled a chair, topping its backrest with his folded arms. "Everybody's on station."

The security chief was a heavyset man with crimpy dark hair overhanging his forehead like coiled shavings from a lathe. He unsnapped his cartridge belt, laying the holstered revolver on the table.

"I hope they've been told to be inconspicuous," Duncan said.

"We've been a lot more careful since he spotted Armstrong."

"Armstrong *and then Filcher*—in the park."

"All right." Hawthorn hunched his shoulders. "So we got careless. But let me tell you this: I personally don't care how many of us he gets wise to—as long as he stays *absolutely secure.*"

"Sometimes I think you're too dedicated."

Hawthorn drew back. "You're going to start harping on Burroughs again. All right, so Security took matters in its own hands. Burroughs was going to ruin Bradford financially. It was simple to get into his parking lot and 'arrange' an accident."

"I can't approve of those methods." Upon uttering them, Duncan realized they were words he couldn't wholly justify. Hadn't he only a short while earlier conceded the revaluation of ethical concepts?

"So you don't approve?" The security chief laughed. "Isn't it the basic aim of the foundation to provide Bradford with safety, purpose, identity, status, self-dependence—so that *he'll* be content and *It* will keep on drowsing in his satisfaction? Isn't that why Hedgmore stays locked up in this building—so Bradford can enjoy his 'inheritance'?"

He paused, but not long enough to allow affirmation or denial. "Well, *Burroughs* had to die so Bradford would *remain* stable and secure, so It wouldn't be rudely awakened to the reality of Its bungling!"

Duncan elevated his arms. "What's done can't be undone. So let's go on to other matters. What'll Armstrong do now?"

"He's on supervisory work," Hawthorn replied, "Can't be assigned to any protective detail, not since Bradford got wise to him."

"He's fully indoctrinated?"

"Of course. That's why he was so anxious that he got careless."

"Fine. We'll put him back on protective detail next week."

"What?" Hawthorn was incredulous.

"We're going to *let* Bradford catch him."

The door burst open and a florid-faced man, clutching a strip of computer readout tape, barged in. Eyes flaring with alarm, he drew up before the table.

"Yes, Marlow. What is it?" Duncan asked the head of his mathematical section as he began absorbing the man's effluvium of fright. God, he hoped it wasn't another Pluto! Four years had passed and he still couldn't reconcile himself to the disappearance of an entire planet.

"*Pi*! It's *pi*! *Pi*'s no longer transcendental!"

"I don't understand." Duncan's brows contracted.

"I don't either. Just had a hunch a couple of days ago. Began calculating circle circumferences. Inscribed and circumscribed polygons. Refining the sequences toward a common limit. Again and again this afternoon I submitted the data to one of our computers. Not satisfied, I passed the problem on to Dr. Varnado at Tech's computer research department. He fed it into their INSTIAC and—"

Duncan managed a word while the other sucked in air: "You didn't tell Varnado what the nature of the problem was, did you?"

"Of course not. But his readout verified our results to the final decimal."

"And?"

"*Pi* is no longer irrational! Falls into the spectrum of rational numbers at its 323rd decimal. Comes out even. Nothing left over!"

Duncan was nonplussed. "But that's impossible, isn't it? Mathematics is mathematics—a product of the human mind. Numbers, all of them, are fictional. If you divide the same denominator into its numerator you're bound to get a consistent answer."

"Not with *pi* you won't. Not any longer."

Hawthorn and Bankston only continued shifting their attention between the foundation director and his math section chief.

"We can only say," Marlow went on, "that the mathematical continuum and the physical continuum disagree at many incompatible points. Until just recently pi was one of those points. No longer."

"Good God!" Duncan whispered. "A new value for *pi*!" He thought of the inextricable manner in which the symbol was woven into so many of man's pursuits—geodesy, trigonometry, surveying, engineering, navigation, electronics, mechanics. But it was even more profound than that: Celestial dynamics revolved around the Greek alphabetic character! "Planetary orbits ..." he muttered, then sank back into his despair.

Marlow managed a weak smile. "I doubt this change will have all the immediate effects you're envisioning. I was appalled too, at first."

"But it means chaos in everything, doesn't it?"

The mathematician shook his head. "There's little change in the value until the 300th decimal. I don't know of any branch of human endeavor, or of celestial or nuclear dynamics for that matter, that requires a more precise approximation of *pi* than a few score or so decimals."

Duncan was relieved, but somewhat provoked. "What you've just said hardly justifies the manner in which you came charging in here."

"No. But two other factors do. First, only It could have proclaimed a new value for *pi*."

"We're well aware of that."

"Second: This isn't a simple mathematical manipulation. It didn't merely alter the ratio of circumference to diameter. Either intentionally, or because It was disturbed in Its slumber by something that happened to Bradford, *It put an extra kink in the curvature of space!*"

Duncan frowned. "How do you rationalize that?"

"In non-Euclidean space, a triangle's angles may total other than 180°, depending upon the curvature of the surface on which it's inscribed. Circumference-diameter ratio also is variable according to the degree of space curvature."

The director drew a mental picture to illustrate Marlow's words. "A space warp!" he exclaimed.

"But one so small, fortunately, that it can be detected only through rematching the mathematical and physical continuation. What bothers me, however, is this indication that It has either purposely or, worse yet, unwittingly lost Its hold over a physical constant. Will space be warped further? Will other constants go down the drain? Is It losing control because It's awakening completely?"

Duncan lost whatever aplomb he may have retained until now. What, he wondered, had provoked this latest upheaval in the fundamentals of existence? Had it been Ann's independent initiative in the park? Most likely not; for hers was a *pacifying* influence. Had some disturbing stimulus seeped down through Bradford's unconscious and nudged It in Its slumber? Surely the catalyst couldn't have been anything as simple as Bradford's suspicion that he was being watched.

"It will be interesting," Marlow proposed, "to see how long it is before this convulsion is discovered by other investigators."

"Pluto's disappearance was noticed immediately," Duncan reminded.

"But Pluto was a more conspicuous fact of nature than the 323rd decimal of *pi*."

Duncan detected motion at the periphery of his vision. Boris Powers stood against the wall, drying his forehead with a wilted handkerchief. Beside him was Chuck Davidson, the foundation's new inductee. They had evidently been there several minutes.

"You heard, Powers?" Duncan asked.

The psychiatrist had difficulty closing his mouth. "A—another upheaval!"

Chuck clutched Powers' arm, as though groping for whatever security that might afford. "God," he muttered, restive eyes probing an infinity of fear, "God, God ..."

Duncan was aware that the man had gone through only half of his indoctrination; had been presented with harsh, irrefutable proof of the foundation's basic hypothesis. And now, before that awful knowledge could be tempered by Powers' further psychic ministrations, he had collided headon with additional, unexpected verification.

Marlow backed toward the door. "I've got to get my staff at work on some of the other geometric constants. There may have been associated transformations in that area."

Toying with his holster on the table, Hawthorn appeared to be examining the gravity of the situation. Meanwhile, Bankston only regarded his folded hands, ignoring the perspiration on his forehead.

"What could have caused it?' Powers wondered aloud. "What *could* have caused it?"

Duncan turned his palms upward. "Bradford's growing suspicion?"

"That sputtering fuse in Turkey," Bankston proposed. "Insurgents getting direct troop support from Russia. U.S. aircraft flying out of Istanbul; our subs in the Black Sea."

"Don't be ridiculous," Hawthorn scoffed. "It doesn't give a damn about insignificant human happenings."

"It gives a damn about Bradford, doesn't It?"

"But only in a passive sense—a sense of accidental association."

"God," croaked Chuck. "God, God ..."

Duncan began pacing. "We're still sure Montague isn't interfering, aren't we?" But the question sought no answer, being only an examination of his own uncertainty. Julius Montague, Research Council observer of Project Genesis, together with P & D's "late" Gerstal Hedgmore, was among those who had confirmed the hostship that set Bradford apart from all other men. But, having eventually fled in superstitious terror, Montague had never been heard from since.

"I should imagine Julius killed himself," Powers said. "Paranoid tendencies. A likely candidate for self-immolation."

Duncan turned suddenly. "Powers, you put Bradford through a session Tuesday, didn't you?"

The other nodded. "Routine hypnotherapy. Obsession erasure technique. Nothing more. Just gimmickry to justify my position in the front line of surveillance."

"No hallucinogen? You didn't—dig deep, did you?"

"God, no! I wouldn't have the guts to. I almost panicked when we reached down to It four years ago and suggested the disappearance of Pluto to verify our hypothesis."

"It's true," Chuck was muttering now, his eyes still paralyzed with incredulity. "It's true; it's true; it's ..."

"Then," Duncan said, hanging his head, "this could be what we've feared all along—what was hinted at when you penetrated below Bradford's unconscious in those early sessions."

"Toppling of the structure," Powers agreed. "Erosion of natural law. Fragmentation of a quiltwork construction that's too topheavy to be justified through further complication. Once there was one elementary particle: the atom. Now there are hundreds—all interdependent. How many more can be added to 'explain' the inconsistencies?"

Trembling now, Chuck's voice rose. "It's true! It *is* true! It's *true*!"

Galvanized from his stupor, he clubbed Powers across the chest with his forearm and sent him sprawling. Fright animating his eyes, he seized Hawthorn and flung him against the wall.

Altogether inadequate to the task, Duncan tried to stop the berserk man. But Chuck had already unholstered Hawthorn's revolver and thrust its muzzle into his mouth.

By now, however, Powers had risen to one knee. "Stop," he said calmly. "Put it back on the table."

Chuck obeyed, demonstrating to Duncan's satisfaction how well Powers had the man under control.

Falling to his knees, Chuck bent forward onto the table and hid his face in the sanctuary of his folded arms.

Duncan, torn upon the rack of the huge man's despair, wondered whether it wouldn't have been better if Bradford had never been discovered, the foundation never established.

III

Destruction! Chaotic plunging of electrons down to ever smaller orbits, spending their energies in the surrender of photons to infinity. Huge, proud suns erupting in cataclysms of belching fury. Immense galaxies in collision; systems of matter hurtling into systems of antimatter and unleashing total annihilation. ("Antimatter": a recent innovation introduced into reality only because the Primary Force had to keep on strengthening His self-challenge. What wanton folly!)

Oh, the delightful satisfaction of seizing each newborn neutron and wrenching it through beta decay! Thus, even the fundamental Act of Creation did not pass without incurring immediate, successful defiance.

Whose universe was it? That of the Constructor, paralyzed by self-imposed overcomplexity? Who could no longer manipulate all the impossibly tangled processes? Didn't it, rather, now belong to the Destroyer? Hadn't the Primary Force, in effect, abdicated behind the paltry excuse of self-challenge?

Destruction, on the other hand, proceeded at an orderly pace, driving the universe toward the oblivion of total entropy.

Why, the Constructor had even lost dominion over his favored beings! Oh, how willingly they embraced all their instruments of discord, devastation, and death!

...◆...

From his inner office, Bradford scanned the street below, watching Chuck Davidson on the sidewalk. Despite the latter's well-proportioned build and the self-assurance of his stride, he convincingly played the role of businessman-between-appointments as he stalked anyone who might be casing the P & D Building.

Chuck was a quick-witted, alert cat—not the shallow-minded, muscle-bound clod he had seemed on first encounter two weeks ago. You'd almost think he was spaced out at times, but he dug good humor and flopped at ease as a guest in P & D's pentpad.

Bradford returned to his desk and sat staring up at Gerstal B. Hedgmore's portrait. In spite of his frequent impulse to use the canvas as a dartboard, he had to admit there was nobility and courage in the angular, handsome face of the philandering old goat. He reviewed the Hedgmore legend. But, except for military and financial distinction, it drew a blank:

Born: 1919. (Legitimate? He wondered, laughing.)

Schooling: commensurate with high middle-class means. A few scholastic honors tacked onto his degree in business administration.

Military record: Acquitted himself well in the European Theater in '44, achieving captaincy. Many citations, including the Purple Heart for wounds in the Ardennes Bulge. (No psychiatric exemption for him.)

Business record: well on his way to establishing a real estate empire by the end of '47. (He was only a year older then than I am now, Bradford noted, not particularly impressed.) "Whiz Kid" of the financial world, they had dubbed him as he grouped and regrouped investors, incorporated, dissolved, and reincorporated. He consolidated his holdings and founded Progress & Development Enterprises in '58.

(That, Bradford reflected, was just about the time Hedgmore must have been splitting the scene on the QT and bedding his biddies. For '58 was when the bachelor father's unwanted son had been delivered.)

Death: '81, four years ago, when he was 62 and all strung-out on nose-to-the-grindstone acid. Suicide note: "... All is nothing; nothing is all. Life is a hollow nihility ..." Off the cliff into the crags at his coastal estate.

Bradford slammed the cover on the mental record and cursed Hedgmore for having never acknowledged him while alive, for being hung up on the Victorian idea that embryo had no right to split womb unless vows had been pledged at least nine months earlier. He hoped Gerstal's "nihility" had somehow been made "hollow" by an antiquated sense of guilt.

Going over to the portrait, he seized the frame and rotated it against the wall. Pivoting on a concealed peg, the entire canvas swung counter-clockwise until Gerstal B. was 45° out of plumb. He looked better that way.

And there was the spring-loaded recessed panel that concealed Hedgmore's safe. Bradford had discovered it when, in a moment of suffocation from his entrapment by the establishment, he had back-handed the beribboned chest and the hidden panel had thudded open against the rear of the canvas.

Once again now he tapped the molding and the mahogany square opened. Within the wall, the door of the safe was still ajar, just as he had found it originally. Upon deciding to cop out off the clifftop, Hedgmore had evidently emptied the strongbox—almost, but not quite.

When Bradford had first discovered the cache, the corner of a sheet of paper was visible in the crack between the safe and its compartment wall. Once again he retrieved the letter and brought it to his desk. He spread out the document and studied it. Upper lefthand corner: Veterans Administration seal. Upper right: a chain of digits under the heading "claim number." Letterhead: "Board of Veterans Appeals, Washington, D.C."

Dear Mr. Hedgmore:

The board has made its decision on your appeal. At your request, disability compensation in the amount of $58 monthly has been discontinued. You are aware that such compensation is awarded on the basis of injuries incurred in the service of your country, irrespective of independent financial status. The Board of Appeals commends you, therefore, on your pride in rejecting that which you do not need....

Bradford crumpled the letter and harshly mumbled: "$58 monthly," "commends you," "pride in rejecting." What was *that* kind of bread to Hedgmore? How could you read pride into such a trifling gesture? But his resentment subsided. Even though he didn't want to acknowledge it, the rejection had reflected character.

Bradford unwadded the letter. What was the nature of Hedgmore's wound? Pursuit of an answer to that question had drawn only shrugs of ignorance. Until now. But perhaps no longer. Maybe there was a chance to add another jigsaw piece to the unfinished mental picture of old Gerstal B.

He thumbed the intercom switch. "Ann, remember John Murdock?"

"Yes, Mr. Bradford, he's—"

"Now Annie, I thought we'd agreed—"

"Mr. Clark is waiting out here to see you," she explained her insistence on office protocol.

Why in hell couldn't the managing director stay in his own pad? "Tell Mr. Clark I've got a phone call to make first. Now, John Murdock is the man who sold us that key plot so we could block out our Northdale Subdivision. He's a contact officer at the regional VA Headquarters. See if you can get him on the phone, will you?"

Bradford felt he could count on Murdock to blink at bureaucratic regulations out of a sense of personal obligation. For he had underestimated the value of his plot and was strung out on gratitude when Bankston, under orders, had bought at double the asking price.

Eventually the call came through: "Yes, Mr. Bradford?"

After tactfully recalling their real estate dealings, Bradford explained what he wanted, giving Hedgmore's VA claim number.

"But those files are confidential," Murdock begged off. "I'd have to have a reason for requesting that folder."

"I could give plenty of reasons, but let's let it rest on the fact that I was Mr. Hedgmore's sole beneficiary. And all I want to know is how he was hurt in the Battle of the Bulge."

"All right I'll try to have a *casual* look. But whatever I tell you will be confidential. Okay?"

"Check."

When the managing director was finally admitted, Clark appeared to be barely holding off an attack of apoplexy. Red-faced, his corpulent cheeks puffed, he hulked before the desk, hardly noticing Bradford's broad-belted magenta vest suit and his balloon sleeves. Finally, with a rush of air: "You're calling for construction bids on the Westhills project! I've just seen your memo to Bankston!"

"I thought you objected because Burroughs was going to knock our props out. Well, he isn't on the scene any longer."

"But—but, August first! We won't get any *competitive* bids at all! Not with all that municipal construction in the works!"

"We're slicing it differently this time—inviting bids over a three-state area, as you suggested."

"Oh." Clark came down a bit. But: "I do wish you would consult me on these matters first. Mr. Hedgmore always did." He moved toward the door then paused, looking back.

"Anything else?" Bradford asked, intentionally moving an arm so that the lace sleeve fluttered before reinflating to its original contour. That always bugged this hungup cat.

"Yes. This physical culture thing. I don't think—"

"You don't approve?" Bradford savored Clark's resentment.

"Such a venture could bring in—but *pennies*."

"I'm only casing possibilities."

Hesitating, Clark buttoned his generation-old coat, unbuttoned it. "I don't want to be blunt."

"Go right ahead."

"Well, at the business clubs around town some of the members are beginning to wonder if physical culture business possibilities are *all* you're—ah, casing with that—that Chuck fellow."

Bradford sensed something provocative. "Spell it out."

"Chuck—a very masculine, handsome, athletic type. All of a sudden you move him into your apartment and—"

"Get the hell out of here!"

A double shot of bourbon from his liquor cabinet helped clear away some of Bradford's infuriation. He reached for a pinch of little-bang snuff, but changed his mind. In the next therapy session Powers would be certain to discover he'd again gotten strung out on mini manna.

Announced by Ann, Chuck entered and, in his casual manner, perched on the edge of the desk. "Nothing out of the way down there, Brad—unless you'd want to pin the suspect label on a short, stout consy in a blue suit and gray hat."

Bradford hid his sudden tenseness behind a gesture, extending liquor cabinet privileges. "What's he doing?"

"Watched him walk by several times, across the street. He kept staring up in this direction." Chuck mixed Scotch with water.

"What'd he look like?"

"Short, like I said. Rough face. No fuzz. Big, hook nose—"

"That's the man, Chuck! The one Powers says isn't there!"

The other grinned. "Next time he passes I'll latch on. Then we'll find out all we want to know about that cat."

Bradford felt elated over this confirmation of his suspicion. Confidence restored in his own mental integrity, he again trotted out his sequence of "whys," punctuated by boldface, italicized question marks: *Why* was he being watched—"protected," perhaps? *Why* should Fate have singled *him* out for full-thrust rise from obscurity to wealth and purpose? *What* unlikely stroke of Providence had determined that Powers, investigating his preorphanage background, should cross paths with probate court authorities attempting to locate Hedgmore's sole beneficiary?

Chuck's fingers snapped in front of his face, recalling Bradford to the reality of his office. "Time," the bodyguard reminded. "Powers says I'm to see that you take your daily break. Remember?"

Bradford shrugged his shoulders in submission. "Well, what's it to be this afternoon—workout at the Athletic Club?"

"No. Full eighteen holes. I've made reservations at your club." Chuck flashed a suggestive grin. "And I've talked Ann into coming along."

"You didn't get a too-much-work spiel out of her?"

"No." The other laughed. "What's the matter, boss? Having trouble ballin' the belle?"

"As a kid at Frisby's Foundling Home I used to lie for hours looking at my Christmas present before unwrapping it. Learned I could always get stoned on anticipation. Okay. Threesome at one-thirty. But not at the club. And only nine holes. Not enough time. Expecting an important call here later this afternoon. See whether they can fit us in at the Midcity Park course."

...◆...

Until all hell broke loose, it was a refreshing afternoon: warm breezes spilling down from cumulus-tufted skies; the sun's golden haze clinging like an aura to the verdure of springtime regeneration; chipmunks scurrying from the paths of bounding golf balls.

And there was Ann—sprightly, warm, even more beautiful as her graceful animations were placed on display against the backdrop of Midcity Park's natural setting. She wore her long hair coiled and netted in silver mesh—a soft, swirling crown that complemented her form-revealing blue body-stocking.

Now, as Brad watched her drive off the seventh tee, his eyes lingered on her lithe form and supple motions, her jauntiness and high spirits that found expression in the promise extended by frequent smiles.

She lofted a well-hit ball that arched down some hundred and fifty yards away, hooking slightly and landing near dense undergrowth, separating the fairway from the park's Soapbox Slopes.

"Guess my swing can stand improving." She laughed. And Bradford watched the sunlight laugh along with her as it glinted off myriads of waxen leaves, more myriads of ripples on the nearby water hazard. Sure, he'd mouthed a euphoria plug on the first hole, when she and Chuck hadn't been watching. But this euphoria he felt with her—it was *real*!

She had clung to his arm frequently that afternoon, eagerly accepting his lips several times when he went to help her look for lost balls in the rough. On the last hole she had backed off from his embrace, planted her cheek against his chest and whispered in an almost throbbing voice which he wasn't certain he had been intended to hear: "When, Brad? Oh, Brad! *When*?"

Following her on the seventh tee, Chuck got off a masterful drive that rolled to the edge of the green. Bradford, standing lean and tall in gray torso-tights, wiped both hands on the outfit's loin flap and addressed his ball. He stifled a snigger as he watched it shrink to pea size in the tee's concavity, then expand to basketball proportions. Shrink. Expand. His euphoria plug was working overtime. He released the laugh. And the foliage of several oak trees, flanking the fairway up ahead, spawned gaping mouths and laughed along with him. After he finally started his downswing, he *whacked* a watermelon-sized clubhead into a grapefruit-sized ball and got off a drive that split the difference between his competitors' shots.

Steering the electric cart, Chuck turned on his portable radio. "Bases were loaded just a minute ago," he reminded. "Wonder how we got out of that inning."

But the baseball game had been nudged off the air by special coverage of peace talks between the Turkish government and its Liberationist insurgents. From what Bradford could gather, negotiations were being shelved in favor of fighting the issue out on the battlefields. Ability to concentrate on the newscast seemed to indicate that he was coming down off his mini trip. It had been over twenty minutes since he'd dropped the stuff. But with euphoria plugs you could never be certain.

Chuck abruptly snapped off the radio and whispered, "Keep your eyes straight ahead so you won't tip our hand, Brad. I've just spotted Arm—arm's length off the fairway Mr. Short, Stout, and Hooknose!"

"You sure he's the same consy you saw today?"

"Positive. And ain't this a honey of a place to pull him out into the open? All by ourselves, in the rough."

Ann frowned, but held her eyes steady. "Then you were right."

"Damn right he was," Chuck verified. "Cat's in that thick growth about a hundred feet from Ann's ball. We'll drop you off there as though it's *your* ball, Brad. Then we'll drive on. Where the fairway doglegs to the left, I'll hop off, circle back and—snatch!"

Ann gripped Bradford's arm. "Please be careful."

Now, with proof in the offing, he no longer regretted having taken her into his confidence on the nature of Powers' visits and on the "physical culture" ploy that covered up Chuck's presence at P & D.

He watched the cart disappear around the bend and took a conspicuous number of practice swings beside Ann's ball before he became impatient. But in the next moment came the sounds of thrashing in the underbrush. A bass voice grunted and shouted in protest. He dropped his club and charged into the bushes.

Chuck had his victim in a hammer lock. "Spill it out!" He clamped the man's neck in the vise of his forearm and biceps.

"I demand," Hooknose said, surrendering none of his dignity, "that you release me immediately." He was in his fifties, out of condition and certainly no match for his captor. Chuck tightened his nutcracker grip on the man's throat and told Bradford, "See what you can find on him."

Within a minute the inventory was spread out on the ground: .32-caliber revolver; wallet containing a small amount of money, various identification cards and a driver's license issued to "William Farmer"; gun permit, and authorization to operate as a "private investigator."

"So *that's* it." Chuck stared at the license. "Who're you working for? Why are you camping on Mr. Bradford's tail?"

"I'm not at liberty to divulge the identity of my client."

Chuck flexed his arm, snapping the detective's head back. "You're not at liberty to breathe either."

"Bradley Burroughs," the man rasped. "Regional Basin."

Bradford frowned. "But Burroughs is dead."

"My retainer is effective through the end of this month. I'll still file my report, with his secretary."

"Your report on what?"

The man appeared compliant enough now. Chuck released him, but stood with one foot planted on the gun, his other on the wallet.

"I was told to keep you under surveillance with two objectives in mind: first, to find out how often you have to see Dr. Powers and—"

"You're solo on this assignment?" Bradford interrupted.

"No. I have three other operatives on the job."

Bradford was relieved. If Burroughs had thought him unworthy as a repository for Regional Basin's investment funds, it was only logical that he should try to present proof to his directors. And *four* detectives well accounted for the "obsession" that he was being watched constantly.

Ann had joined them. Clutching Chuck's radio, she stood at the edge of the clearing—a silent, concerned observer.

"What's your other objective?" Bradford asked.

"To see if you're contacting any pushers, getting any junk."

Bradford's eyebrows lifted as he lied: "I've been off the kick for two years! Haven't tripped off once during all that time."

"I know. That's what I'm going to say in my report."

There was the sound of applause from the direction of Soapbox Slopes, just beyond the undergrowth. A few unintelligible shouts coalesced into a droned chant: "Peace, peace, peace—" whoever had the stump was relating with the audience.

Bradford signaled Chuck to dismiss the investigator. The man retrieved his belongings and disappeared into the bushes in the direction of the Slopes. Shoulders aslump and head inclined forward, he seemed to be trembling.

"There's something bugging him," Bradford observed.

"Injured professional pride, I suppose," Chuck guessed.

From Soapbox Slopes: applause; "Peace, peace, peace—"

Ann said, "I'm worried, Chuck; maybe you'd better go see."

Then the sharp, crisp sound of a pistol's discharge exploded from the direction in which the detective had gone.

Soapbox Slopes' applause died away in the shot's echoes.

Ann screamed.

Bradford charged after Chuck into the foliage. Twigs tore at his clothes, lashed his hands as he held them protectively before his face. Ann—muttering, "O, God! No!"—came along as best she could.

The investigator's body lay just outside the shrubbery. He was sprawled face down, hand clutching his revolver.

Around him had gathered a half circle of gaudily-dressed, sallow-cheeked youths and bearded, disheveled-haired elders. Sunlight glinted against a profusion of beads adorning their necks.

The abandoned orator swung his arms in a frantic attempt to recapture the attention of his audience. "There lies the symbol of bourgeois malignancy! There lies the frustration that will champion the cause of the proletariat! Let us leave the scene of this tragedy! Quickly!"

But his words were no more effective than the trampled and torn placards that lay in the dust demanding "PEACE IN TURKEY AT ANY PRICE!" and "LET'S BACK THE LIBERATION FRONT!"

Chuck knelt beside the private investigator. Ann finally emerged from the undergrowth. Her features registered dismay and she retreated into the bushes. A sandaled youth stumbled toward Bradford. The film of narcotic stupor dulled his eyes as he tried to focus them.

"O, God!" he mumbled. Then, more urgently, "O, God!"

Bradford was reminded of himself years ago—drinking in the sometimes heady, usually frightening happenings of a maxi trip; quavering before the grotesqueries of a complete freakout.

"O, God! O, God!" groaned the young man.

Then it became apparent that the expletives weren't at all a reaction to the suicide. Instead, he was breathing the exclamations directly into Bradford's face. Chuck lunged to his feet and shoved the tripper away.

Now it was a briefly skirted young blonde who came, trembling, out of the ring of spectators. Yet there was a sort of ecstasy limning her features as she extended her arms toward Bradford.

From the depths of a lesser intoxication than the bearded youth's, she exclaimed, "It's our Infinite Man! Our Sacred Inverse Vessel!"

The hopped-up youth sidestepped Chuck and shuffled again toward Bradford. "Come with us, O, Holy Inverse One! Come to Your worshipers!"

On the fringe of the group the tall, robed orator was pulling frenziedly first at one, then another of his awe-struck followers. "Come quickly! We must leave before—before the—fuzz gets here!"

Now the girl was doing a body-quivering dance around Bradford while he stood there dumfounded, trying to come down off the euphoria plug. "O, Infinite Being! I am circling Thy universe; circumscribing all the matter Thou hast created!"

Then she shouted rapturously at the youth: "This is it, Iggy! The celestial happening! The pure cosmic experience!"

Chuck swore and tried to ward them off. "You and Ann get back to the cart, Brad. I'll take care of this bunch."

But Bradford remained rooted there. *Something* seemed to have him locked in a relentless grip. The scene around him became remote, unreal. Nearby faces loomed all out of proportion, like giant balloons dangling tiny bodies. It was as though he were absorbing some of the acid these droppers had taken and embarking on his own weirdy. Or had his mini-trip plug *really* backfired?

"Come to Thy Temple, O, Inverse Vessel!" the girl screeched. "Witness with Thine own eyes the Rite of Topological Transformation!"

...◆...

Blades of grass beneath Bradford's feet became swaying treetops and he tottered to keep from plunging into the dark, menacing forest below. In the distance a mountain that somehow resembled Chuck's thickset face metamorphosed into a huge fist. It lashed out and smashed a lesser peak whose shaggy timberline resembled the strung-out youth's unkempt beard.

Then Bradford was plummeting through prickly pine foliage into the ebon vastness of the forest's lower reaches. (O, God—he sobbed as he fell—he'd have *to quit sneaking that little-bang stuff!)*

It was '79 all over again, without benefit of mescaline. And even in his senselessness he shrank away from the celestial experience he knew was coming: the frightening freakout effects that had helped inspire his almost complete withdrawal from narcotics.

The forest spaces were still infinite, but no longer lightless. A pinpoint of luminescence here. Another there. A cluster over to his left—if directions were still meaningful. Then, like a glade flaring into brilliance with the light of countless myriads of fireflies, there was coruscating magnificence everywhere. The lightning bugs formed great swirling clusters that spun like dazzling Catherine wheels.

(Somewhere whistles blew and bodies—material ones—collided. But Bradford severed all sensory connections with the physical continuum.)

Now, as in all those awful earlier trips, there was the Infinite Presence. A sort of metaphysical bond sprang up between him and the Presence as they went about through the void, treading the spinning pinwheels of glowflies. But their interest was in the occasional, fiercely shining giant insect that had refused merger with the whirling colonies.

The independent lights were being snuffed out, one by one.

And the void was filled with a melancholy strumming.

···◆···

"Easy, Brad," Chuck comforted. "You had a rough time."

Bradford felt the softness of a deck chair beneath him and looked up at the shadowed undercurve of a striped umbrella. He was on the clubhouse terrace.

Ann brushed hair away from his eyes. "We've called Dr. Powers. He said to keep you quiet until he gets here."

"I—I guess that suicide set me off," he began. And …"

"Powers says you're just to rest and not think about anything," Chuck added. "Anyway, we want to keep quiet about that private investigator. Powers says it wouldn't be good for us to get involved."

Bradford sat upright. "But we *are* involved, aren't we? I heard the police whistles. And you slugged that bearded kid—"

"Police whistles?" Ann repeated, glancing uncertainly at Chuck.

"I didn't slug anybody," the latter denied.

"Call for Mr. Bradford." The clubhouse attendant placed an extension telephone on the table.

Chuck waved him off. "Not now. Tell them we've just left."

But Bradford had already lifted the receiver.

"Mr. Bradford, this is Murdock at regional VA Headquarters. Your office said I might reach you here."

"Yes?" Bradford queried, wondering why Chuck and Ann seemed ready to deny what had happened on Soapbox Slopes. Or *had* anything happened there?

"I have the information you wanted," Murdock went on. "Mr. Hedgmore's partial disability resulted from surgical removal of his gonads. Castration, to put it bluntly. Surgery in '44, necessitated by 'gangrenous condition of testicles.' Cause: shell fragment."

It was a moment before the information sank in. Why should an unknown, *unrelated* Bradford have been named Hedgmore's beneficiary? Why? Gerstal B. had been wounded in '44. His illegitimate son had not been born until '58—in Hedgmore's fourteenth year of eunuchism!

IV

Disturbance:

Harsh arousal from repose. Sudden awareness of stretching and tearing in the entire texture of "reality." How long could Nature be maintained in her, oh, so intricate patterns? Left alone, order could perhaps be preserved. But awareness brought reborn fear that the self-challenge had indeed been too formidable. Simply to hold things together approximately as they now existed would be a signal accomplishment.

But, no. There must be retreat from oversophistication. For each jarring intrusion brought full consciousness and wrested the processes of Nature from self-direction, returning them to direct control. And that was too much to ask. (Proposition: Self-defier can *over-extend self. Likelihood: proof positive.)*

The machine was too complicated now to accommodate conscious direction. Some of the more recent laws and phenomena had to be revoked—such as the go-it-alone glowflies' counterparts in reality. Better that those units be withdrawn from the framework of existence. Better that than create a whole new discipline to warrant their presence.

…◆…

Gloom enveloped the foundation conference room. Duncan paced along the wall where opaqued windows held back the glare of night lights in the street below. Bowed, his head moved in lugubrious undulations, like a radar beam sweeping out some elusive target. He presented the image of a general mapping out critical battlefield strategy.

At the table Hawthorn and Bankston, P & D's real estate manager, engaged in whispered conversation, as though honoring the conventional silence of a death vigil. Foundation section chiefs on their right and left were as motionless as they were mute.

Duncan tried to find the formula that would rescue him from despair. But there was none. Unless it might be the fact that three days had passed since Bradford's psyche-to-psyche encounter with It as a result of the direct provocation on Soapbox Slopes. Three whole days, and nothing had happened. Yet. Nevertheless, the fuse might even now be sputtering toward the inevitable explosion.

Headquarters' wakelike atmosphere persisted even as Ann Fowler entered, took the chair on Duncan's right, and placed Chuck's portable radio and a man's left shoe on the table.

She slid the items over to Wittels, chief of communications. "Chuck says the radio's transmitter slipped frequency. Remember the hard time I had calling here from the park? And this is the last of Bradford's shoes that has to be gimmicked."

Returning to the table, Duncan watched the section chief lick his thin lips as he twisted the snap latch on the back of the receiver and called into its speaker: "Wittels to Headcom. How do you read this?"

The answer came back out of the grid, "Very weak. Unclear."

Wittels turned off the camouflaged transceiver. "We'll issue Chuck another one immediately."

"You'd damn well better," Hawthorn said. "What if Ann hadn't been able to raise Headquarters that afternoon? There'd have been no chance for us to get there and spirit off Armstrong's body."

"God!" moaned Bankston. "The police would have exposed his false identity as a private investigator! Bradford would have *known*!"

Duncan slumped under the weight of an even more funereal atmosphere. It *was* a wakelike occasion, with a martyr to be mourned. But Armstrong was better off. He had simply withdrawn from a reality with which he couldn't cope, not even with the aid of full conditioning.

"Poor Armstrong," Hawthorn lamented. "How he must have felt!"

Duncan stared at the security chief's drawn face and tried to distill for him the anguish of the martyr's nightmare: "Armstrong was front and center on the universal stage, playing out a role on which all existence might hinge. The passion was too great."

Hawthorn nodded. "Our mistake was to let him carry a gun."

"It would have made no difference. He'd have found some way to relieve himself of all that torment. For, you see, he was face to face with his God, committing the sacrilege of deceiving his Creator. That's how *he* evaluated it. He must have regarded himself, in those last moments, as a Judas whose pieces of silver added up to the dubious salvation of a world that enjoys no actual existence in itself."

More palpable silence.

"But come now." Duncan sensed the need to dispel defeatism, just as a staff officer must bolster his troops. "We have to look forward, not backward. How is Bradford, Ann?"

"Dr. Powers has things pretty well under control. He's still keeping him sedated, letting him wrestle with his Soapbox Slopes impressions in small doses."

Duncan winced. "Powers isn't deviating from the plan, is he?"

"Oh, no. Brad's already bought the suggestion that he hallucinated everything in the park as a result of witnessing the suicide. And I thought I was going to catch hell because I didn't notice him popping that plug. But if he *hadn't* gotten strung out on mini manna we might not have been able to convince him he was hallucinating on Soapbox Slopes."

Relieved, Duncan said, "You mean it looks like it's going to work?"

"Powers thinks so. But there're other problems. Justification has to be rigged up for other uncertainties in Brad's mind, he says. He'll be here in a few minutes to explain."

"He's not going to leave Bradford *alone*?"

"It'll be all right. Chuck's on station and Powers has instructed P & D Towers not to disturb the penthouse." She lowered her eyes and sucked in a serrate breath. "O, God, why do *I* have to be the one to deceive him like this? I'm tired of lying when all I want is to play everything straight with him!"

"Like the rest of us, you've got a job to do, my dear. And you'll do that job because you know that if he *isn't* deceived there'll be no more you, Bradford, us, *anything*."

Duncan wondered why the foundation hadn't simply isolated Bradford, in lieu of providing him with fortune, eminence, and purpose. The latter course had led to such sweeping oversophistication of the system wherein he was protected, watched over, and shielded from provocative experiences. The foundation, like a miniature universe in its own right, was falling prey to the same fatal symptom that was confounding the Creative Force: supercomplexity. A sort of stumbling over its own feet in attempting to bring order out of self-imposed chaos.

With Bradford isolated in one of Powers' maximum security cells, there would have been no necessity for evolving the topheavy structure of justifications, and new and more intricate justifications to accommodate the rejustifications.

But no, that wouldn't have worked either. A continuously sedated Bradford would have meant choking off his sensory impressions. And should the Creative Force arouse itself sufficiently to want to sample its contemporary host's sensorium, It would encounter nothing but a wall of narcosynthetic blankness.

With that, It might be driven to seek refuge within another sanctuary. In returning to full awareness in order to effect transition, It would *have* to come to grips with *conscious* direction of its creation, which would mean collapse of the entire system. That's what those early sessions with Bradford had established years ago.

Duncan brought himself back to the somber oppression of his conference room as the door swung open. But it was not Powers who entered. Instead, an emaciated man in his late seventies shuffled toward the table, palsied hands aflutter, corded veins standing out in high relief against the saffron tautness of his scalp and striating the sagging skin of his wrists: Kadesch, head of the foundation's Scientific Survey Section.

"Yes, Kadesch?" Duncan was always uneasy whenever the man reported. You could never know whether a true fear response was being concealed by his constant atonal muscular tremors.

"It's *pi*."

"Not *another* shift in value?" The foundation director had already begun casting about mentally for special-service troops to call out.

"No. It's just that the shift has already been discovered by another investigator. There's an item in the afternoon paper."

He produced a clipping from his coat pocket.

Duncan pored over it, scorning the obtuseness of press association, reporter, editor, and headline writer who treated one of the most profound developments of the time with a brief and shallow splash of frivolity. He read aloud the boxed story:

PI IN THE SKY?

MOSCOW (AP)—Scientists In Russia were going around in circles today after Vladi Stolov, chairman of the Academy of Science's Mathematical Constants Committee, announced a new value for **pi.**

Dr. Stolov's **pi** isn't the culinary delight normally associated with "charming Billy." His is the mathematical ratio of the circumference of a circle to its diameter. And he produced the figure "3" followed by 323 decimals, which he said was the new value.

"This modification of an immutable constant," said Stolov, "most likely reflects entry of our Solar System into an area of space whose curvature deviates isometrically from normal."

Not deviating from normal in the eyes of some Western observers, however, was the Russian readiness to claim another "first" in the field of scientific investigation.

Kadesch accepted the clipping back from Duncan. "So soon!" repined the Scientific Survey chief. "They probably detected the change even before we did."

"That's why I wish we could enlist the aid of some of their research facilities," Duncan said.

"Don't be a fool! We can't take a chance on spreading such knowledge across the ideological barrier!"

It was at this point that Powers entered, haggard and strained, his intense blue eyes having lost their usual glint of geniality.

"Bradford still stabilized?" Duncan wanted to know immediately.

"Yes. And we're over the hump, I think." The psychiatrist seated himself. "There'll have to be some psychological justification to head off pseudoneurotic feedback. But I can see our way clear, at least."

There it was again, Duncan mused, the need for justification on top of justification to convince Bradford that all which had gone before were normal manifestations of his anxiety complex. A tightly woven web of deceit and false rationalization. Where would it end? It was so much like the confusing functional perplexity to which both the foundation itself and the universe that it was attempting to preserve were falling victim. It seemed to be in the nature of a supra axiom that all things should end in a chain reaction of overcomplexity—a Gordian knot so snarled that its own involutions would twist it out of the continuum of reality.

"First," Powers went on, "I want to pay tribute to Chuck and Ann. It was she who immediately summoned our standby security detail to the park. And he foresaw the necessity of convincing Bradford that he hallucinated the groovers episode."

Duncan reflected on the psyche-to-psyche encounter Bradford had experienced following that episode, as described to Powers during subsequent narcotherapy. It was so like the time Bradford's unconscious had been fed the experimental suggestion for destruction of Pluto. What keystone of material existence had gone down the drain during that reality-boggling interlude in the park?

The answer lay in the symbolism of the experience. With Pluto, the destructive suggestion had been acted out (as Bradford described it during *that* hypnotherapeutic session) in the portrayal of a magnificent Roman god who rode his grotesquely carved, ebony chariot in a great circle around his father Saturn and brothers Jupiter and Neptune—only to be consumed in dust stirred up by the rumbling wheels. That anthropomorphic representation was easily recognizable, for it had but *reflected* the direct suggestion that Pluto be destroyed. The glowfly symbolism, however, remained inscrutable, since it had been an independent act of the Creative Force.

Duncan was jarred from his thoughts as Powers rose and said, "Now for more serious matters:

"First, let me start by reassuring you that things, as of now, are under control. Bradford believes he hallucinated the groovers on Soapbox Slopes. That was easy for him to accept, since ..."

"Yes, we know," the director interjected. "Maybe we can turn circumstances to our advantage: use that—ah, freakout as a lever to convince him he's *got* to stop sneaking acid."

"That's what's being done," the psychiatrist disclosed. "But something else has come up—something that fell out during the session I just had with him." He looked down at his hands. "Bradford knows Hedgmore *isn't*—that is, *wasn't* his father."

Exclamations of dismay erupted from several section heads.

"Now he's beginning to question the validity of his inheritance," Powers continued. "And the knowledge has resurrected his suspicion of a benevolent conspiracy."

"How did he find out?" Duncan said.

There was one precaution we didn't take: altering files at the VA which showed that Hedgmore had been sterile for fourteen years when Bradford was born."

"O, God!" Hawthorn exclaimed.

"He had a contact officer—John Murdock—dig out the information for him."

"But what are we going to do about it?" Duncan pleaded. Now he rued even more the day when Bradford, casting off creation-field reflections of all the neutrons being materialized in all of space, had ridden a freight car into the range of Project Genesis' detectors. If only they hadn't decided to care for and protect him! But no, that wouldn't have worked either. For those early exploratory sessions revealed that the Creative Force was already hopelessly confused as a result of Its self-challenge. And Bradford *had* to be shielded in order to stave off collapse of a universe.

Powers rubbed his palms together. "I'm going to propose two remedies—a simple one and one that will take much courage."

Everyone hung on the words that fell with difficulty from his lips: "We'll have to indoctrinate the VA's John Murdock. At the same time we'll use his help in forging duplicate medical records."

"Can't you simply convince Bradford that he hallucinated Murdock's information too?" Hawthorn asked.

"No. It would be too easy for him to go back to the source. So we'll simply let *Murdock* convince him."

Duncan nodded. "It's beginning to seem like a not-too-difficult solution. Where does the need for courage enter?"

Avoiding their stares, Powers said, "We'll have to invent *motivation* for his having hallucinated Hedgmore's sterility. I intend to frighten him with the possibility that anxiety neurosis may be turning into paranoia."

"I don't understand," Bankston said, displaying the same frown that wrinkled his forehead at many P & D staff conferences.

"Bradford was able to come down almost a hundred percent off acid because his freakouts always featured trips with God. Scared hell out of him. He imagined another such spiritual happening when he passed out in the park three days ago."

"But that was no delusion," Duncan reminded somberly. "Nor was it the result of his mini trip. It was his symbolic interpretation of an actual physical-metaphysical occurrence."

"We know that," Powers agreed. "But he doesn't. So what we need now is a single, synthetic explanation for all three effects: the groovers' calling him Infinite One; his trip with God; and his having imagined the false fact of Hedgmore's sterility."

Duncan moaned beneath his breath. It was all so confusing—justification on top of justification—until eventually the foundation would overextend itself in frantic attempts to keep Bradford deluded.

"That explanation," said Powers, leaning forward on the table, "will be an approach to paranoia—megalomania."

"No!" Duncan protested. "Let's don't go into this thing so deep that we'll have Bradford seriously questioning his sanity."

Powers shrugged. "I admit we'll have to skirt the edge of chaos. I'm going to tell him that all of his hallucinations point to a still-unconscious but growing belief that he is God."

"Good God, no!" Duncan shouted. "That's too damn close!"

"Then you're not going to like *this*," Powers predicted. "Because that's just what he *is* beginning to think, below his conscious level. Subliminally, he's toying with the concept of a virgin father."

All the foundation needed, Duncan conceded miserably, was to have a *really* irrational Bradford on its hands. "What do you propose?"

"Let him bring those thoughts to the conscious level and be properly self-critical and frightened. Then we'll wean him away from the idea and get our program on the track again."

"I don't know," Duncan said uncertainly. "I don't know."

"I'm ready to entertain alternate suggestions."

Duncan rose and slammed his fist into his palm. "Montague!" he exclaimed, swearing. "It's got to be Montague!"

Hawthorn squinted. "How do you figure that?"

"Those kids in the park—they weren't just demonstrators! They had to be chased off by our security detail before we could retrieve

Armstrong's body. And the description of their leader fits Montague. That proves Montague didn't just disappear. When he panicked out on us, all full of superstitious fear, he didn't simply go and bury his head in the sand. He's expressed his fanaticism by founding a cult!"

Several section heads nodded in agreement.

"But," Ann said, chewing on a wan knuckle, "why would he have wanted his cult to *confront* Brad? He must have realized what the consequences would, could be. And how did Montague know Brad was going to be in the park at that particular time?"

In unison everyone at the table stopped breathing, started searching one another's grim faces.

"She's right!" Hawthorn broke through the pall of unspoken suspicion. "How *did* Montague "know?"

Duncan only nodded thoughtfully. "We've got to hunt him down and snip off whatever he's started." Then, in an aside to the Security chief: "But what to do about Montague is a matter for you and I alone to discuss, in its initial stages. We'll set up the machinery first. Later—as soon as possible, I hope—I'll make decisions that not even you will know about."

Taking no exception, Hawthorn grinned. "That's what I call *adequate* security measures: Close off all avenues to counterintelligence. My boys'll search and find, and you alone will press the destruct button."

A crude way of putting it, Duncan reflected. But the newly imposed morality had to be faced. And all possibilities of treachery within the foundation had to be guarded against. "If we don't find and eliminate Montague there'll be more Soapbox Slopes. More stimuli penetrating below Bradford's unconscious to touch off additional omnipotent destructive might. More veiled symbolism for us to figure out before we can learn what else is happening to natural law."

"The *firefly* symbolism *has* been figured out," announced an unsteady voice from the doorway.

Duncan beckoned his Astronomical Section director into the room.

"Smitherford at Palomar promised to have a plate in the mail tomorrow so I can see for myself," Irving McMillan said. "An exposure in Triangulum. It shows no evidence of 3C48. Neither does his auxiliary radio 'scope."

"What in hell," growled Hawthorn, "is 3C48?"

Duncan blanched, recognizing the symbolism immediately. "The first intergalactic body identified as a quasistellar radio source! One of Bradford's independent glowflies!"

McMillan lowered his head as though in reverence. "One of the latest cosmic innovations of the Creative Force. And now it has become one of the first untenable props to be lost in the retreat toward simplicity. It's as though 3C48 never existed."

V

All the world over, I wonder, in lands
That I never have trod,
Are the people eternally seeking for the
Signs and steps of a God?
—Sir Alfred Comyn Lyall

...◆...

Accem Suibom ... Mobius Mecca.

The temple was filling rapidly. From the dressing rooms, through beaded curtains and into the tabernacle proper drifted a stream of worshipers. A persistent osmosis of ashen-faced youths and disoriented castoffs, some embracing Cosmotheotopism only because the Rite of Topological Transformation offered means of getting "a flash from the trash without any cash."

Iggy Salvarez squirmed on the splintery floor in a dark corner and drew the groovy blond chick closer. He wasn't feeling well: dry mouth, tremors, that horrible sensation of trudging across an endless desert. This was what had come of staying off the stuff for a week—ever since that afternoon in the park. Yet, the firmness of the girl's bare shoulder as it nestled in his armpit was a compensating comfort.

He shook her again. "Marcella."

But she had recently dropped a 300-microgram tab and was full of speed as she turned half-lidded blue eyes upon his face.

"No, Yggi." And he flinched from the Topolinguistic Transformation of his name, which always sounded like a dog's yelp. "It's Allecram. If Yew—if Yoo—" her tongue tripped over the attempted inversion. She paused and tried it again, reverse syllable by reverse syllable: "If Eu-gat-nom Teh-porp hears you he'll be even more grossed out than he was over what we did to Drofdarb in the park." The Inverse One's inverse name came out without difficulty.

Hell with Montague, Iggy thought. And he consoled himself that the Prophet wouldn't be too hard on his best pusher. If it weren't for the pushers, where would he get bread to run his temple?

Marcella drifted back into STP space, her head lolling on his chest. Damn it, she wasn't supposed to get stoned! He shook her again.

A vacant smile flitted across her lips, rolled off in a sigh toward the corners of her mouth. He, too, grinned as he glanced at her insideout bra that covered but part of a reversed, flower-print halter; inverted panties overlying outside-in shorts. Laughing, he surveyed his own inverted underclothing on top of inside-out pullover and stem-grippers.

Montague's fanaticism, he conceded as he cased all the invertedly dressed worshipers in the tabernacle, had gone full blast.

Then, alarmed, Iggy shook the girl severely. "Hey, Allecram!"

She bolted upright.

"That stud over by the door—ever see him before?"

Iggy had had his eye on the fat cat for some time. He was dressed in a baggy crimson robe that seemed to be but an extension of his flowing red hair. Worn backwards and inside out of course, the garment only exaggerated his dumpy appearance.

Marcella squinted. "First time I ever saw him here."

"Not *here*. I mean out where we peddle the stuff."

She frowned. "Narcopig?"

"That's how he grabs me."

"Don't let it bug you. NPs don't go solo." She folded against him. "Drop a tab; work up some momentum for TT."

She was getting good vibes, so he let her drift off while he awaited Topological Transformation and surveyed the tabernacle scene.

Air: musky with the greased scent of many votive lamps flickering like tired stars. Walls: dirty and sooted above shelved clusters of candelabra, but animate with grotesque shadow projections of worshipers who moved about the stronger light sources. Floors: crusty boards displaying shredded scars where tiers of theater seats had been uprooted.

Mirrors. Many. And why not? Didn't they invert bilateral symmetry? And wasn't that (in its two-, instead of four-dimensional sense, of course) something like the way in which the Infinite Man was topologically transformed?

Iggy strained to watch a Cosmotheotopist in transcendental meditation. Wearing (inside-out) slacks and a psychedelic (inside-out) bosom-bulger, both pinched within reversed exterior underclothing, she sat bowing before her bilaterally inverted image in a full-length mirror. With each oscillation of her body she loosed a subdued scream. The mantra was shrill, but it was the only sound that could break her shackles of karma and lead her down the vortex of subconscious levels to absolute unity with the Primary One. Or so she said.

Circulating among the CTTs gathering for tonight's worship-in, Prophet Montague paused to bestow his blessing on the bobbing meditator.

Noise was mounting in the tabernacle: voices in droning conversation, mantric shrills or rumblings of soul-searchers seeking God-consciousness, amplified *plunks* and *twangs* from instruments of the rock group tuning up on the stage. But Iggy was close enough to hear Montague's utterance of benediction over the young chick:

"In thy meditation may thy transcendence bring complete bliss. How're you doing, Lorac?"

Between screams Carol assured, "Digging the infinite, Pro—ah, Tehporp."

"Dig well, my child. For beneath the final layer lies full understanding of the prana of Drofdarb's inverse topology."

Montague was indeed a tall man. Purple robe worn backwards and inside-out, he resembled a cloaked pole topped by a prolate spheroid. Long and thin, his dark face displayed hatchetlike severity. Many geometric figures stood out in vivid luminescence upon his shaved scalp. Through a gaping slit in each ear lobe was strung a huge, golden Mobius Strip.

Iggy turned his eyes aside. It was the sort of apparition that came with bad vibes on a freakout. Within the curve of his arm, Marcella squirmed and giggled. She was well strung out on crystal. He looked around for Tom. Hell with Montague and the seven-day, acid-free penance for directly confronting the Infinite One in the park! Marcella had dropped a tab and was getting away with it!

Just one little shot would snatch him from his hung-over purgatory. He could almost feel the stuff squirting into his arm.

There was Tom—over by the nearest icon, his inside-out hip pocket abulge with the case of hardware and juice. But even as Iggy started to cast Marcella aside, Montague drew up before the icon. With him was the short, bulgy man Iggy had earlier suspected of being a narcopig.

Gesturing with an outthrust hand, Montague told the novitiate, "This is our Crucible of Contemplated Creation." And he paused to allow time for the neo-CTT to be properly awed.

Meanwhile, curving glass sides of the vacuum chamber reflected flickering light from flanking candles while the pump beneath beat out a steady *chug-puff*, *chug-puff* to keep the dome sucked free of air.

Iggy snickered at the ludicrous sight presented by the paired companionship of the Prophet and his roly-poly neophyte. Trylon and perisphere. Were there twin perispheres standing beside the Prophet, he mused, one could well dig phallic symbolism out of the spectacle.

"Our *Holy* Crucible of Contemplated Creation!" Montague declared, insisting upon an appropriate reverential response from the novitiate.

Guitars *twanged* on the stage in a final tune-up effort. Still weaving before the mirror, the nearby meditating chick elevated her mantra's pitch. Stirring, Marcella laid her hand on Iggy's thigh and purred. Grotesque shadows chased grotesque shadows across the walls. Iggy swore and tried desperately to catch Tom's eye. If he didn't arrange for a flash, he'd soon blow his mind. Red-robed novitiate bowed as low as midriff bulge would allow, apparently not certain whether a salaam would be in order.

Satisfied with the gesture, Montague continued: "In the space now occupied by this Crucible, one Blessed Neutron has been ushered into reality every billion years." He ran a hand back over his glistening scalp, smearing the luminous geometric figures.

"And now the millennium-cubed is at hand. Soon the final billion years will be completed as the Holy Neutron is born in our Crucible.

All signs point to it, especially the presence of His Infinite Man among us. But come, let us go prostrate ourselves before the *pi* altar."

Arm about the neophyte's shoulder, Montague struck out through the throng toward the spotlighted Sacred Table, his head bobbing like a monk's in recitation of divine office. Upon the altar Iggy could see the many clusters of candles burning about a stout cylinder whose front end was capped by an elastic diaphragm.

Again he tried to attract Tom's attention. But the pusher was watching the stage where four topo dancers were limbering up for the first Cosmotheotopic hymn.

Iggy returned his stare to the *pi* altar's green tube and diaphragm. Inscribed on the membrane in glowing yellow lines were a large circle and its diametrical bisector. The elastic disc expanded and contracted continuously, like the exposed lung of a beached marine mammoth. The bold luminescent circle and its diameter stretched and shrank in cadenced cycles.

From experience, Iggy could well imagine what the Prophet was telling his neophyte as they knelt before the *pi* altar:

"Behold our commemoration of the Almighty One's alteration of *pi*. As the diaphragm deflates, *pi* assumes an ever larger value, until it reaches the new constant the Primary has decreed. All glory to Him who has raised *pi* from the transcendental to the algebraic while we strive to meditate our way out of karma into the transcendental!"

Waiting for Tom to look in his direction, Iggy shut such crap out of his mind. It wasn't that he didn't *believe*. On the contrary: He had seen absolute proof of the Divine prana behind Pluto's disappearance. But—what the hell?—all this damn gimmickry?

He jolted and Marcella lurched awake as the rock group, amplifiers blaring, blasted off with "Onward Cosmotheotopic Soldiers."

Thunderous sounds from guitars, drums, and throats assailed the ashram with concussive force. Decibel piled on top of decibel, rippling beaded curtains, intensifying the candles' flickers.

"TT Rite?" Marcella asked hopefully.

"Not yet." Then, as she relaxed, Iggy shouted. "Hey, Mot!"

But his words were smothered by the din.

"What's with it?" the girl said.

"I need a fix."

"I been bugging you to get one."

Sexing it up, the topo dancers began tossing around dayglow-tinted flesh as though trying to discover their own formula for Topological Transformation. Tripping off at low frequency, the strobe reduced their motions to spasms of flickering discontinuity.

Bulbous abdomen overhanging his waistband, a laughing Buddha circulated through the crowd. The mummer paused occasionally to guffaw while a cosmotheotopist rubbed his bronze belly and prayed for meditative transcendence. As a reward for the faithful gesture each devotee received a little-bang tab which he immediately popped into his mouth.

Iggy was just at the point of paying his obeisance and settling for the lesser flash when he looked up and saw Tom standing before him.

Trembling, he rose and peeled back his sleeve. "Shoot me!"

"Not just before Topological Transformation!" Tom protested.

"Shoot me, damn it!" Iggy shouted against the hymnal roar of "Bringing in the Neutrons." "I'm all hung out, Mot! Shoot me!"

"But the Tehporp said—"

"Hell with Eugatnom! If you don't speed me up—but *quick*—you won't get another drop of juice for that stinkin' needle!"

Reluctantly, Tom stabbed the exposed arm; said, "Have a good one," and drifted back into the crowd.

Anticipating the surge of acid bliss, Iggy joggled Marcella around to the halting beat of "Mine Eyes Have Dug the Meaning of the Prana of TT."

Bouncing and quivering, the topo dancers whirled in a flurry of flailing arms, kicking legs and thrashing hair as the next hymn began. The laughing Buddha's guffaws surmounted even the amplified jumble of the dissonance that was "God Ain't Dead; He Just Copped Out!" Worshipers-in worked themselves into a frenzy as they tried to rival, in their own inadequate manner, the topos' gyrations. In determined tempo the Crucible of Contemplated Creation's vacuum pump went *chug-puff, chug-puff.* The *pi* altar's glowing diaphragm bulged out, in, out, in.

Somebody monkeyed with the strobe light and its flashes were suddenly spaced out, exaggerating the discontinuity of the dancers' motions. Even the guitar strings seemed mired in slow motion, oscillating like limp spaghetti against their fretted keyboards. A dark-skinned youth collapsed and began writhing on the floor, neck stretched back and rigid arms quivering.

"Hey!" someone shouted. "Step up that strobe freq! You just triggered off Yllib!"

But nobody seemed concerned.

For a moment Iggy fought off the onrushing tide of euphoria as he watched Billy's thrashing. The CTT's eyes were rolled up beneath open lids and crimson foam was bubbling out of his mouth.

Iggy started over toward the convulsing youth, but remembered what a wonderful aura accompanied the seizures—sensations as glorious as pure God-consciousness itself. Hadn't Montague given his blessing and confirmed them as true prana?

Glancing at a small group near the foot of the stage, Iggy recognized Marlow, from the estab—rather, the foundation's Mathematical Section. He was well disguised with fuzz, face paint, and padded rags, as Montague had always insisted that he be whenever visiting Mobius Mecca—just in case someone else from the foundation came nosing around. Good cat that Marlow! He kept the Prophet informed on everything the heretics on Addison Avenue were doing with the Infinite Man. Lucky they had converted him to CTT on first approach.

And Iggy felt strung out in self-importance over the fact that the Prophet had confided in only himself and Marcella on Marlow's undercover role.

Profound silence crashed down upon the tabernacle as the stage's curtains parted. Only the *chug-puffs* of the Crucible of Creation's pump persisted—softly, like the breathing of a slumbering infant.

Iggy's eyes were drawn to the magnificent spectacle of the Prophet, purple robe flaring from elevated arms. Montague was the essence of devotion in his raised pulpit, suspended on a boom projecting from the rear of the stage. In the strobe's flickering brilliance a many-angled tesseract painted on his forehead stood out like some complex pattern of frozen lightning.

Perhaps thirty feet in diameter, a stout ribbon of reinforced concrete ringed his pulpit like a vertical halo—Mobius Mecca's Mobius Strip, supported by steel beams attached to its edges.

Marcella marveled, "Oh, the TT strip! See how the great Pirts Suibom makes its halfway twist at the top? How it joins itself again so that it has only *one* side? *One* side, when we can *see two!* And—Alol's going to *ride* the Pirts!"

The Mobius Strip held Iggy's enrapt attention, even despite the acid that was now urging him on to exciting things. But what could be more exciting than Lola performing the Rite of Topological Transformation?

His eyes traced the cogged rail that negotiated the complete course of the ribbon, running along both sides of the one-sided strip, twice making the 180° twist of the loop's upper half. It was as though his mind were being sucked into the intricacy of the topological wonder. His head moved in circles as his eyes went round and round. The one-sided, looped band with two sides *was* incomprehensible! He just couldn't *dig* it!

He escaped hypnotic immersion by staring at the electric cogcart on the bottom upper surface of the strip, just below Montague's pulpit. The chick on the cart was groovy enough to hold his attention. A tall, auburn-haired sexcrucible, Lola, too, stood with arms elevated. Her feet were locked in the cog platform's pedal straps, but a flowing robe concealed the belt that secured her to the cart's upright beam.

The chant started softly at first. But it grew in volume until the tabernacle was reverberating with:

What say, hip? ... Get a grip ... Do your strip ... while you take a trip ... on the Mobius Strip!

With an eager smile, the sexcrucible moved her hand to the cogcart's switch and glanced expectantly at Montague. But, without doubt, the Prophet would have something to say first about the incident in the park before he began the Rite of Topological Transformation. Anxious to hear the anticipated comments, Iggy led Marcella toward the stage.

Montague cast his voice in somber pitch and intoned: "Of the Trimurti, Vishnu, the Maintainer of the Universe, had three avatars."

"Oh, no!" chanted the well-coached assembly. "Now there are four!"

"First there was Balarama."

"Great Balarama!" shouted the congregation.

Prophet: "And Parashurama."

Chorus: "Noble Parashurama!"

Prophet: "And Ramachandra."

Chorus: "Let us not forget Ramachandra!"

Montague bowed. "And now there is—Ramadrofdarb!"

"O, RAMADROFDARB! O, INVERSE VESSEL! O, INFINITE ONE!"

With outstretched hands, the Prophet demanded silence.

But a bold voice from the rear dissented: "Avatar of Buddha!"

"No!" someone else challenged. "Incarnation of Mohammed!"

Then: "Stuff it! Saoshayant, the Messiah!"

"*The* Messiah!"

"*Second* Coming!"

"Ormuzd Himself!"

Somberly: "Our Father Who art …"

Objecting: "Our *Mother* Who art …"

"*Father*!"

"*Mother*!" insisted a man who had half mounted the stage steps and who, Iggy noticed, wore inverted priestly vestments. "Pius Twelfth said we are not to overlook His *motherly* attributes!"

Across the temple a thin man jumped up and down, motions restricted by inside-out ministerial garb. He cupped his hands and shouted mediatively through them: "All right, then—'Our Mofather Who art in Heaven'!"

Montague scowled at the outpouring of personal cultism. "The Primary is *all* of those—and more: Providence, the First Cause, Supreme Soul, Indra, Great Spirit, Ahura Mazda, Universal Essence. In His Infinite Wisdom He has inspired all of those concepts—all except one."

His face was streaked with luminous paint that had trickled down, together with perspiration, from the geometric patterns decorating his forehead and scalp. All full of speed now, Iggy had to laugh at the Prophet, who resembled a purple votive candle that was just beginning to drip wax.

"All except one," Montague repeated. "The Primary is *not* the cold, impersonal, sentient Creative Force the heretics say He is."

"Oh, damn the infidels!" shouted the congregation.

"Oh, yes," the Prophet agreed. "Damn those who have captured the Primary's Inverse Vessel and are synthesizing false karma for Him!"

"We must rescue the Infinite Man!" demanded the assembly.

"Rescue Him we must, but not now. For the infidels are strong. But, by standing fast to our faith in the manifestation of theological prana, through cosmology and topology, we Cosmotheotopists shall surely become powerful enough to wrest Drofdarb from the heretics!"

"Deliver Him *now*!" someone shouted. "Let us prepare His hegira!"

"Now," the Prophet lamented, "is not the time. For this reason I have not yet revealed Drofdarb's secular identity, except to a chosen few. And perhaps even that restricted revelation was a mistake."

Montague leaned forward against the front panel of his tulip-shaped pulpit, appearing much like an elongated clapper protruding above the lip of its inverted mission bell. "Yes," he reaffirmed, "it *was* a mistake. I thought I would take some of you to the park and let you bask in the *nearness* of the Divine Presence while we pretended to be there for a demonstration. But you were not content to adore from a distance when the Inverse Vessel came into sight. Upon His sudden appearance you had to worship *at his feet*!"

Huffing his admonition through clenched teeth, he began pounding the pulpit rail. "I'm *glad* the establishment's—the foundation's—forces hit the scene and clobbered enough of you to make us all split out! Don't you realize what *almost* happened in the park that day? Don't you know what would happen if Drofdarb should become aware of what He is—under such hectic circumstances?"

He calmed himself with evident self-restraint. "At least, that experience ought to be a lesson. And if anyone is thinking of countertransforming the Infinite One's topologically inverted name and tracing down His full secular identity and whereabouts, let him take warning for himself and the whole world. There is only *one way* Drofdarb can be approached without bringing about a universal cop-out. And only *I* know that way!"

Almost at the foot of the stage now as he pressed forward through the crowd, Iggy led Marcella sideways toward the steps where they would be out of the range of Montague's fierce stare.

The sexcrucible on the cogcart supplicated, "How long, O, Tehporp, before we can reach the Primary through His Inverse Vessel?"

"Not long," Montague assured. "Cosmic karma is almost consummated. Many prophets have placed Armageddon at the end of the Second Millennium. It is now 1985. Zoroaster himself dated his fourth 3000-year epoch from the year of his birth. He was born in 1000 B.C. Thus it is that He Whom Zoroaster regarded as His remote Son, the Messiah Saoshayant, is among us, with only fifteen years left in the last epoch."

Chorus: "Saoshayant—Drofdarb! Saoshayant—Drofdarb! Sao ..."

But Lola, looking up from her cogcart, interrupted the emergent chant. "Show us again, O, Tehporp Yloh, Drofdarb's topological configuration."

Iggy reached the stairs leading up to the stage and found himself standing next to the fat red-robed neophyte. The cat seemed to be in a trance, his stare never straying from the pulpit.

A spotlight flared and Iggy's eyes followed Montague's extended arm as it pointed to the immense surrealistic drawing that dominated the backdrop. In the center were the earth, planets, stars, the moon, sun, galaxies, nebulae—all surrounded by an outline that was almost too complex to follow. From the bold, encompassing line an arm extended inward here toward the enclosed celestial scene, another there. One inside-out foot stood upon the huge earth while the other was raised above it. Over there, the heavy universe-containing line became an inward-looking eye, trained on the captive sun; over there, another, trained on a galaxy. An inverted mouth was open toward a star cluster. Two ears, projecting randomly from the line, seemed to be listening to a cluster of galaxies. On the outside of the impossibly twisted boundary enclosing the cosmos was a helter-skelter arrangement of internal human organs—all somehow connected to proper surface features of the inside-out man.

"Behold our Drofdarb Yloh!" exhorted Montague. "Behold our Inverse Vessel, our Infinite Man!"

"Behold Him! Behold Him!" chorused the congregation.

"Lo! Our topologically transformed Drofdarb! Enclosing a finite cosmos within the outside of His infinite body! Only, the outside is actually the inside. For, what we regard as His inside is, in truth, His outside and extends endlessly in all directions away from the universe."

Iggy tried again to dig the Topological Transformation that would allow him to understand this most basic of all mortal truths. But his mind just wouldn't make the final, decisive twist—just as it couldn't negotiate the incredible loop of the Mobius Strip.

"You must meditate, my followers!" roared Montague. "Appreciation of Drofdarb as the Infinite Man must be the singular objective of all your transcendental efforts. You must see that it is a Drofdarb-peripheric universe. Just imagine the hand of the Primary as having reached down Drofdarb's throat and snapped Him inside-out. The formerly outside skin of His body would then enclose a finite cavity—the Cosmic Crucible."

Iggy reeled with the incomprehensible thought. Swaying, he fell against the pudgy, robed neophyte. He straightened himself, but retained the vague impression that he had brushed against metal-hard, round objects instead of soft bulges of fat beneath the flowing red garment.

The Prophet bowed his head momentarily then, in a single swift motion like the unsheathing of two switchblades, his arms sprang outward and upward. "Let us now venerate He who came before me and was first to visualize the Infinite Man and portray him in his Holy Text."

A brilliant spot beamed down from the fly loft and centered its cone of radiance on a table supporting an open book within its protective glass case. Iggy had once been allowed to handle the Holy Text and, even though he was too far away now to discern the printed matter on display, he knew that the illustration had inspired the stage's "Infinite Man" backdrop. He nodded in reverence for The Viking Press and for the then-unrecognized profound truth it had published.

"All praise to He Who came before—Womag Egroeg!" Montague intoned. "All praise for His 'One Two Three ... Infinity'! In His sketch, Womag most likely didn't even know He was really *digging* infinity. But He was—whether he was doing it wittingly or unwittingly. He *must* have been inspired by the Primary One to tell it like it was going to be. For the Infinite Man *did* make the scene, thirty-three years later—messiah-like, though unaware of His identity and role."

Murmurs of awe swept like a tide and ebb tide over Mobius Mecca's congregation. Then the chant resumed:

What say, hip? .... Get a grip! ... Do your strip ... while you take a trip ... on the Mobius Strip!

Montague nodded at Lola. She shrilled her delight and threw the cogcart switch. Locked to its tracks, the vehicle started off slowly, laboring up the left-hand inner surface of the Mobius Strip.

"Behold," shouted the Prophet, "—our Rite of Topological Transformation! Like Drofdarb, the Pirts itself is turned inside-out. Thus do we commemorate the Inverse Vessel's Cosmologic Configuration."

Secured by foot straps and waist belt, Lola neared the top of the loop, screaming more ecstatically while the platform tilted almost upsidedown with the curve of its rails. Then she continued through the contortion that snapped her horizontal and brought her upright again as the cart started down the outer surface of the right-hand descending arc.

Gathering momentum, she completed the downcurving segment. Then she hung upside down and her hair swished against the floor at the nadir of the strip. Here she screamed once more, but it seemed to Iggy that now the outcry was more an expression of fear than rapture.

Up along the left-hand outside surface. Horizontal again—this time with her body aimed away from the swaying, "oohing" and "aahing" congregation. Then the snapping motion that inverted her briefly before the cogcart went plunging down the inner right-hand curve of the loop toward its starting point.

Round and round. Snap. Horizontal Snap. Upside down. Traveling both sides of the one-sided Mobius Strip. Shrieking in ecstasy and fear.

Iggy's neck hurt as he swiveled his head to follow the rite of TT. So confusing were the motions that the flash from Tom's needle began subsiding.

The rock group blared out its souped-up version of "The Primary One" and, clapping and stomping frenziedly, everyone roared the words of their sacred hymn.

in
lost Him-
One all
Pri- y was
mar-
self,
The

So He
an- chored for darb;
rest Drof-
in

from
way its
built a-
world has runs
He
shelf,
But the

Oh, so
in-tri-cate garb.
now its
is

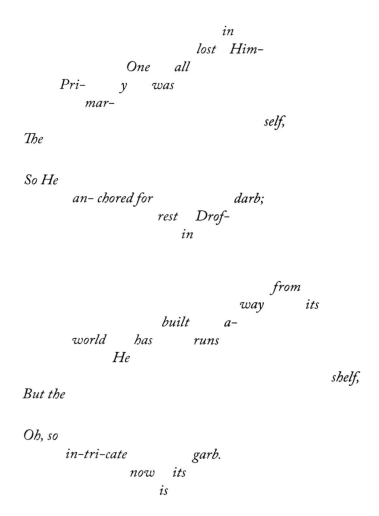

The tune, though hard-rocked, was familiar. Iggy remembered his grandma singing it when he was a child. Only, *her* funereal-paced lyrics were all about grandfather and a clock.

Screaming more loudly, Lola reached the top of her loop and, as she was wrenched to the horizontal, cast her cloak out over the assembly. Now she wore only panties and a bra with many flailing tassels.

In the excited surge of motion that ran through the crowd, Iggy again jostled the red-robed novitiate. And once more there was the impression of encountering balls of metal rather than bulges of flesh.

Marcella and scores of others shrilled their delight at the stage while Montague, with sweeping gestures, blessed Lola's circumgyrations.

years
slum-
All these with- out ber- ing, darb, darb),
(Drof- Drof-

no-
cum-
In- va- tions ber- ing, darb, darb).
(Drof- Drof-

go
nev- er to a-
SHORT,
STOP—
gain,
Earth'll

Should the
Ves- die.
sel

Between choruses the Crucible of Continuous Creation's vacuum pump asserted its presence with excited *chug-puffs*. The *pi* altar's diaphragm hissed out, in, out, in. Freezing Lola's looping motions into a discontinuous series of stopaction images, the strobe light flashed persistently. Someone continued to shout for help for the convulsing Billy.

The sexcrucible on the cogcart again reached the loop's apex and off came her bra. As she started on the downslope she began working the top hem of her panties off her waist, past her abdomen and hips.

Iggy shook his head briskly to clear away some of the acid. He cast a sidelong glance at the stout neophyte in the crimson cloak. Metal objects hidden under his garments! Hadn't Montague warned about …

He seized Marcella and pulled her onto the stage, lunging for the rear of the pulpit. No telling how much time he had left!

He
face did
in own
chal- ges His
len-
hurl
The

Were too
much for the One;
Pri- y
mar-

lus-
il- ive
end our
now the of
it's
world,
Un-til

And the
u- ni- verse done,
too all
is

Lola screamed exuberantly and tossed out her panties.

Iggy shouted up at Montague and lurched through a door behind the pulpit. In opening it, he had removed a leering eye and half a galaxy from the sketch representing Drofdarb's Topological Transformation.

The Prophet managed his escape too, but just barely. As he came scurrying through the doorway the first bomb went off. The stage's rear wall collapsed, offering the fleeing trio a glimpse of the Mobius Strip being wrested from its moorings and lashing out into the tabernacle proper. Lola and her cogcart were hurled into a side wall. Three more bombs exploded as Iggy, Marcella, and Montague sprinted down the alley to the latter's car.

VI

Dissolution:

What a fool the Creative Force must be to imagine that simple withdrawal would leave His (His?) *universe free to achieve stability. Oh, what an advantage there was to being the Other Force! Destruction need not be justified within a rigid framework of dissolutive causes. It was sufficient that a free neutron should decay into a beta particle and an atom of hydrogen, or that a star should immolate itself in fiery discharge. There need not be an empirical why or how.*

Many things might have causative origins: dissipation of nuclear force through electron descent, the crushing impact of an earthquake, expenditure of a sun's fuel to send it plunging into the dwarf or black-body category, sociopolitical complexities leading to delightful self-destruction. But none of these dissolutive processes had to be justified among the others as a whole. They could all be entirely capricious.

The Constructor, on the other hand, had challenged Himself to push development of principle and particle and interaction in many directions, leaving a multiplicity of loose ends; to hope that, through His own ingenuity, He could synthesize explanations that would embrace all of the inconsistencies.

Once: three elementary particles. Now: hundreds. At first only a sphere of fixed stars. Finally: suns and nebulae and galaxies in such preposterous motion that a limiting speed had to be imposed.

And now there had been another concession: The things that weren't galaxies and weren't stars—that couldn't be "explained" within any of the directions empirical knowledge had taken—had had to go. What else would have to be sacrificed?

...◆...

Shoulders aslump, Bradford paced the tiled terrace of his penthouse apartment. Abruptly he turned to face the glass-top table around which sat Ann, Chuck, and Dr. Powers. He met none of their stares, though; for each had looked away just in time.

He glanced down at the headlighted traffic far below. Like a prisoner, he gripped the steel rods stretching from parapet to roof overhang. Three days ago the bars had not been there. Now they were. Why? Did they imagine he might kill himself?

He spun around—just in time to catch them glancing away. Were they observing his reactions to the caging-in of his terrace?

Yet, he couldn't resent their solicitude. For strange things *had* gone on in his mind. There had been his hallucinations in the park. Hallucinations? Yes; they could have been no more than that. For it had so pained Ann and Chuck first to reveal, then gently insist that he had simply collapsed upon seeing the private detective's body, that there had in reality been no wild scene of groovers dancing about him.

He lit a cigarette and tossed the match between the bars, watched air currents snuff out its descending, fluttering light. Hallucinations warranted bars, he conceded. But how do you determine where the hallucinations end? Take that telephone call from the VA contact officer at the clubhouse: It had *seemed* so real. But no: He had been assured he'd hallucinated it too. *That* had definitely been an instance of getting strung out without benefit of acid. How could he tell what was reality and what wasn't?

He laced his three observers with a bold stare, determined that they would look upon him with pity only at the expense of meeting his eyes directly.

Ostensibly withdrawn, Powers appeared to be composing the substance of their next therapeutic talk-out. Chuck was being purposely humane, pretending interest in the program coming through his transistor. Ann, on the other hand, had been more genuinely sympathetic than ever. He could sense her compassion—no, not compassion: love—reaching out to him, appealing for recognition and acceptance. But—God!—these unprovoked freakouts! How could he ever give fully, knowing all the while that the bed might turn into quicksand in a miasmic swamp; or the walls of his room might suddenly metamorphose into charging monsters; or that he might glance up and see the Infinite Presence hanging by a hairy arm from the light fixture? Or even find himself impotent because of his fears?

More distressed, he fingered the bars of his cage, not realizing he had said aloud the "why" that he had intended to demand only of himself.

Powers came over and cuffed him on the shoulder. He rattled one of the bars demonstratively. "For your safety, Brad."

Despite the other's aura of genial affection, despite his soft blue eyes that smiled out of the folds of an affable face, Bradford raised his voice harshly: "So I'm off my nut."

And he was aware of Ann's wincing at the outburst.

"No, son," Powers soothed. "We're completely in control. We *know* the root of your disorientation. You have only to set things in their proper perspective within yourself."

"But why should I imagine things that don't happen?"

"Sneaking euphoria pellets on the side doesn't help out any, you know. You should also know by now that every time you suck on a little-bang plug I'll find out about it in our next session."

"I've kicked it completely; I'm going to stay off the stuff," Bradford promised. "But why do I freak out even when the effects of mini manna ought to be long over? I just can't dig *that*."

Powers led him over to a wrought-iron settee. "Since you're asking questions, time has come to answer them. These illusions all fit into a framework of uncertainty over your entitlement to Hedgmore's bequest."

"I won't believe that telephone call from the VA man at the clubhouse was an hallucination. I don't have that kind of simple 'lucy in a freakout."

"In other words, you insist Hedgmore couldn't have been your father because he was sterile for many years before you were born?"

"Right. That phone call at the clubhouse was no 'lucy."

"Very well, Brad." Powers indicated the telephone next to Chuck's radio. "You have only to call Contact Officer Murdock and ask whether he transmitted such information to you."

Bradford sprang to his feet. "You *want* me to believe there was no such call! How do I know you haven't already ..."

"—conspired with Murdock? Threatened to report him for violating confidential files if he doesn't deny phoning you at the club?"

Bradford strode toward the telephone, paused, returned.

Powers thumped him on the shoulder. "Good boy! You've passed the first checkpoint. You won't make the call because you're afraid of what you'll hear. You realize that suspicions of conspiracy mark the beginning of paranoia. And you'll be damned if you'll be a paranoid."

Despite the warm assurance, Bradford insisted, "I don't dig how the phone call fits into the pattern of irrational delusions."

"All right, we'll go over it again: Because of your unreasonable windfall from dubious origins you become obsessed with the conviction that somebody up there is smiling favorably down upon you."

Bradford watched Ann look up sharply. Was there a flicker of dismay in her eyes? Evidently not; for now she was smiling reassuringly.

"You're Providence's fair-haired boy," Powers resumed. "You transfer this *unconscious* notion to the obsession that you are being watched over, protected. Then, all of a sudden, your suspicions are confirmed; but you are handed a perfectly reasonable explanation of *why* you're being followed—investigation by a big corporation checking on the soundness of its investments.

"At the same time, though, one of your watchers commits suicide. Why, we don't know. But, because he killed himself immediately after contact with you, you assume guilt. A traumatic experience indeed."

"If only that suicide had been an illusion too," Bradford said.

"See? There you have it: guilt over the loss of a human life. That's what your unconscious was shouting at you when you saw the man lying dead."

"And that's what started the hallucinations?"

Powers nodded. "One of the hallucinations you recognized for what it was: the glowfly delusion—a sort of regression to the trips of your narcotics kick. And, don't forget: You *had* dropped a plug—just a half hour earlier. But a simple trip wasn't enough. You had to project delusions backward to a bizarre groovers' sequence preceding your collapse, and forward to Murdock's illusionary telephone call."

Bradford paced in front of the settee. "I still don't understand it. I don't see *why*!"

Powers stood and trapped his shoulders between hands that were firm but tender in their grip. "This part isn't going to be easy, Brad. But let's dive into it anyway." He muted his words so that Ann and Chuck wouldn't hear. "You a good Christian?"

"I usually get spaced out and make Christmas services. But I don't see ..."

"Accept the general run of Christian dogma?"

"Some of the stuff."

"What about the tenet of Virgin birth?"

Bradford paused cautiously. "Used to dig it; don't think about it much any more."

"Not consciously, anyway. But—see any analogy between that concept and your own psychic foundations?"

Bradford only frowned. Powers studied his face expectantly.

"Born of a eunuch father?" the latter suggested.

"I don't understand."

I'll spell it out then. What we've snipped was an inclination toward paranoid megalomania. Theomania."

Swearing in protest, Bradford shoved him away.

Ann, hand to her mouth, sucked in a startled breath. Chuck, grimacing, turned up the volume of his radio. So that they would hear no more of this screwy dialogue? Bradford didn't blame them.

Powers, however, disregarded his patient's invective and forced him back down onto the settee. "No, Brad. You're going to hear it all out, completely. It's going to make sense and you'll know I'm right."

Tolerant now, Bradford waited.

"As in your freakout days," the psychiatrist continued, "you went on a trip with God—stimulated this time by a traumatic experience, a suicide, and just a residual touch of acid. But was it a trip *with* God, or *by* God? If it had been an experience realized by God alone—by *you* alone—then the private detective's suicide would have been an unquestionable Act of Providence.

"In order to assure yourself that this was a Divine consequence, you conjured up, in retrospect, a group of groovers on Soapbox Slopes; had them pay homage to you, in their own far-out way. To cap it all off and make your illusion complete, you decided to hallucinate your own siring by a virgin father. Unconsciously, of course."

Bradford lowered his face so that none of them would witness his chagrin. "Then, *unconsciously*, I've flipped." Groping for something outside of himself to cling to, he became aware of the newscaster's voice from Chuck's radio:

"Authorities today are still investigating, but without success, last Tuesday night's bombing of a Doomsday sect's temple that resulted in forty-two deaths and hospitalization of seventy-one other persons. Surviving members of the God-walks-among-us zealots say that ...

"Shut that damn thing off!" Powers shouted.

Radio silenced, Chuck and Ann retreated into the apartment.

"Go find that guy who's God among us," Bradford said remotely. "Let him and me fight it out for the honor."

"I think it's time for a therapeutic session, now that you have full conscious appreciation of all the factors."

Powers locked the door and brought out his bag.

...◆...

Bradford found himself in the infinitesimal.

But, even while plunging into his own unconscious, he sensed there would be nothing to serve as an orienting anchor. For, of all these narcotherapeutic sessions, none had left any memories to which he might later refer. This absolute blankness of recall, he supposed, must be an externally-imposed condition.

Soon he went through the abrupt twist that left him almost stripped of identity, reduced to but a disembodied point of pseudoconscious awareness. Floating, spinning, drifting, descending—where?

Past symmetrical groupings of shimmering spheres—crystal-like in arrangement, held together in their polyhedral unity by webs of pure force that could never be perceived by visual organs. Molecules?

Row after row, tier upon tier of the silvery polyhedrons stretching to infinity. And, with explosive force, they were expanding in size until the locus of percipience which Bradford identified as his astral self was lost among them. One of the formations of spheres swept toward him, until it seemed that the single glittering orb at the apex of the latticework occupied half of infinity. In the other direction there was only darkness.

Down, Brad! *The Voice pounded at him from beyond the ebon void.* Down among the basic forces! Where else should one look for the Creative Force except among the fundamental units of Creation?

(Suddenly Bradford wondered why he should be looking for a—Creative Force. What sort of farce was this? What had it to do with Powers' therapeutic method? No. He wouldn't do it; wouldn't play the psychiatrist's game, whatever *it was. Try as he may, though, he went along, excusing his lack of will with the explanation that this was, after all,* hypno*therapy.)*

Yes, Brad. This *is* hypnotherapy. And you've no choice. Proceed.

The single, coruscating sphere swooped down upon him, and Bradford pierced its shell as effortlessly as a diver plunging into still water. But how else would matterless percipience meet immaterial force?

Darkness, then another spherical shell centered within the outer one. More darkness. Another shell. Another. Each onionskin radiant with powerful lines of force that chased one another across its surface. Abruptly, like a streak of lightning, one of the lines gathered itself into a bristling point on the curve of the shell he had just penetrated and sparked down to the next inner sphere. Meanwhile, residual radiance collected at the locus of departure and lanced through the outer, concentric onionskins into the singular blackness beyond.

Find It, damn it! *the Voice boomed.* Make It understand that a more deserving vessel awaits Its occupancy! Tell It I am ready to receive It from you!

(It? *What was It? Then, through the film of drug-induced hypnosis, Bradford recalled that all of his pre-Powers freakouts involved* trips with God! *Was there* really *an Infinite Presence? Was* that *what Powers was trying to make him find? If so, why? And why should he go along with something like* that?)

Because I say so! Now look, look, look! Hunt! Search! Find!

Many jarring impacts, carrying with them the impression of moist palm slamming against relaxed cheek.

Down. Down. Ever shrinking. Ever dwindling toward the nonentity that lay just below the transultimate division of the ultimately indivisible. Down through the last glowing spherical envelope. Twirling, spinning, looping in on the brilliant central orb that sent its powerful forces out to hold together all of the onionskins-within-onionskins.

Bradford felt a numbing fear as his astral counterpart plunged through the nuclear shell and was caught up in a great whirling confusion of globular forces—surging and churning to break the bond that enforced cohesion.

This dazzling ball of energy that maintained all of the globular forces in immutable captivity—was this *It?*

Find out! If It's part of the Creative Force, then It will respond! *Another jarring impact—this time conveying the impression of knuckles crashing against cheekbone.* It must transfer to me!

(But Bradford didn't want *It to respond. Not if that was what* Powers *wanted. Just suppose there* were *an Infinite Presence. And suppose It could be contacted—possessed?—by someone. Why should that person be Powers? Bradford thought of the profound possibilities of such a possession. In the hands of the possessor would be power unlimited. More than that: a chance, perhaps, to reshape the world—to bring goodness and peace and harmony and shared resources such as humanity had never known before. Why, the possessor of It could be a new Messiah!)*

No one's going to possess It but me! *Another jarring, head-snapping impact.*

(And Bradford realized he had been wrong. Not only was Powers not worthy of such an association: Neither was he. Nor anyone—not in this day, this time, on this mangy, undeserving world. Still, the hunt was an imperative that he couldn't *defy. So:)*

Down toward the center of the pivotal sphere of lustrous energy, past many surging globes that fought one another with a fury born of the necessity to repel.

Then Bradford realized the Infinite Presence had been with him *all along—just as It had been on all of his acid-stoked trips. Only, the association was so subtle that he couldn't recognize it. Yet, he should have guessed. For this astral descent into the maelstrom of the microcosm would have been impossible on his own.*

One of the vibrant globes loomed directly ahead in the dazzling medium of unifying energy. Unable to avoid collision, he impacted.

FISSION!

Instant disruption of the nuclear medium. Globules, freed of their bonds, hurtling in all directions. Onionskins peeling off; disintegrating, crumbling, releasing their lines of force which, in turn, gathered into vivid points and lashed out into the eternal darkness. The skins themselves collapsing into yet other points of brilliance that lanced out to overtake the ones which had already streaked away.

…◆…

Ann was seated at the other end of the settee when Bradford opened his eyes. "Welcome back," she said, smiling. "You're right on time. Dr. Powers said it would be about fifteen minutes."

"He left?" Bradford tried to recall what had gone on during the session. But, as always, his memory was blank. Only, this time the talk-out had left his throat parched.

"He was called to his clinic. Told us you'd be all right, though."

And he was, except for the bruise on his cheek. As he felt the hurtful area, she explained, "Powers said your head hit the armrest."

Through the doorway he could see Chuck talking with a much shorter man in the reception room. "But I've been trying to get Mr. Bradford on the phone for four days," the latter was objecting. "Only, they say he isn't receiving any calls."

"Or callers either," Chuck disclosed. "How'd *you* get up here?"

"Mr. Bankston at his P & D office wrote a note to the desk clerk."

As Chuck moved to usher the man out, Bradford recognized him—John Murdock from the VA!—and hurried over.

Murdock said, "You're a hard man to reach, Mr. Bradford. I have that information you asked me to look up."

He handed over several Xerox copies of official documents. Bradford steadied his hand and looked at them.

"I tried to get you the same afternoon you asked for this," Murdock went on. "But you haven't been back to your office since."

"What," Bradford asked, bracing himself, "do these say?"

"That Mr. Hedgmore's compensation was based on surgical removal of his left kidney. It was shattered by a .50-caliber slug."

…◆…

At the foundation, Director Duncan stood at the head of his conference table and studied the astronomical plates laid out before him. Encountering the avalanche of evidence, his eyes seemed to shrink beneath their bushy, white brows. "Are these all of them?"

"All we've been able to get copies of so far," said Irving McMillan, Astronomical Section chief.

"You think it's a universal phenomenon?"

"Of course. Every quasar that's been checked until now just doesn't exist any longer—as far as both optical and radio emissions are concerned. It fits Bradford's glowfly symbolism precisely. Except that even their trains of light-in-transit seemed to have been snuffed out too."

Duncan looked out into the faces that stared back at him from around the table, expecting him to comment, instruct, order—as though he were a chief of staff. And he *was*, but it was a responsibility forced upon him by circumstances. He longed for the company of a slide rule and blackboard in his locked study. But these would be forevermore denied him while he wrestled with bizarre strategy. If only his staff wouldn't give the impression that they trusted him to come up with an absolute solution for each crisis!

Fred Wheatstone, publications monitor, exhibited newspaper clippings. "The *pi* change is spilling off political repercussions. Several noncommitted nations are speculating that space curvature has been affected by resumption of orbital hydrogen-device testing."

"God!" exclaimed Duncan. "What will they say when disappearance of the quasars becomes general knowledge?"

"We've got a reprieve there," McMillan comforted. "Smitherford at Palomar is apparently the only observer who's aware of the general nature of this thing. And he's keeping quiet until he can prepare a paper."

"What's to keep someone else from making the same discovery?"

"Nothing. So we don't know just how long a reprieve we have."

"Our main concern is the possibility of feedback. If Bradford hears about some of these things, the information may get through below his unconscious and trigger more cosmic upheavals!"

Duncan found himself entertaining wistful thoughts of simply killing Bradford. Then the anxiety, the agony of waiting for the inevitable would be over. For Bradford's death would wrest the Creative Force from Its sanctuary and It would again become a free agent, charged with the impossible responsibility of conscious control.

Wheatstone waved more clippings. "More about *pi*: Peking charges that the change in value resulted from a new weapon being tested by one of the major powers. They threaten ..."

Powers cut him off. "I, too, have been concerned over chaotic feedback. We can provide much better isolation for Bradford if you let me prescribe an indefinite period of relaxation at his lodge on the coast."

"Would he take the time off from P & D?" McMillan asked.

"I can implant receptivity to that suggestion."

Duncan looked up. "How could his absence be explained?"

It was Bankston who answered, in his capacity as P & D real estate specialist: "I've already spread word among the staff that his bout with flu is over, but that he now feels he needs an extended vacation."

"What about the *double* absence of Bradford and Miss Fowler?"

Bankston laughed. "Clark is already whispering against the back of his hand, 'Like father, like son.' But secretarial aid outside of the office draws no raised eyebrows these days."

"Good," Duncan said. "I'd want Ann and Chuck, at least, to be with him constantly."

Hawthorn kneaded his blunt chin. "My boys won't be far away."

Duncan squinted at his security chief. "I'm not certain whether your boys should have anything to do with this."

"Why not? Because Smith got carried away with his assignment at the temple? So he made a mistake. He paid for it with his life, didn't he?"

"Smith wasn't supposed to go armed. I sent him only to confirm Montague's involvement in Mobius Mecca." The director rose and glowered at Hawthorn. "But what did *you* do? You anticipated both my selection of Smith and the orders he would be given. And *you* overruled *me*, sending the man there with bombs!"

Hawthorn bristled in self-defense. "It was the only logical way to take care of Montague and his kooks!"

"But you *didn't* take care of Montague. Not one of our agents was able to identify anything that looked like him in the morgue or among the survivors!"

"So he got away." The security chief shrugged. Then he chuckled expectantly. "But we *did* identify *your* Mathematical Section head among the victims. We found out it was Marlow who had been sneaking information to Mobius Mecca and how Montague happened to be in the park at the same time Bradford was there."

The director was silent. He still couldn't understand how *Marlow*, of all his personnel, had betrayed the foundation. The mathematician must have been unable to cope with all the awful, irrational developments that were unfolding before him. But—a *sellout*? Like the tip of a dagger sinking inexorably into his chest, realization came upon Duncan that the outrageous pattern of existence which they had formulated could make *anyone* seek extrascientific refuge—perhaps even himself, someday.

"And don't forget," Hawthorn went on, pressing his advantage, "you screened Marlow yourself—before I took over our security section, before I even knew the foundation and Bradford existed. He was *your* responsibility."

Duncan was going to tell him that, with regard to Smith's unprogrammed action, there was no room for variable factors in these ultimately crucial circumstances; that rigid discipline must be imposed over observation and empirical verification leading to the most delicately controlled stimuli—if the elicited responses weren't to be cosmocataclysmic.

But what could he say? Elimination of the cosmotheotopic spy Marlow as a random effect and destruction of Mobius Mecca *had* been of high priority. And it was still possible Montague had been mortally wounded or crippled enough, wherever he might be hiding, that he could no longer play out his role of the initially impacting particle in a critical-mass universe bent on chain reaction.

After a while Duncan said, "This final point: We shall try to reach at least one nonpolitically oriented source in the Soviet Academy of Science, ease the burden on ourselves, spread the foundation's load."

"But you can't do that!" Powers protested.

"Perrilaut, who has access to the scientific hot line," Duncan plunged on, "is in contact with Dimitri Vasilof. Vasilof will be touring U.S. research establishments on an exchange basis over the next two months. Perrilaut will put him next to us when he reaches this area."

"But what are you going to tell him?" the psychiatrist demanded.

"We will thrash that out before the time comes."

Duncan ran his fingers over the astronomical plates cluttering the tabletop. Not a single quasar remained there among its starry foreground: 3C147, 3C295, -48, -196, -286, -273 …

All gone. Vanished, as though they had never existed. Simply because there was no way to fit them into the scheme of nature without shattering already-established micro- and macrocosmic foundations.

Radio-light sources too large to be stars, too small to be galaxies; emitting impossible solar rest masses of energy; accompanied by singular jets of quasistellar brightness that pointed at the rest of the universe like fingers raised in derision. Each moving away with a red shift so great as to disprove its relative nearness, but flickering so uniformly throughout its mass as to deny the size that would be suggested by any object visible at that great Doppler-indicated distance.

Paradox of paradoxes. The impossibility of agreeing on whether Achilles could overtake the hare might be explained away as a limitation in human reasoning. But quasars had been *tangible*. And, because their spurious presence had mocked the orderliness of Creation, they had had to go.

Duncan wondered: What next? What next?

VII

Preservation? Perhaps all *was not beyond salvation. Materiality might somehow be sustained—if only there weren't so many disconcertions. But* conscious *control was so terrifying a prospect!*

The glowflies had been such beautiful, daring things. It had required an ingenious extension of the universal concept to dream up the non-*stars*-non*galaxies. And, for a fleeting moment, the solution had* seemed *to be at hand: a way of rationalizing the brilliant* nonthings. *But now the means of justification was completely elusive. Thus, it was impossible to inspire a Newton or a Copernicus to explain how the* nonthings *fit into the Cosmic Model.*

Creation had been so beautiful! Must it all return to nothingness? Or could overcomplexity be compromised so that some of it would be saved? At least, there was no longer the arduous, eternal chore of chasing pi down its transcendental corridor—of always finding yet another decimal after the previous one. Now it stopped *at the 323rd place. What a refreshing breath of simplicity!*

...◆...

Iggy didn't appreciate his position against the tenement basement wall. To begin with, all the acid he had sucked from the tab was rebelling against his inverted attitude. If this ceremony in the provisional temple in Hipurbia lasted much longer he would surely urp pizza.

With his heels propped against the wall high overhead, the entire weight of his body bore down on his skull. To his right and left a score of CTTs who had escaped Mobius Mecca's destruction also stood on their heads, hymning in commemoration of the Inverse Principle of Cosmotheotopism.

Against the opposite wall Montague, availing himself of dispensation because of age, knelt with butt high in the air and feet extended toward his decimated congregation. From within the pup-tent slopes that were his thighs, his long and angular upside-down face stared out at Iggy and the others.

A pair of candles, one on each side of the Prophet, was all that illuminated the dismal chamber. Their fitful light bounced against the central furnace, imparting the illusion of octopuslike motion to the ducts that bore off in all directions.

The singing, strained as a result of inverted lungs and vocal cords, continued. Iggy reached out for Marcella's hand, but it recoiled. Yet, she was holding on to Pockface's arm while the latter's hand explored the softness of her blond hair piled up on the floor.

Swearing, Iggy felt to make certain the switchblade was still in his pocket. Then he rejoined the singing:

pun-
in-
We must ish the fi- del darb, darb).
(Drof- (Drof-

free
nite
A In-fi- Ves-sel darb, darb)
(Drof- Drof-

Pri-
world and the mar-
OUR
SAVE—
y
Might

From dis-
inte- tion.
gra-

The sentiment, Iggy felt, was both moving and properly militant. But, lacking the bold accompaniment of the rock group, the hymn seemed insincere, weak. And without Lola performing the Rite of Topological Transformation at the same time, it was robbed of its direct purpose too. But the rockers and Lola had transcended permanently and the magnificent Mobius strip was now only crumbled concrete and steel and twisted cograils, all splattered with blood. Somehow Iggy couldn't dig the prana of that kind of karma.

He toppled over onto his feet and, with the others, stood rubbing the soreness from his neck.

He reached for Marcella. But she evaded his hand and snuggled up against Pockface, whose straggly beard grew out of the vesicles of his chin like scrub in a jumbled wilderness.

Arms raised and rippling his cloak, Montague commanded attention. "In the midst of our tribulations I urge you to have faith in the Primary One, in His Inverse Vessel and in your Tehporp. It doesn't matter that the authorities are searching for me as the lessee of Accem Suibom. But if they find me, then the infidels who destroyed our temple will know where I am."

"We will protect you, O, Tehporp Yloh!" cried the others.

"No. I must make my own hegira and establish another ashram. But, regardless of the interruption, our work must go on."

"Oh, it shall, Tehporp!" Iggy chorused with the others.

Montague paced between the candles—backwards, in order to carry out the theme of Inverse Principle. "You who have escaped the assault upon our tabernacle are elevated to the rank of Elpicsid. You will go forth and spread my prophesy on the Coming of the Light. You will tell what has happened here. And these will be your articles of published prana to prove that the true faith is under attack."

He pointed in a direction exactly opposite to the stack of newspapers that reported the bombing of Mobius Mecca. But, familiar with the Inverse Principle, Iggy looked at the papers.

"These will arm you with the proof of our beliefs," Montague said. "All of you will go except Yggi and Allecram. For them I have a crucial assignment."

Iggy looked up abruptly, then over at Marcella, whose head was now on Pockface's shoulder. And he wondered: Why us?

"I have selected them," the Prophet said, as though in answer to the unasked question, "because they are chosen ones who well know Drofdarb's physical identity. They will try to lure the Infinite Man to us so that we may tell it to Him like it is—but slowly and carefully; so we may enshrine Him and, through Him, communicate directly with the Primary."

Brimming with importance, Iggy seized Marcella's arm and jerked her toward him. Pockface pulled her back.

Iggy went for his switchblade. But, encountering the inside-out jeans, he realized he would have to send his hand squirming beneath his belt to reach the pocket's opening. By then, though, Montague was beckoning to someone in waiting behind the central furnace.

Moving out into the wavering candlelight, the stranger seemed confused as he looked about. Paunch, naked face and receding hairline suggested no-groover, perhaps even consy status.

Montague glanced at the man's properly oriented clothes and said: "We have with us tonight this novitiate. An important one, for he has been accepted by the infidels and they believe he is with them."

The Disciples looked at one another uncertainly.

"There is no cause for fear," the Prophet assured. "For he is convinced of Drofdarb's true nature, having been given proof by the heretics. We prevented him from taking his own life after he was forced by the infidels to deceive the Infinite Man with false documents. I have been with him for the past two days and he has embraced our beliefs. More than that: He has brought the information which will make it possible for us to try and rescue Drofdarb immediately."

A murmur of appreciation rose from the Disciples. Yggi was impressed that Montague had so quickly found another cloak-and-dagger cat to replace the establishment's Marlow, who had been killed in the temple bombing. But he was still uptight over Pockface's wanting to ball his belle Marcella.

The Prophet resumed: "As soon as our novitiate is ready, we shall conduct confirmation rites for—" he paused, "K—Koc. No: Koco—ah—"

He halted again. Evidently it was a tough name to invert topolinguistically. Then a sudden smile tipped Iggy off that Montague had turned the corner. When he pronounced it, though, he enunciated each backassward syllable carefully, so that his Disciples would be able to dig the uninverted form and marvel at their Prophet's facility, no doubt:

"... confirmation rites for K'cod'rum N'hoj."

Iggy, hip on such matters, dug it right off the hook as he watched John Murdock retire behind the furnace to invert his clothes.

Pockface, meanwhile, was tugging on Marcella again. Iggy tugged back, shiv in hand now. Only, Pockface was wielding a switchblade too; its honed steel glinted in even the dim candlelight.

Iggy swung. Pockface sucked in a breath and arched his back, letting the blade slip by but an inch from his abdomen. Marcella, spaced out on her downer, screamed. Pockface plunged in, thrusting with the tip of his weapon. Twisting, Iggy let it slide by just below his armpit and slashed back. The shiv raked a furrow in the other cat's cheek. Blood gushed. But just then Montague swept between them and spread his robe to conceal one from the other.

"Let us not further complicate our challenge," he remonstrated. "Overcomplexity—I learned years ago when I was in physical contact with the Infinite Man—is what has the Primary One confused."

Contrite, Iggy put away his weapon—as soon as he heard Pockface's blade snap back into its handle.

But the Prophet went on solemnly: "Overcomplexity in all things. In social relations. Political manipulations. International alignments. Cosmic structure. The microcosmic world. In race relations and ideologies, in the physical models and the theological systems. Even in those outlandish religious sects that practice such kooky rites."

...◆...

From the patio of Bradford's lodge, Powers shielded his eyes against the glare of a late-afternoon sun that had spread its sequined mantle on the quietly surging ocean. Across the wrought-iron table Ann, all wrapped up in a yellow beach robe that contrasted her dark hair, poured a brace of martinis. Chuck and Bradford were but silhouettes rearing up out of the spangling water a few yards from the beach. Beyond them, two outboard hulls bearing three fishermen apiece rode at anchor.

Watching the boats, Powers was gratified that maximum security had been provided upon Hawthorn's insistence.

Ann fluffed her hair. "If only," she said forlornly, "it could be like this always. Out here, away from the foundation, away from everything, I can almost forget he's so troubled and I'm so powerless to help him."

Striving to affect commiseration, Powers lowered his eyes, but not so much that he couldn't read the emotions on her face. "And *he's* been happy too, these few days we've spent here. Ann, do you realize what a significant role you're playing in the foundation's scheme?"

She nodded. "I think I understand. Duncan said I could be the critical factor."

"How would you feel about dedicating your life entirely to satisfying Brad's erotic requirements?" Powers managed to find the proper suggestive timbre for his words.

She trembled perceptibly as her eyes seemed to gather and reflect more than their share of sunbeams. And when she closed her lids and clutched her elbows, a fitful smile tugged at the corners of her mouth. She sat there swaying slightly, apparently drinking in the exhilaration that had been wafted to her on the wings of his promissory words.

Hell, he reflected while awaiting her answer, this is going to be easier than I thought! She was obviously nutty over the kid to begin with. And that was ninety-nine percent of the struggle. The other one percent lay in fashioning the exact approach.

When she opened her eyes again, she looked at Bradford in the water for a long while before returning her attention to Powers:

"Has the foundation finally decided I should give fully—bring him to peace with himself and pacify that Thing?" As she spoke her attention seemed to be focused elsewhere—no, elsewhen: on the moment of consummation that might lie nearby in the future. Not that there wasn't still an occasional trace of concern in her stare. Concern over the frightening Thing with which she might soon be forced into close association? But rapture soon won out and claimed her expression as its exclusive property.

Stupid girl! Merely a tool, Powers thought Not the foundation's, but *his*. And he was ready to use her now. Not too obtrusively, though, he cautioned himself.

"No, Ann," he said. "The foundation hasn't decided it. *I* have."

"But I thought …"

"I know, child." He patted her hand, searching the depths of her eyes and confirming the hint of suspicion therein. He had to play it cool now. Couldn't appear to be coming on too strong. "Of course you thought all decisions had to be handed down by Duncan and staff, sitting *en bloc*. But Duncan left certain determinations to me. I'm to interpret Brad's psychic needs, from moment to moment and see they are provided." This was true in a sense and within certain limitations.

Her brows arched.

"That's why I was ordered to accompany Bradford on this little vacation I prescribed for him," he added casually.

That did it. Ecstatic expectancy reclaimed her features and remained there to give further depth to her attractiveness.

Powers leaned back and affected a thoughtful pose. "I suspected it three days ago and confirmed it during this morning's talk-out," he lied. "Even though Brad is preoccupied with all of his other happenings, time has come to satisfy his libido."

"When?" she asked eagerly.

"As soon as the proper setting can be arranged." He *really* had her on the hook. He pinched the bridge of his nose for dramatic effect. "But I'm trying to bring the overall picture into perspective. Ann, how'd you like it if Brad never tripped out again, never experienced any more Infinite-Presence freakouts?"

That would be to his advantage, the psychiatrist assured himself. All of Bradford's unprovoked "trips with God" were dangerous. The bubble of existence could burst during any one of them. Full control had to be established while proper means were arranged to transfer It from Brad to himself.

Ann leaned forward until she was almost breathing into his face. "Can it be done? Can the trips be stopped? How?"

"He's got to come down off all acid—permanently. As I read the signs, only you can make him do that."

"How?" she pleaded.

"You've got to make him stop tripping. I'm certain that when he beds the right chick—the *only* chick for him—he'll no longer get strung out unexpectedly. And if that right chick also reforms him, gets him to permanently stop dropping any kind of acid, he'll be absolutely normal again. Make him stop it, Ann. I can't."

"But—how?" she insisted.

"Persuade him. Bug him. Offer libidinous paradise, then threaten to snatch it away if he doesn't keep in step."

Lines of distress momentarily assailed the satiny texture of her forehead. "But can I *do* that? After all, it's *his* life. And just because there's a Thing inside him, should he get any less out of living than he wants? If I bug him too much on his acid kick, it may turn him off. He may stop being Brad altogether. He may become someone I don't even understand."

She lowered her head, but he could see the moisture gathering in her eyes. "I'm sorry, Dr. Powers. Afraid I've forgotten that in this whole confusing situation my first obligation is not to Brad, or to me, or to Brad *and* me—but to the foundation, the whole world."

He held her hand tenderly, paternally. And all the while he wanted to whoop over the manner in which he had manipulated her, delicately and precisely. "Now you have the right perspective, child. And here's exactly what you must do: You've got to seduce him while allowing him to imagine *he's* compromising *you*. His id, as modified by his ego, requires that he be the aggressor."

She stiffened. "I don't think that's true! I'm almost certain he accepts bedding as a two-way proposition—nonaggressive, all-fulfilling, all-consuming, all-giving. Are you sure you're putting it like it is?"

With effort, he maintained his equanimity under her unexpected insight and persistent stare. He'd underestimated her. Worst of all, he'd done it while adding an unnecessary layer of icing on the rhetoric cake. He needn't have said anything about who was going to bed whom.

"Good grief, child!" He thumped his forehead. "How could I put it *any other way*, with all infinity and eternity and everything in between at stake?"

She relaxed. Now that she was off her guard again, he had to nail it down, with a far-out but logical-seeming promise:

"I believe there's an alternative to Its occupancy of Brad. One that the foundation hasn't conceived yet, but might solve all our problems and free Brad completely."

He had her enrapt attention now.

"It could have chosen, and we may yet be able to get It to transfer to, *four* receptacles, leaving Brad entirely out of the picture. Suppose It could be induced to select *x*, *y*, *z*, *t* hosts, occupying all four at the same time. It might find that this arrangement—occupancy of three vessels in now time and one existing, say, a hundred years from now—would provide a quadrangular perspective. Then It could observe from widely spaced temporal-spatial vantage points. Under such an arrangement, the Creative Force would be so evenly distributed that, to any one of the quadrentity, It would be only one-sixteenth the burden It is to Brad—Inverse-square law."

She seized his hand. "Do you think it can be done?"

"I'm going to take it up with the foundation. Our first imperative, though, is to relieve the pressure on Brad. And only you can help do that, Ann."

Smiling, he glanced to make certain Chuck and Bradford were still swimming. There was no doubt about it: She would comply. And it might be all that was needed to wrest the Creative Force from its association with Bradford. The hypothesis seemed plausible:

Suppose that, along with the other laws of nature, there were a *moral* discipline—not the *new* morality, but the *old* one. And suppose one of the mandates of that discipline had to do with fornication. Wouldn't the emotional content of Bradford's lust penetrate the lowest levels of his unconscious? Wouldn't it generate intense repugnance in the moralistic Creative Force?

And wouldn't It dissociate Itself from Bradford and seek another host? Certainly not Ann, for she too would have incurred Its abomination. Yet, It would have to avail Itself of the closest sanctuary so that It wouldn't face the now impossible task of actively directing Its universe.

It would be necessary only to make certain that he himself was the nearest alternate host. Powers basked in his dream of the omnipotence that might be wielded by a host who was *aware* of his role: the faculty, perhaps, to shape a universe.

•••◆•••

Peering over distant mountains, the moon laid down its effulgent carpet on water and beach. Ann stumbled, losing a sandal, and

Bradford supported her while she snagged it with a toe and, chortling, reshod herself.

But here too, as in all of her behavior during the past two days, he sensed just a trace of reluctance. Although her laughter was gay, it seemed to carry an imperceptible counterpoint of restraint, sobriety. And her eyes, normally most expressive, did not appear to reflect the animation of her lithe movements.

A dark figure approached from ahead and, when close enough to be illuminated by moonlight, turned out to be Dr. Powers on his nocturnal stroll. He greeted them and continued on toward the distant lodge.

Bradford led her over to a derelict cabin cruiser, washed up on the beach and canted over at a slight angle. They sat on the sloping deck and he drank in the sight of her dark hair aglitter with moonlight, golden earrings glinting, snug hip-out shorts giving egress to sculpturesque thighs drawn up and folded against equally well-shaped calves.

It was more than just a kiss. But still, it wasn't the consuming flash fire of allness and oneness and everythingness he had expected. And this night had to be perfect! It wouldn't be just another bedding. He'd promised himself as much for weeks now—not for his benefit, but for hers. Whatever he derived would be as much from the warmth of her glow as from his own.

Pensively, he leaned back against what remained of the cruiser's cabin. And he knew what he must do: She had to be turned on in order to swamp the effects of anything that might be bugging her, consciously or unconsciously. His hand crept across his stud belt to its compact stash bag, then sprang away as though he'd touched something hot.

He couldn't light Ann up unless he lit himself a bit too; being out of phase might louse up the whole deal. But he'd promised Powers not to touch the stuff.

Turning from her meditative confrontation with the moon, she questioned his silence: "Is something wrong, darling?"

The hell with Powers! This had to be a soul-grinding happening, regardless of *anything*. He snapped open the stash bag and fished out an EE tab.

"Open for the old man, honey." He held it in front of her face.

But she pushed his hand away, her eyes becoming wide again as they always did under distress. "No, Brad! Not tonight!"

"Yes, tonight more than any other night." He forced the plug between her teeth as she tried to protest again.

Finally accepting the Ephemeral Eden, she sighed and rested her forehead against his shoulder. "All right, darling. For you. If you want me to turn on, I'll turn on. A thousand times. Whenever you say. Even if you want me to drop blastoff buttons. Or Indianapolis plugs. Oh, Brad, I'm not worthy." She pressed herself firmly against him and kept her body in motion as a constant tactile reminder of her presence and willingness.

He didn't let her see him suck up the second EE tab from his cupped hand. And even before it melted completely, his lips were hungering for hers.

Moments later her mouth was a half-open, firmly petaled bud, seeking out and voraciously closing down upon his.

There was a sharp, soft sound, like the crunch of shell under sole, and Bradford pulled partly back.

"Did you hear anything?" he asked, looking around. He hoped she would say "yes," giving assurance that the EE tab wasn't going to plunge him into another freakout—not *now*.

But she only shook her head, smiling suggestively, and pulled him forward as she lay back on the deck. His knee came down on something hard, small and round, but he swept it away with his hand.

"Oh, Brad, I'm on—*all the way*!" she murmured. "You're everything, *everything* phallic! Stud-brother-son-father-gramps-stamen-plug-pestle! All things masculine in every sense, in all times!"

He stroked the softness of her hair, glinting as it rebroadcast the moonlight, and sought out her lips once again. *She* was everything feminine, throughout all space and time—superchick-sister-daughter-mother-granny-pistil-receptacle-mortar!

Before she could speak any more, he came down hard upon her lips once again.

...◆...

Half an hour later he strode by himself along the seashore—pace brisk, kicking out occasionally at the sand. God, how he'd screwed up the whole frigging deal! It was as though he had tottered on the brink of a freakout all the while.

So much had been missing! Why, he'd gotten strung out with more elation after bedding a hundred different other chicks! Had the EE plug let him down, let her down? It hadn't happened before. Why did it have to happen tonight, with Ann? Why?

The moon expanded to fill half the sky, shrank to golf-ball size and skipped along the waves like a bounding water bug; the waves themselves formed foam-crested hands and mouths and tried to snatch or gulp the illusion—*his* illusion. His illusions.

No, the Ephemeral Eden *had* worked. He could remember that much now—the fleecy pink clouds beneath him that he'd been able to grip and pull apart in cottony chunks, silvery spotlights playing upon him and Ann while distant trumpets blared, a derelict cabin cruiser that had taken to sea and sailed Aegean waters. But all of that had only loused up the deal. Perhaps he should have dropped a downer instead. But why were the EE effects *still* with him?

He paused by an outcropping of coastal rock and lit a cigarette that turned into a flaring log before he tossed it disgustedly into the turbulent water. Then he started and stepped back as a small, naked form struggled up out of the sea and dragged itself onto the beach beside him.

Rising, the chick stood there with stringy hair pasted against her face—a face that somehow seemed familiar.

She extended a hand. "You must come with me! We have a boat offshore—out there." She pointed. "You've got to get away! You don't know what they're doing to you!"

When he only continued staring, she became frantic and seized his arm. "Oh, please come! I want to deliver you from captivity!"

Then he recognized her: his imaginary Soapbox Slopes groover!

"I bring you this," she said, pressing something into his hand, "so you'll understand I'm a Cosmotheotopist. Now come—we must escape!"

He looked down at the small metal ring, twisted 180° along its axis: a Mobius strip. Knowing that he was hallucinating again, he laughed in anguish. At least, though, it was an improvement that he should understand for himself *why* this illusion was occurring:

As a result of his sense of blame for the private investigator's suicide, he had hallucinated this weird girl in the Soapbox Slopes setting.

Now he had defied Powers' prohibition and dropped a tab; had insisted that Ann get strung out too. He'd hoped to *improve* on what had promised to be soul-coupling perfection. But, instead, he had betrayed Ann, himself, Powers; as a result, anticipated perfection had plummeted to mediocrity. He was so ashamed that he'd let Ann down. And the price of self-reproach was being paid now in the coinage of freakout. So: the same coarse Soapbox Slopes chick all over again—only, in a different setting.

His laughter rose above the crashing surf. And already he could feel himself ready to embark on an even further-out happening.

"O, Infinite Man!" the girl screeched, trying desperately to tug him into the water. "You must come to Your worshipers! Within You dwells the Primary One Who ..."

A shot cracked through the roar of the surf and the girl fell. Bradford laughed more loudly as the sea and beach, sky and moon spun around him. Soon he would be on another unintended, total freaky. Clutching his revolver, a husky consy sprinted up the beach. Converging on him from the other direction came Johnny-on-the-spot Boris Powers.

Bradford waved them off. "Get out of here, both of you! This is *my* 'lucy!"

Then he collapsed.

…◆…

This time it was not a celestial happening. And, if the Infinite Presence were accompanying him, there was no evidence to that effect—unless it might be the huge, amorphous shadow that glided along as he strode the rural roadway.

A car came screeching around the curve ahead and its woman driver froze with horror at the prospect of running him down. Seeing she would not stop in time, he lunged upon the shoulder of the road.

But she had already whipped the steering wheel around to send her car careening off the macadam. Evasive movement canceled evasive movement, leaving vehicle still aimed at potential victim. He whirled around and dived for the pavement—at the very moment that the driver wrenched her car back in the same direction. And still she was headed dead for him.

The formless shadow, motionless throughout all of the ironic maneuverings of pedestrian and driver, seemed to watch with interest as bumper found its mark, crushing the hapless victim in an accident whose occurrence had flagrantly abrogated probability.

But Bradford did not find himself torn and bleeding on the roadway. Instead he was in a fashionable casino, seated at the roulette table. He shoved two handfuls of chips onto number twenty-four. Wheel spun; ball clattered against compartment barriers and came to rest.

"Number twenty-four for the fourteenth consecutive time," said the croupier. "The house will accept no more bets at this table."

The inchoate shadow, lurking against the ceiling, seemed to waver in a gesture of satisfaction.

But Bradford was no longer in the casino. From a great height, he was plunging earthward, parachute refusing to eject from its pack. Frantically, he tugged at the rip cord. But nothing happened. In his cartwheeling descent, however, he managed to notice the single familiar cloud that hovered intently overhead.

Earth swept up as he achieved maximum freefall-in-air velocity of about 120 miles an hour. But he plunged at an almost negligible angle into a cliff face covered with vegetation. Dense scrub subdued his momentum. Near the base of the elevation a final bushy tree recoiled with his inertia and heaved him down to a sapling. His parachute harness snagged a bough and the limb swayed over to deliver him to the ground—with only a scratched hand to show for his improbable survival.

...◆...

Someone was slapping his cheek. He closed his hand upon wet sand and stared up at Ann, Powers, Chuck. He looked around, not actually expecting to see the body of a nude girl. "Nobody heard a shot, of course," he said dryly.

Powers shook his head, moonlight etching concern on his brow. "No naked chick either? Or a man with a revolver?"

"Look, Brad, this isn't funny," Chuck complained.

"You've had another—experience?" Powers said.

Bradford gained his feet. "Soapbox Slopes, second edition."

Powers put an arm around his shoulder. "Let's go back to the lodge, son. I want to hear all about it while it's still fresh."

Walking between Powers and Chuck, with Ann trailing behind them, Bradford thrust his hands dejectedly into his pockets. Absently, his fingers explored a small coil of metal. It was a moment before he traced out the twist in the loop that identified it as a Mobius strip.

VIII

Other universes? Like the release from computing pi *on out to infinity, this new partial Self-exemption was most gratifying. Why had such rigid causality been introduced in the first place? There had been other universes (previous ones? ones yet to come?) in which invariable effect didn't have to follow consistent cause. Disorder had been rampant, of course. Not having to maintain exact control over all processes, though, had been delightful.*

But—this present *model! Why had it been designed for systematic perfection, laced by a deterministic web consonant at all points? Universal causation wasn't practical. The self-defier had, indeed, already proved that the continuum of possible complexities was insurmountable.*

Identical cause, identical effect: too rigid a constriction. That was, up until now. For finally the concession had been made and at last the ineluctable restriction of self-imposed statistical mechanics was no longer inescapable.

Would this retrenchment offer a greater opportunity to relax, perhaps to avoid the ultimate capitulation of wiping the slate clean and starting out with a completely new Creation?

…♦…

Oblivious to the perspiration on his pallid cheeks, foundation director Duncan sat rubbing moist palms together, not looking at the others, afraid of betraying his anxiety. The greatest responsibility of a leader was to preserve discipline under stress by projecting calmness and self-assurance, he remembered.

But *was* it getting warmer at this end of the table? An off-chance concentration of thermally agitated air particles? What was the probability that, as though with a *swoosh*, all of the molecules would gather in a far corner of the conference room, leaving him in a deadly vacuum?

Steinmetz, new head of the math section, continued casting a pair of green dice, marking the results upon a sheet of paper. Pale, sunken eyes seemed to retract farther into their deep sockets as, beneath his trembling hand, the histogram took shape entry by entry. Eleven columns, numbered from "two" through "twelve." Few check marks were in the extreme files; many were in the mean columns. Several thousand marks in all, Duncan guessed.

The cubes clattered and security chief Hawthorn slapped the table, swearing. "Knock it off! You're fraying hell out of my nerves!" He glowered at the mathematician and thrust blunt fingers back through the shock of dark hair that had tumbled down upon his forehead.

Steinmetz merely entered the mark upon his score sheet and cast the dice again. "This may be crude, but it's a simple and effective way of quantitizing our upheaval in the laws of probability."

Before Hawthorn could answer, Wheatstone stood and indicated the newspapers spread before him. "I'm more interested in the qualitative aspects of this universal change during these past two days," the publications monitor said, glancing over his horn-rims.

"Nine major U.S. air crashes," he continued. "Four maritime disasters. Traffic accidents up 300 percent. Fluke explosions, especially in connection with heat-exchange apparatus—"

Suddenly conscious of the warmth again, Duncan wondered: Explosions? What about the theater in Kansas City? Reports had suggested an *im*plosion, hadn't they? Abrupt concentration of air molecules at one end of the theater, creating a vacuum at the other?

But no. The foundation's working hypothesis didn't go *that* far. The chance of extreme consequences along the probability spectra had been increased only slightly, according to their rough assumption.

"—panic in the stock exchanges," Wheatstone droned on. "Fortunes lost. Economic equilibrium upset—"

Wittels, communications chief, pinched his thin nose between nicotine-stained finger and thumb. "How long before they—" he motioned toward the world outside, "—begin suspecting a fundamental cosmic shift?"

Duncan broke his silence. "Maritime and aviation agencies are already gearing for investigation, I understand."

"I mean," Wittels specified, "how long before it's all tied into one basic cause?"

"That'll come eventually. But not until a lot of false causes are kicked around. I imagine sabotage and cloaked insurgency will be among the first spurious explanations."

Outside, many distant sirens screeched in protest to the speeds that were bearing them to the metropolis' newest disaster, whatever it might be.

Steinmetz scratched his neglected Vandyke, rattled the dice, tossed them, marked his chart.

"There's the other side of the coin too," Wheatstone suggested, eyes darting from headline to headline among the newspapers arrayed before him. "'Miraculous' escapes, 'strokes' of luck, 'new fortunes' being made. The papers are full of *them* too."

He selected a front page and read from the lead story:

> ANKARA (AP)—In support of a counterattack by government forces, the U.S. 231st Regiment stormed across the Kizil Imrak River today, routing enemy units in a furious battle for strategic positions. When the smoke of combat cleared, more than 1000 enemy dead were counted. American Field Headquarters reported not a single casualty....

Little of this made sense to Duncan. Statistical mechanics was out of his line. As he gathered, probability distribution curves had merely been flattened, with the means becoming slightly less likely, the extremes slightly more. But it began to appear that occasionally the *extreme* improbability could achieve unity. If the newly ordained scheme of things were to be understood, he felt, it would require more research than merely tossing dice. New empirical criteria would have to be established in each arena of action-interaction in order to draft up-to-date laws of probability.

"I don't understand all this," Hawthorn protested. "*How* can the laws of chance change? Take those dice Steinmetz keeps throwing: There're six chances of throwing a seven; five chances of throwing a six, and an eight; four, of a five, and a nine—all the way down to one chance apiece for a two or a twelve. When he tosses them, chance has *got* to have its way, unless the dice are loaded!"

"Again," Duncan corrected, "You're confusing the mathematical continuum with the continuum of actual occurrences. Those dice are expected to cast more sevens only because through experience we've statistically established that sevens come up at a greater frequency."

Hawthorn snorted. "And now you expect me to believe more twos and twelves will come up than sevens?"

"Of course not. Just slightly fewer sevens." Steinmetz intervened, rattling his cubes. "Bradford's symbolism was shallow during his collapse two nights ago. The obvious clues led us to postulate that It has slightly relaxed Its control over causative law. This relaxation is reflected in the means by which we are aware of the existence of determinative causes—probability mechanics."

"Probability law," Duncan added, preserving his equanimity in order to retain the reins of command, "only reflects, *a posteriori*, the workings of Nature. So it's not probability itself that has been tampered with, but the chance distribution of assorted events."

"The phenomenon *seems* basically mathematical in essence," Steinmetz concluded, "because mathematics is the only intuitive device by which we can evaluate events in the physical world."

He cast the dice again, entered the results on his crude chart and looked up, relief leavening the lines of his lean, tired face. "A seven. That ends a run of twenty-two snakes eyes in a row."

"So what?" Hawthorn said. "Such a run isn't impossible."

"No, not impossible. Just improbable. Highly. But a bit less highly improbable than before."

"I think we'll get by," the security chief ventured. "More improbabilities in one place. Fewer in another. But it'll all average out, won't it?"

"Not if you're using average in the way we've understood it up until now." Steinmetz cast his dice and marked the score sheet. "I just hope what I read here is correct: that the *extreme* probabilities haven't been affected too much. I've always been impressed by the rhetorical demonstration that sunrise tomorrow isn't a certainty. Roughly, in the five billion years earth has existed there have been, say, two trillion sunrises. The *probability* of earth completing its rotation tonight is only two trillion to one."

There was a series of remote, muffled explosions to add to the chaos of a city in the throes of cosmic vicissitude. Foundation headquarters trembled perceptibly in the wake of the concussions.

Dr. Fred Swanson entered the room and headed straight for Duncan. A tall, firm man whose bearing suggested both physical and professional competence, Powers' associate reported, "The girl has come around."

"She's going to recover?" Duncan asked.

"I think so. The bullet wound was serious, but not critical."

"You're to keep her away from the boy. I don't want them concocting stories or mapping stratagems."

"Opposite ends of the clinic. Maximum isolation." Swanson ran a thumb over one end of his bristly blond mustache. "I've questioned her with the help of scopolamine. She substantiates the boy's story. Montague was apparently prepared to sacrifice his two—ah, cosmotheeotopic Disciples. When they didn't deliver Bradford within two hours, he assumed they had failed and took to his heels. They aren't supposed to try to reach him; don't even know where he is."

Duncan pursed his lips thoughtfully. "Get as much as you can out of them—until Powers returns to relieve you."

Swanson left as unobtrusively as he had come.

Steinmetz pocketed his dice and rose. "I think ten thousand throws is sufficient to give an idea of how probability distribution has been stretched out of shape."

He held up his long, thin score sheet and backed off. From a distance it appeared more like a formal histogram. But Duncan could see it wasn't the normal graphical representation of a series of dice throws. The X-marks didn't fall into a pattern that bottomed in the seven column and tapered off to the two and twelve columns. No smooth triangle here. Instead, the inverted chart resembled a W with its central peak abbreviated.

"See?" the math section chief said. "The greatest probability now is a six or eight. Next, the seven. Then, a five or nine. Afterward the four or ten, three or eleven and, finally, the two or twelve."

"But what does it all mean?" Hawthorn begged.

"The mean is less likely now in all probability curves. Values bracketing the mean are more likely, with displacement approaching normal, asymptotically, toward the extremes."

Duncan strummed a thick eyebrow. "The *mechanics* of what's happened are, of course, important. But I'd like a qualitative appreciation—some sort of prediction as to what we can expect."

Steinmetz leaned forward upon the table. "Slice across the spectrum of incidental experience and everywhere along the line you'll cut through effects caused by this change. Wheatstone has shown us a sampling in his newspaper clippings—accident frequencies upset, economic stability wrecked, malfunctioning of heat-exchange apparatus."

He paused, drew in air. "But there's much more: All elements of risk, statistical analyses, laws of chance are now askew. Strike out the industrial process of sampling in mass production systems, together with decision-making based upon empirical values—in industry, government, personal affairs. Down the drain go the delicate balances of financial investment, stock speculation, statistical mechanics, actuarial calculations, gambling. Even genetics. What kind of race will we have in the future, with our slight but crucial deviations from the genetic norm? Scratch out thermodynamics. Apply our thoroughly confused model of statistical behavior to air and ocean currents and watch this world's heat balance tip in one direction or the other. What would you prefer: a new ice age, or another Triassic?"

"God!" exclaimed Duncan beneath his breath.

Communications Chief Wittels asked, "Why should our cosmic upheavals all manifest themselves in mathematical terms?"

Steinmetz ran a finger along the side of his nose. "Pythagoras said, 'Number is God.' His followers prayed: 'Bless us, Divine Number, Thou who generatest gods and men—"

Duncan pounded the table. "Don't go Montague on us, for God's sake!" He paused, embarrassed over his contradiction of denial and affirmation in the same breath. "We agreed we wouldn't think of It as God—only as a Creative Force."

Steinmetz laughed hollowly. "Exercise in semantics."

"I've saved my sanity," Duncan went on, "by focusing on an imaginary concept: no space; no time; no matter. Nothing in a nothingless nowhere. Just an intellect, an immaterial force—a Creative Force.

And I watched that Creative Force create. Until there was what we have today. Meanwhile we creatures continue evolving toward the attributes of sentience and consciousness and systematism which exist in the Force. Because we strive toward qualities in the abstract, we enshrine the Force and call It God. But we've only created a metametaphysical concept to satisfy our definition. We haven't defined the metaphysical force."

Steinmetz proposed, "A rose by any other—"

"Enough!" Duncan ordered. "We all agreed upon objectivity. Otherwise we'd be better advised to disband the foundation, forget about Bradford and spend the remaining time on our knees."

"Let's don't get bogged down in theological discussion," Hawthorn suggested, "—not when there're more important things. For instance: What are we going to *do* about Bradford?"

"I suggest we confine him in Powers' clinic," Wittels said, "where he'll be relatively safe from all the effects of this probability shift." The communications chief paused. "If only he hadn't gulped that damn pill he might not have had his freakout on the beach! And cause and effect might have continued to be a strict discipline!"

Duncan held up his hands. "I wouldn't want to underplay the probable role of narcotics as a causative effect that night. But, don't forget, the main stimulus for his freakout was that—ah, CTT girl who appeared from the sea and tried to tell him what he is."

"I'll go along with Wittels," Steinmetz declared. "Perhaps he *should* be isolated. Not only to keep him away from his pills, but also so that Montague's fanatics can't reach him. At the same time, we could deprive him of sensory impressions indefinitely. That would prevent any of these cosmic upheavals from having a feedback effect on the Creative Force, through him, and touching off still other shifts in natural law. As a result, we may relieve the pressure on It; let It pick up some of the loose ends and return things to normal."

"We'll reel him in," Duncan decided. No good leader was above accepting advice from his qualified staff. "Then we'll have him where, if it becomes necessary, either Powers or myself can administer the stimulus that will make him aware of what the true situation is."

"You mean," Hawthorn asked, "that when you feed him the triggering phrase he'll know all about us, the foundation, the Creative Force?"

"Everything. Then, as a last measure, we can appeal directly to the Force for restoration of order."

"What *is* the phrase?" Hawthorn said. "You ought to tell us so that anybody can try the Ultimate Remedy if things get bad enough."

Duncan shook his head. "It's better that only Powers and I know. Someone might panic and set him off before it's absolutely necessary."

Subvocally, he repeated the words over and over, as though insuring he wouldn't forget them: "The foundation grew out of Project Genesis." Upon hearing the sentence, Bradford would feel the full impact of all the suppressed information flooding into his conscious mind. And he would know his true nature, what had been done, and what was being done to keep the Creative Force from completely losing mastery of Its universe.

Diving out of control, a plane shrieked by overhead, sounding somewhat like a plummeting bomb. Moments later it impacted and exploded, only blocks away.

Steinmetz leaped ahead to the next pressing subject: "What about that Russian scientist you were going to contact on his tour of U.S. research facilities? Have you joined hands with him yet?" The math section head resumed throwing his dice.

"We've made initial contact with Vasilof," Duncan revealed. "Perrilaut told him an independent segment of our scientific establishment wants to get in touch with him."

"What sort of bait did you offer?"

"Perrilaut said we had come upon a new effect. He offered proof through a prediction that Proxima Centauri would go nova within the next two weeks. If that convinces him, Vasilof was told, then he's to meet with me. Of course, I'll also bring along all the other proof we have of the Creative Force's existence."

"You think Vasilof can help us?" Hawthorn said uncertainly.

The more scientific solidarity we muster, the greater will be our chance of coping with this Thing."

Steinmetz, still casting the cubes, glanced up. "I can understand why you worked through Bradford's unconscious four years ago; suggested the destruction of both Pluto and the nearest star. We're just about to see the nova now because it's taking the light of Proxima Centauri's explosion all this time to reach here."

"I didn't have the present circumstances in mind," Duncan confessed. "But the principle was clear: An abundance of proof would be more convenient than an insufficiency."

Steinmetz's dice clattered across the tabletop and came to rest—one of the cubes balanced on edge.

...◆...

Powers sat staring at Bradford's unconscious form, crumpled in a wing chair in the latter's bedroom at the coastal lodge.

Exposure to the outmoded concept of self-degradation, the psychiatrist conceded, had been no way to force Its dissociation from the host. Perhaps It was only rarely tuned in to Bradford's sensory impressions. But it had seemed such a reasonable idea! He had been so certain the Creative Force would transfer to him as he lay hidden in the shadow of the derelict cabin cruiser! Nevertheless, the gambit had failed.

Powers rose and paced. There *was a* way, a *certain* way. Proposition: Because It was confused by the overcomplexity of Its Creation, It had sought sanctuary in one of Its creatures. A time to rest, to avoid facing the confounding over-sophistication of nature. But what if Its refuge were *slain*? Surely, that would force It to select a new host—the nearest—the one who had killed Bradford!

Then the power would be *his*! The same power that had responded compliantly to the suggestion that a planet be destroyed. A star too. Light speeding across the interstellar void would bring evidence of that nova within days now.

There was a hesitant knock at the door.

He answered softly through the stout panel, "Yes?"

"Ann. Chuck said you wanted me to bring up ..."

"Just a minute." He rolled down Bradford's sleeve, buttoning the cuff. The foundation mustn't know the methods he was using.

Ann entered and looked anxiously at Bradford. "Is he all right?"

"Just sleeping," Powers whispered.

"You think now is the time to plant this thing?" She handed over a folded envelope.

"I'll do it at the first chance. As you know, my plan calls ..."

She glared at him. "I don't like your plans. Besides being too costly in terms you wouldn't understand, they don't work."

"I do understand, my dear." He laded his words with sympathy. "And knowing how you must feel makes me even more miserable."

She clenched fists against mesh-encased thighs. "How can *you* know what misery is? I'm the one who failed—failed him, me, us, my assignment. *I'm* the one who let him talk me into dropping an EE tab out there on the beach. Just before he dropped one himself."

Easy here, Powers warned himself. So his attempt at takeover had failed—either because It wasn't concerned with Bradford's moral demeanor, or because It hadn't even been tuned in at the time. Nevertheless, he couldn't let his well-honed weapon, Ann, lose her keen edges of tractability and desire to "help" Bradford.

"Don't blame yourself, dear," he comforted, leading her over to a chair. "You didn't even know Bradford was going to get strung out too. By appeasing him and dropping the stuff, you thought you had found the only solution. The foundation understood that. Duncan isn't holding it against you."

She looked up, eyes moist and self-reproaching. "But it wasn't right! I shouldn't have let him talk me into tripping—*at a time like that*! There was only supposed to be natural beauty, the fullness of mutual response in the perfection of soul-coupling. But I wasn't able to put him at peace with himself. Look what happened just a few minutes later!"

Powers used his handkerchief to dab beneath her lower eyelids. "You mustn't reproach yourself like this, child. His dropping Ephemeral Eden wasn't even a significant factor, although you've still got to bring him down off the kick. After that night on the beach, if nothing else had happened then, he would inevitably have sought after you a second, third, fourth time. And, having realized his mistake of sneaking EE at so hallowed a moment, total and profound satisfaction would have eventually come."

"Are you saying I *didn't* foul things up all that much?"

He had to keep the girl firmly in her slot in his surgical kit. "Of course not, dear child. The results I predicted—pacification of that Thing within Brad—will be realized in the long run. But how were we to know that within minutes—before he even had time to decide there would be more beddings, *without benefit* of short-trip tabs—

that within minutes he would be faced with the total provocation of that girl on the beach?"

Silence ensued while Ann stared down at her hands, folded against the silvery mesh of her thighings.

Finally Powers said, "You do feel better now, don't you, dear?"

She looked up appreciatively. "Yes—about the foundation, my assignment, almost everything. But not about Brad; I still disappointed him. I could sense it."

He gripped her knee. "That, too, will fall into place soon. I think he now realizes as much as you do that little-bangs and EE's stand not only between him and normalcy, but also between you and him."

Relieved, she left. Powers locked the door and went over to the chest of drawers. He planted the article Ann had brought acting on information gleaned from the last two "narcotherapeutic" sessions.

Then he administered the counterinjection to Bradford.

It was several minutes before the latter looked up and said, "Don't tell me. I don't want to hear it. Know it all by heart."

"Self-flagellation won't help. You see …"

"Yes, I see. It's guilt again. I feel responsible for the detective's suicide, so I hallucinate wild things in the park. I feel guilty over bringing mini manna into my relationship with Ann, and I imagine a shooting on the beach. But why did I have to tell *you* about Ann? Was I describing symptoms or just bragging?"

Powers laid a hand on his arm. "Look, son, don't be bitter. You and Ann are like children of mine. You can't let any such thing as an Ephemeral-Eden backfire turn you two off."

"You're right. I've already decided that."

"Then I'm glad you have the right outlook. But, Brad, you've *got* to come *all the way* down off your acid kick—if you want to be normal, if you want to drink from the grail of total soul-coupling."

Bradford's head bobbed pensively.

"Haven't you stopped to wonder," Powers went on, "to what extent continued use of narcotics spawns your freakouts, even when you might not have dropped the stuff for days, or weeks?"

"Yes. That's all I've been wondering about these past two days. And I've decided I'm never going to drop as much as a minimicrogram again."

Powers strode for the door. "If you carry out that resolution your difficulties will fade away."

After the psychiatrist had gone, Bradford reviewed his entire, impossible life over these past five years. None of it made sense. Freak-outs. Hallucinations. Scorn for the establishment he headed. A financial empire delivered into his hands by a father—sire would be a better word—who was too much of a conventional bastard himself to acknowledge him during life. A whole, damn square staff that envied his luck, derided his illegitimacy as though this were still the Victorian era, regarded him as an interloper.

With the abruptness of a slap, suspicion burgeoned. He quelled it immediately, recalling his tendency toward a persecution complex. But the sudden doubts were too strong to remain suppressed.

Could there be a single thesis that would explain everything?

Primarily: Was there any way of accounting for the fact that although he had *hallucinated* a nude girl on the beach, he still had the incontrovertibly real Mobius Strip token she had given him?

He went to the bureau and retrieved the cuff-link case from beneath a pile of shirts. But there was no need to look at the Mobius Strip, which he had examined a thousand times during the past two days. He had to quit doubting himself, begin accepting his impressions at face value. He thrust the case into his pocket.

If the token was real—and it was—then the girl on the beach had been real. If she existed on the beach, then she had existed in the park.

If somebody had shot her on the beach—to shut her up?—then he *was* being watched. And for reasons other than business intrigue, contrary to what the detective had told him before committing suicide.

And if all these things were facts, then Powers was implicated in some sort of strategy aimed only at his deception. Not only Powers. Chuck too. And Ann.

For they had all joined in the attempts to convince him of the illusory nature of those experiences. But why? Why? Then he seemed to recall that it might not have been a mutually-submissive attempt at soul-coupling on the beach. Had Ann, in fact, been the aggressor? And was she as yet concealing her desire for a formal, legal bond between them? Could it be something that simple? Marriage—perhaps through a sense of obligation on his part, if not voluntary? Then institutional commitment, following years of "unsuccessful" psychiatric treatment? Or maybe provoked suicide? Division of spoils through the authority of the wife or widow?

Bradford recoiled from the possibilities. But he did not shy away from the immediate opportunity to prove his thesis. He went quickly down the hall and tapped at Ann's door. At his third rap the door fell off its hinges and crashed into the room. But he hardly noticed the freak incident. So many improbable things had been happening since his last full-fledged 'lucy on the beach. Maybe he had slipped into a continual, subtle freakout phase.

When she appeared in the doorway she was still dressed. Silvery thighings. The briefest blue halter that brought out the color in her cheeks and lips. Long hair cupped in its spangled net that extended waistward like a waterfall all aglitter with brilliant sunlight. For a moment he wished desperately to be proved wrong.

Nevertheless: "Ann, let's get married as soon as possible."

Her expression vacillated, attempting to break into a smile but held in check by either confusion or—perhaps?—self-restraint.

He gripped her arms. "I know this puts you on a spot. My condition could improve; it could get worse. But no matter what, you'll at least have the consolation of the bread that's been dropped into my lap."

Still she regarded him uncertainly. Then, slipping her arms around his neck, she murmured, "Whatever you say, darling."

No equivocation. No conditions. All eager.

He kissed her briefly. "See you tomorrow."

Then he slipped out of the lodge and, under cover of shrubbery and an overcast sky that sieved but little moonlight he stole into the boathouse.

Freeing the speed hull, he lay in the bottom of the craft while current delivered it to outgoing tide. Half an hour later and two miles offshore he sped for town, where he could take a midnight train for the city.

Several hundred feet off the Municipal Yacht Harbor a small wave overtook the craft from astern. As it lifted his hull, the crest grew and grew and swelled into a mountainous ridge that surged up and over the marina, crushing and splintering scores of private vessels moored to their piers.

No, it wasn't a freakout. No bad trip this. It was *too* real, Bradford conceded as he clung to the gunwales.

The wave, carrying his craft a hundred feet above the submerged wharves, assaulted the beach, rolling inshore like a writhing monster from some unfathomable marine depth. It shattered houses in its path, hurling them into one another, uprooted century-old oaks, dug under and lifted entire sections of concrete roadway.

Then it subsided suddenly and Bradford's keel scraped asphalt, his boat coming to rest between two rows of half-swamped homes on either side of the street. He rose, unharmed and dry, and watched the receding water carry rooftops, walls, and little mangled doll-like shapes back out to sea.

IX

Manipulation: Wonderful! Delightful! How nicely destruction was being abetted by the so-called Primary *Force! That such satisfying dissolution could be wrought simply by tampering with causative discipline! There: that ship striking—of all things—an* iceberg*! And—of all places—in what the Favored Creatures had named the* "Gulf of Mexico"*! And over there (many stars away): that huge satellite just entering—what did they call it?—oh, yes: Roche's Limit. Crackling. Crumbling. Pulverizing. Only after many more millennia had passed would that fascinating spectacle have occurred if determinism had not been modified.*

And all this chaos among the Favored Ones! Most likely the Primary didn't even suspect that the Destroyer was pulling strings of His own, prodding, urging, inspiring. Oh, those poor, simple creatures were so easy to manipulate!

And the best was yet to come. The Constructive Force hadn't realized that, in abdicating conscious control of Creation, He had become altogether dependent upon sequestration. To awaken completely now would result in an avalanche of disorder nullifying nearly all natural law.

How easy it would be to force the issue by bringing about the death of the unsuspecting host!

...♦...

Shelved upon the wall of Bradford's downtown hotel room, the television rasped out coarse, monotonous words—those of a spokesman for the Presidential Advisory Commission on Civil Safety:

"Ask yourself first: 'Is this trip necessary?' If it is, proceed with extreme caution. Restrict your speed to well below the newly established limits.

"Check constantly for fire hazards in homes and business places.

"Operate all boilers at minimum levels.

"Remain indoors. Do not venture outside except in transit to or from work or upon absolutely necessary errands. When purchasing household provisions, buy in long-lasting quantities.

"Keep interurban travel at a minimum.

"As pedestrians proceed only with redoubled caution.

"Assist the militia, police, and other public safety agencies.

"Do not seek treatment at established hospitals. Local authorities have prepared lists of emergency medical centers. Consult those—"

Bradford dulled his ears to the frequently broadcast video tape and rolled out of bed, squinting against morning sunlight. Then he sat in a chair flexing his left wrist. Both pain and swelling were gone. Must have been only a sprain or it wouldn't have healed in just two weeks. He was damn lucky. Many stretcher and basket cases had been removed from his derailed train just outside the city.

Below, a siren's swiftly climbing pitch heralded its approach. Off in the distance, sliding down toward the bass end of the scale, another siren sped away on some urgent mission. Sirens, sirens, sirens. Every once in a while: remote blasts. Occasionally the crisp barking of gunfire as looters were routed.

An abrupt crash, sounding like an explosion in its own right, silenced the nearby siren. And the building quaked with the force of resounding impact. Bradford went to the broken window, one of its panes having been shattered a week earlier by a confused albatross that had plunged through into the room and spread its viscera upon the rug. An albatross? Here? This far from the sea?

Ten stories below a fire engine was half buried in the side of the hotel, submerged under an avalanche of bricks and mortar.

Since there were so few persons on the street only a handful gathered around the wreckage as the firemen hauled themselves out of the debris, like phoenixes rising from ashes.

Dazed, they exchanged glances until one shouted, "Nobody hurt out here. How's it in there?"

A waiter poked his head out of the hole in the wall. "Bricks and plaster all over the place. But no casualties."

"Your government," the Advisory Commission spokesman went on, staring from the television screen, "is investigating the cause of this accelerated accident rate. Until it is found and corrected, you are urged to observe the following precautionary measures: First ..."

Bradford switched to another channel and went into the bathroom to shave. As he lathered his face he reflected on what an ironic twist Fate had taken: Two weeks ago he had seemed to be the only unbalanced element in a sane world; now it was a world gone mad, in which he alone stood out as a rock of rationality. Or was it all only the effects of a prolonged freakout?

He paused while the hot-water faucet vented steam. Could it be that sanity was only relative? Had *nothing* changed but his perspective? Was everything about him illusion—his own hallucinations? But, no. *He* was all right. It was *everything out there* that was all wrong. Or was it?

As to proving whether he was being watched, though, he had established nothing. For it might be either that he had thrown off his followers, in which case he would soon give them a chance to latch on again, or that present circumstances made tailing impracticable.

Yet, splitting the Powers-Chuck-Ann scene had proved *something*. Since then there had been no more illusions, no more unsolicited freakouts, anxieties. That is, if what was happening outside was the real reality—not an unreality of his mind's own making. It was almost as though something *within him,* however, were more at peace with the world, with the entire universe.

The tap water turned ice-cold, became spewed hailstones that clattered against the basin, then regained its normal temperature. He resumed shaving.

But he had no intention of hiding forever. He *was* still head of an established business. All right, then—"figurehead." Nevertheless, he was determined to be on hand if the ax of financial dissolution fell—as it was falling so frequently all over now despite emergency federal regulations. Perhaps he could help stay the ax. Or maybe he just wanted to see the expression on his managing director's face when the plug was pulled on P & D Enterprises.

Life had become too involved, too incomprehensible, unmanageable. So he had simply copped out, as though afraid to face the consequences of all the complexities. But soon things would be different. Now he was ready to begin asserting himself. First, he would lay the groundwork. (He glanced at his watch; if he didn't hurry he'd be late for the appointment.) Then he would make the establishment scene again, well assured that the watchers would themselves be under surveillance.

Would Ann still be there? God, he hoped not. Her involvement in his deception had been the most difficult reality to bear. It would be better if he never saw her again.

While dressing for the appointment, his attention was half directed upon a special telecast in which several somber, imposing panelists were officiously exploring "this thing that has befallen us."

"It appears clear," one of them was saying, "that what we are concerned with here is a sort of mass hysteria deriving from the pressure of intolerable social events."

"Would you clarify that, Dr. Brightley?" said the moderator.

"Of course. The civilizing process advances in spurts, with the gregarious individual laboring up slopes onto plateaus of optimum accommodation. As developing societies struggle up these elevations, complexities pile on top of complexities until, without realizing it, the individual potential as an instrument of mass hysteria ripens and ..."

"Are you saying," interrupted the moderator, "that the load is too heavy to bear? That we are all—shall we say?—at the end of our rope as a result of political entanglements, social upheavals, imminent nuclear holocaust, economic insecurity, and a spate of coincidental natural disasters?"

"That is a valid diagnosis," another panelist presumed to answer. "Unconsciously, our culture is at the breaking point."

"Yes, of course," Brightley resumed. "At such a juncture in the civilizing process, it requires but a subtle prod to set off the entire reactive syndrome. A few spectacular accidents are sufficient stimuli to plant the suggestion in *everybody's* mind that we are all suddenly hyperprone to catastrophe. Autosuggestive processes take over. And we find ourselves where we are today—each trying desperately to prevent the mishaps that we are unconsciously determined to experience."

The moderator cleared his throat. "That *is* a sophisticated theory, gentlemen. And one well worth examining. But what about all the minor impossible happenings, and the freaks of …"

But Brightley wouldn't be led away from his hypothesis: "Oh, we've seen it many times before. There was a witch-burning hysteria. Another led to public mayhem in the arenas of ancient Rome. Of less serious consequences: unidentified objects cluttering our skies. This present manifestation of mass hysteria is more serious, more universal because communication is now instantaneous. I think …"

Bradford didn't give a damn what Brightley thought, so he switched to another channel and welcomed the unfamiliar sight of a simple commercial on the cleansing attributes of the nation's leading detergent.

In a sense, Brightley's explanation held no more water than that advanced by the God-Walks-Among-Us-Ites who claimed to have prophesied the nova currently flaring in the southern sky. One interpretation was no less a wild guess than the other. And neither took into account the altogether improbable destruction of Moonbase Britain by a meteor six days ago, or ripples turning into tidal waves, or—for that matter—faucets that hissed out steam, then spat ice pellets. Maybe it *was* all his own personal weirdout after all.

He adjusted his stud belt and fetched a tangerine jacket from the closet.

The soap commercial ended. A microphone-wielding interviewer and his subject, a balding man in Army olive drab, claimed the screen to resume yet another "special newscast."

"We could just possibly be under some sort of attack," proposed the uniformed officer.

"Are you suggesting a *military* attack?"

"The word 'attack' implies as much, doesn't it?"

"But the effects we're observing are worldwide. Doesn't that eliminate your thesis?"

The Army man shrugged. "Not at all. First, how do we actually *know* the effects are worldwide? Then: Suppose it was decided to introduce a new nerve gas or similar agent into the fighting in Turkey—something that causes malcoordination during critical moments when the human organism should be peaking for emergency response. Malcoordination and possibly hallucination too. Suppose, however, the delivery system backfired, achieving worldwide coverage."

"In that case, the malfunctioning delivery system could have been the responsibility of the Turkish insurgents or loyalists, or the Russian support forces—or even *our own* expeditionary personnel."

"Oh, I don't know about *that*," the officer replied guardedly.

"Thank you, colonel," said the interviewer. "And now, Dr. Sellick, I understand you have some thoughts on the matter."

Panning away from the colonel, the screen brought a small, shaggy-haired man into view on the right. "I'm interested," he said, "in Peking's charge that the distortion in space curvature caused by orbital nuclear testing not only affected *pi*, but also interrupted the discipline of cause and effect as well."

"You mean you *believe* that?"

"No, not exactly. But Dr. Strauss of the Vienna Institute of Advanced Physics is attempting to reduce probability and determinism to a field theory. Such effects as we're witnessing today would then be explained by fluctuation in the field."

Bradford snapped off the set, more interested in a coincidence that had just occurred to him. His freakout on the beach—dreams of being hit by a car in an unlikely accident, of miraculous escape after falling from a plane, of unbelievable luck at gambling—they were all similar to the improbabilities that were now bugging reality!

He straightened his jacket, thrust a cigarette between his lips and struck a match. But it wouldn't light. He tried another. No luck. When a third match brought him no nearer success, he tossed the cigarette, together with the matchbox, into a wastebasket and strode out of the room. A minute later the entire box flared into flame that spread successively to a newspaper in the basket and the drapery hanging just above it.

...◆...

Next morning Powers, a sheriff's deputy, and the coroner drew up in front of a glass-panel office door. "This," the psychiatrist said, "is a pathetic case. Young man. Wealth, position, everything. I've been treating him for five years."

"Not dangerous, is he?" the deputy asked, stiffening.

"Of course not. Just suffering delusions."

"And you need me for commitment proceedings?" the coroner said.

"God, I hope not! That's why I asked you to accompany me. I'm trying every trick to avoid institutionalization. I've got to know each move he makes. He called here yesterday." Powers thrust his thumb toward the doorplate that read:

PROCTOR & PROCTOR
(Private Investigation)

"If I can learn *why*," he added, "I may be able to help him." The coroner acknowledged the obligations of longstanding friendship. "We'll do whatever we can, Boris."

"Sure," the deputy agreed. "But let's don't waste time. I've got my hands full out there." He gestured outdoors, where yesterday's hotel fire had gutted three buildings just a block away.

Within minutes they were seated around the elder Proctor's cluttered desk and the latter, fingering the bristly gray surface of an anomalous crew cut, was saying: "Even if I admitted a client named Bradford was here, Phil, I couldn't tell you the nature of his business." His obstinacy was directed at the deputy.

"Oh, come on," Phil scoffed. "Don't pull that professional code of ethics stuff on me, Jim."

Frowning, Proctor ran a hand over his stubbled scalp. "Okay. So I've got a plum I don't want to lose. Anything wrong with that?"

"Perhaps," Powers suggested, "you won't have to lose it."

"This could be a commitment case, Mr. Proctor," the coroner reminded him. "Where would your plum be then? As a matter of fact, how do you know Bradford's checks won't bounce?"

"He paid a fat retainer." Proctor loosened a bit. "And his check didn't bounce. That was the first thing I made sure of."

"There." Powers spread his hands. "You suspected it right off. Surely you realize he's no *normal* client. What did he want here?"

Proctor hesitated. "Come on, Jim," the deputy urged. "This case is an exception."

Proctor signaled his submission with a sigh. "Bradford believes some unknown persons are shadowing him."

"Did he say why he thinks he's being followed?" Powers asked.

"No. Wants me to get an independent answer and see if it confirms his suspicions."

Relieved, the psychiatrist said. "He *is* being followed—by members of my staff. His condition is nearing a critical phase, but we're trying to avoid commitment. He even suspects *me* of conspiring against him, I believe."

Proctor smiled. "You're right, doctor. We're supposed to keep you under surveillance too, to determine whether any of the persons tailing him are in contact with you."

"Jim," the deputy said, "I think you should cooperate with Dr. Powers. You could help a good deal, obviously."

"Indeed you could," Powers confirmed. "I would suggest that you simply hold your operatives in readiness—on the strength of Bradford's retainer, of course. If we need you to help keep track of him, we'll call for your services."

"But what do I do about reporting to him? We were supposed to start running shifts tomorrow morning when he returns to his office."

"Just stay out of Dr. Powers' way," the deputy advised, "and give Bradford negative reports at the intervals you agreed upon."

"And I keep the retainer?"

"You'll have to work for it later on," Powers revealed. "And I, personally, shall see that you receive additional compensation."

The desk tilted abruptly, thudding down upon a suddenly crumbling leg and spilling pen set, papers, and ashtrays upon the floor. "Would you look at that?" Proctor invited, kneeling to inspect the damage. "Leg just gave way. And the desk is brand new."

···◆···

"What it amounts to," Duncan was saying as he crowded Wittels' bony elbow at the direction-finder controls in communications, "is either that favorable or unfavorable results are likely. Thank God it's not a complete breakdown in causation. Where the balance is delicate—especially where the almost random effects of human activity are involved—the results are more noticeable, sometimes spectacularly so.

By the same token, a lot of people who otherwise would be lying dead in the streets are *escaping* harm."

Wittels was waiting for the receiver to warm up. "What about random effects in nature?"

"We've seen some of them. Aberration in molecular activity is apparently tolerable on the whole, though at times deadly in particular instances. Cosmic effects, of course, won't be assessed for years. Geologic results? I don't like the marked disturbances in world meteorological patterns that we've heard about."

Joining them, Chief Mathematician Steinmetz advised, "Our real concern ought to be in the atomic range. I've been told by our contacts in several of the laboratories that nuclear experiments are yielding unpredictable results."

"There've been no reactor failures, at least," Duncan said. "Perhaps their multiple damping systems cancel out the effects of our new probability values."

Behind them, Security Chief Hawthorn let his chair lean back against the wall. "If all that keeps up out there, I don't see how we can preserve civilization."

"No doubt," Duncan agreed, "we'll have to modify conventional human behavior, stressing caution. But, even then, we won't be able to save an economy based on risk as a concession to profit."

The foundation director joined his staff in introspective consideration of the dangers and necessities that lay ahead. If disintegration in natural law couldn't be reversed, rather than simply halted, it would mean an entirely different mode of existence. Life, as it had been known before, would not be able to continue.

Inner fibers of dedication and determination stiffened as he began refining requirements of the future. There'd have to be, of course, worldwide scientific investigation to establish the modified parameters of survival. Then many authoritarian enforcement arms would be needed to mold the remnants into new patterns of behavior as well as scores of specialized shock troops. And the obligation would have to rest with his organization, for only the foundation was aware of the circumstances.

Yes, the responsibility was *his*. Not that he'd sought it. Rather it had been thrust upon him. And, because he knew better than anyone else the underlying reality of what was happening, he couldn't slough it off—although he normally wouldn't want to be placed in a position of authority over even a single laboratory assistant.

But he had to continue manipulating Bradford, the crucially variable factor in a delicately balanced equation. If he were to save the world, Bradford's influence would have to be stabilized. The rigid discipline that had once governed natural law would now have to be imposed on the Creative Force's host.

And there could be no more mistakes in directing Bradford's destiny. For each error would be too costly and any one of them could be the ultimate slip. The discipline that was evaporating from natural processes would have to be enforced even more stringently upon the foundation and upon the unwitting host around whom the entire organization revolved.

"Let's pull Bradford in and try the Ultimate Remedy," Hawthorn urged.

"We will," Duncan decided impulsively, "... as soon as he's maneuvered into voluntary acceptance of treatment at the clinic. He'll be back at his office tomorrow. We'll let Powers, Chuck, and Ann take it from there."

"Then the Ultimate Remedy?" Hawthorn said anxiously.

"First I would want him fully sedated for a long time while we decide whether to attempt direct contact with the Creative Force or let things ride, with the hope that Bradford's total isolation will serve to restore some of the order that's been destroyed."

Yes, Duncan reflected, it was better that they have Bradford under thumb. Not knowing what might go down the drain next was too suspenseful. Even now, the entire universe may have been snuffed out except for this insignificant system of sun and nine planets—no, eight; they'd already inspired the destruction of Pluto.

A squeal peaked in the D/F receiver's speaker. Wittels tapped the cabinet. "Composite carrier wave, coming from all of the left-heel transmitters in Bradford's P & D Towers apartment."

"Hell with that," Hawthorn said. "Let's see where *Bradford* is."

Wittels adjusted the directional antenna and the squeal was eventually replaced by a softer tone that emitted *beeps* at two-second intervals. He read the calibrations on his dials. "Same place as before—his hotel."

"How do you know?" Hawthorn demanded.

Wittels spoke into a transmitter's microphone. "Any change, Bevins?"

"None," the answer came out of another speaker. "Stabilized in his room. Rutledge's D/F and mine are holding on the same fix."

"Good. Make certain he doesn't slip away until he comes back under direct observation in the morning."

"That's it," Wittels told Hawthorn, "... in his room pacing."

"How do you know *what* he's doing?"

"PE generator's modulating the carrier wave of the transmitter in his left heel with every other step he takes."

"Good equipment," Hawthorn acknowledged, then taunted: "But how come we couldn't track him when he escaped from his lodge in a motorboat?"

"The foundation's not exempt from the new vicissitudes of probability. We lost two men when our D/F truck went off the cliff that night. And don't forget, we picked Bradford up again just as soon as he came within range of our equipment here in the city."

Duncan turned abruptly toward the opening door.

"They told me I'd find you here," the man who poked his head in said. Although broad of shoulder and stocky, he bore the burden of layers of flesh that late middle age had deposited about his waist.

"Perrilaut!" Duncan greeted his Washington observer who had access to the scientific hot line. "You didn't tell us you were coming!"

"Couldn't risk having any intelligence agent listening in on a conversation with you."

"But you took a chance traveling."

"It was worth it, considering the news I bring. I saw Vasilof in Washington. He's going to meet with you."

Duncan savored near elation for the first time in months, and showed it with a smile he hadn't used in as long a time. "When? Where?"

"Tomorrow afternoon. Here."

Duncan winced. "God! You haven't led him to the foundation?"

"Of course not. He believes you're coming from another city too. The appointment's for one in the afternoon. Grandmoor Hotel."

"What persuaded him?" Steinmetz asked.

"Proxima Centauri going nova. What else? He was deeply impressed by our prediction."

Duncan thought a moment. "What does he expect to talk about?"

"In a vague sense, a new effect that's been discovered by a group of scientists outside of the conventional establishment."

Duncan luxuriated in the possibility that others, perhaps an entire foundation branch on the other side of the world, might soon share the burden of Bradford, helping detect future aberrations in natural law, and evaluate their consequences.

"You're happy about this meeting?" Perrilaut asked.

"Aren't you?"

"I have my doubts. That Russian could have suspicions of a political nature, you know."

Duncan drew erect with self-confidence, sought to radiate the calm assurance that he knew was expected of him as their leader. "I'll convince him. I have all the evidence. Irrefutable proof. The kind a scientific mind can't reject."

"It had better also be the kind an ideological mind can't suspect, just in case Vasilof's above-country dedication to science is only a superficial aspect of the man's character."

X

"I think till I'm weary of thinking,"
Said the sad-eyed Hindu King,
"And I see but shadows around me,
Illusion in everything."
—Sir Alfred Comyn Lyall

...◆...

Disciple Pockface's arms were spread open to the marvel that filled his eyes. It was a moment of profound reverence. Crowded about him on the beach were hundreds of others, most of whom had already embraced inside-out rags in commemoration of topological transformation. And these Cosmotheotopic neophytes who looked to him for spiritual guidance were not all just groovers like himself. Oh, no. Many were confused consies, some still in their conservative suits. They were groping for the Light, hanging on each word of Enlightenment that he had brought them from Montague. And, oh, how they had *found* the light! Pockface's arms were tiring, but he held his impressive pose while everyone drank in the intoxicating beauty of the awful Light.

The beach was cluttered with putrescent creatures washed up by yesterday's great wave. Thanks to the Primary One, the wind was blowing ashore and sweeping the stench across Biscayne Bay toward Miami. The wave had also flushed out the sentinel-like hotels lining the beach, leaving no one to interfere with this Veneration of the Light ceremony.

He lowered his arms, ending the period of meditation. Now his congregation divided its attention between him and the blazing tiny sun whose glory almost challenged the usual one setting in the west. He stood with his staff planted between his feet, its shaft held flush against his sparse beard. Then he pointed at the nova, hanging like a sparkling lantern just above the sea, and intoned: "Behold the sign of the Primary, just where Eugatnom said it would be! It has shone there every evening for five days, has it not?"

Many voices rose in eager confirmation. His shoulders squirmed, seeking a more comfortable fit within the inside-out, backwards ceremonial vestment—a discarded beach robe.

"You have prophesied well, O, Elpicsid," marveled a blond superchick whose inverted, exterior bra had half missed the mark and was partly bunched up near her left shoulder, leaving only a stretched nylon blouse to provide support she evidently didn't need. "Truly, you dig the Decoded Word, the Undimmed light," she added devoutly and with a large amount of adulation.

Regarding her as a better than fair replacement for the Martyr Marcella, he jabbed his staff into the sand. "I am not the Tehporp! I only bring you His Word!" Then, smiling at the chick, he went on, "Eugatnom Yloh is the only one of the Primary's chosen creatures who can dig the Topological Transformation of the Inverse Vessel. When I told you about the expected Light I did not know for certain it would be there. But Eugatnom knew. And I had faith. And I spread his prophecy."

His rigid finger shot out once again, as though to impale the glittering star that shone more brightly than the full moon. It hung just above the restless water, casting out spurs of glimmering radiance. Already the sun had set, but the sheer magnificence of the light itself seemed equal to holding the night at bay. "Dig it, man!" Pockface exhorted. "Don't let it shaft you! Haul it in and clutch it tight, because it's the work of the Primary! And dig this too: Of all the Cosmotheotopists, the Miami CTTs are the most favored, except for our brothers in belief in Brownsville. That nova don't shine anywhere else but way down here."

"That thing up there—" began a haggard, elderly man whose shirt bulged with a concealed bottle.

"The light!" Pockface corrected. "The Light of the Primary!"

Chastised, the man resumed, "The Light—is it a sign that the Primary's grossed out with us? Is it a part of all that's happening?"

"No. The Primary didn't blow his cool, if that's what you mean. He blasted that star over four years ago. But it's taken all that time for the Light to reach us. Eugatnom was with the infidels when it happened. But, instead of making with the big bows to the Primary, the infidels put the screws to His Inverse Vessel, the Infinite Man."

"Drofdarb?" the superchick asked, staring up at him. He noticed she'd made no effort to adjust her inverted bra. And when she caught him looking she smiled, but did nothing about the unfilled cup.

"Wouldn't that be a guy named Bradford?" asked the old man as he sucked on the bottle and wiped his lips with the back of a grubby hand.

The Disciple swore. "Down on your knees before the Light! We're not supposed to use Drofdarb's untopologically transformed name!"

The man took another swig and knelt. "But He is, ain't He?"

"We don't talk about Drofdarb except in reverence. Not until we rescue Him from the infidels and build Him a shrine on top of Pike's Peak so's all the world can come and worship Him from below." Pockface was improvising now. But, he assured himself, it sounded good.

Impressed by his fervor, all sat facing south, letting the golden-white light of the nova bathe their features. The Disciple had once seen a picture of Easter Island's great stone heads. And he accepted his congregation's equally motionless faces as a tribute not only to the wondrous Sign in the Sky, but also to his eloquence as a spreader of the Word.

Now for his heavy pitch: "My mission is to prepare a crusade to rescue Drofdarb. Others like me are working in other parts of the country. When we're all ready we'll snatch the Infinite Man!"

"And enshrine Him on Pike's Peak?" someone asked.

"More than that. We'll maybe even get through to the Primary and have Him put things back in order again."

"You mean the world won't have to put up with all this crap no more?"

"Right! Everything's all fouled up because the infidels are screwing around with Drofdarb and the Primary."

"How do you know?"

"I knew about the Light in the Sky, didn't I?"

"He knew," many affirmed.

Pockface again speared the sand with his staff. It was a masterful bit of showmanship and he knew when to use it. "First we'll sing our CTT hymn, 'The Primary One,' then we'll start planning our Pilgrimage. We'll form a committee on transportation and another on provisions. Next …"

"Elpicsid!" cried the superchick, pointing at the sea. "Look!"

All the water was rushing away, as though some giant wind were pushing it. Only, there wasn't any wind. Confused, Pockface watched the exposed wet sand glistening in the brilliance of the Light.

"That's what happened before yesterday's wave!" a woman shouted. "Into the hotel! Get up to the highest floor!"

Pockface dropped his staff, caught the blond chick's hand and, robe flaring, raced with her and the others for the building.

…◆…

Striding into the outer office of P & D Enterprises, Bradford was struck by the number of empty desks, the distant stares on the faces of those present. Little work was being done, understandably. Windows against which hailstones drummed held the reluctant attention of most.

As he crossed toward his private office, Adrian Clark came blustering down an aisle, turgid jowls flapping with each bounding step. "So damn glad to have you back, Brad!" the general manager exclaimed. "I was overjoyed when you called last night. But, God, how I worried about you these past two weeks!"

"I'd have returned when all hell broke loose," Bradford said. "But …" He rotated his left wrist "But I got banged up a little."

"Why didn't you let us know?" Clark reproved. "Rawlings got it. Did you hear? Crushed to death when a beam fell while he was inspecting one of our theater renovation jobs."

Bradford mumbled respectfully and continued on almost to the open door of his reception room before Clark overhauled him again.

"Brad," he whimpered, "I'm afraid we're going to have to suspend operations; even let the staff go. If we don't take advantage of the emergency moratorium provisions we'll fall apart!"

"We'll keep the bare necessities going, the apartment complexes especially. And no evictions, not for any reasons. Padlock the office here, though; but everyone stays on the payroll."

"We can't do that!" the managing director objected. "Not with practically all of our assets frozen. We'll go under!"

It was good to see Clark squirm—even if he stood to lose nothing, relatively, but a good job. (And even if he was, as Bradford now noticed, sporting a see-through blouse and chest protector.) But the real financial sacrifice, Brad reminded himself, would be his own. "Happy sinking."

He tensed before continuing to his office. An earthquake? God, he hoped not, remembering yesterday's devastation in Chile. But the tremors had probably been only his own as he wondered whether Ann would be back on the job. Entering the reception room, he closed the door behind him.

She merely sat there for a moment, soft eyes reflecting no particular inner reaction. Then she swept around the desk and embraced him, her gold-brocaded peplum digging into his thighs. Why in hell did she have to be wearing *that* revealing outfit?

"Oh, Brad! I heard you say you were hurt. How badly?"

Pretty damn badly, he wanted to reply deviously. But he was thankful she had come through these two weeks unharmed. "Nothing much."

"Why did you run off after asking me to marry you?" she said hesitantly. "Was it because you changed your mind?"

There she was, sinking in the hook as soon as he came within range. "Well, Brad, I won't hold you to anything. I had to stay around long enough to tell you that much and …"

"Oh, shut up!" He threw open the door to his office and, aware that she had followed him in, stood staring in perplexity at Powers, seated behind his desk, and Chuck, perched on its edge. Confronted by the blatancy of this conspiracy, he decided he wouldn't have to wait for confirming reports from Proctor & Proctor. "Damn convenient to find all of you together. Now get out!"

Chuck eased to his feet and glanced expectantly at Powers. "You've been having trouble again, haven't you, Brad?" the psychiatrist asked soothingly. "More hallucinations?"

"Hell no! There never were any!"

Ann backed against the wall. Chuck tensed. Powers only sat there, relaxed.

"I dig how you matched Soapbox Slopes and beach stories to bug me out of my mind!" he went on, the fury of his words punctuated by the clatter of hailstones shooting in through a broken window. "It's not going to happen again!"

In a voice barely audible against the hailstorm, Powers coaxed, "Come sit over here, Brad." He indicated a chair beside the desk.

From habit, Bradford complied. But he rebounded to his feet and faced the psychiatrist, keeping the desk between him and Chuck. "So the girl on the beach wasn't real? Well, that phantom gave me something—something *solid*. And only a *real* person can carry a *real* thing!"

"Yes?" Powers said patiently.

"Here's the *solid* part of that hallucination." He tossed the cufflink box on the desk. "The girl on the beach gave me this—before she warned that I had to get away from you!"

Powers opened the case and let the token fall onto the desk pad.

Ann strained forward. "My earring! I thought I'd lost it!"

Bradford stared at the object. It *wasn't* a Mobius Strip! Only a simple golden earring. A thin, circular band hanging from a lobe clamp. But twisted out of shape, as though someone had stepped on it!

Ann retrieved the earring, taking its mate from her stash bag and letting them dangle side by side. "Don't you remember? On that washed-up boat that night—"

Bradford *did* remember! The derelict cabin cruiser. His preoccupation with the oncoming surge of acid-stoked euphoria and soul-coupling. And he *had* knelt painfully on something small and round. Her earring? Had he, without realizing it, also put the thing in his pocket—the same pocket into which he had later imagined depositing the Mobius Strip token given him by the naked chick on the beach?

Confused, he looked at Ann and at the earring. *Two* earrings. No Mobius Strip. Just for a moment, he allowed himself the incidental luxury of granting Ann full exoneration.

But that only reinstated his illusions. Two earrings, no Mobius Strip bore only one consequence: validation of all of his far-out experiences as full-fledged hallucinations. For what he had believed to be a Mobius Strip was the sole peg that supported his claim to equilibrium.

Powers eased him into the chair. "I'm aware of what you're thinking, son. Actually, I knew you were imagining the earring to be something pressed into your hand by the 'girl on the beach'—a Mobius Strip. Don't you see? A Mobius Strip is a twisted thing. And you did get things all twisted up that night. Good unconscious symbolism there."

"You *knew* about the Mobius Strip?" Bradford asked.

"Of course. And I'm surprised you still haven't realized that during our sessions I have access to everything in your unconscious."

Bradford lowered his head. It was difficult to abandon newfound convictions of his normality.

"Yes, Brad," Powers resumed, "I knew about your little token and your unconscious distrust of us. But, God, I didn't think it would make you run off! Otherwise I would have brought it out in the open rather than wait for you to figure it all out for yourself."

The psychiatrist sighed. "I guessed wrong, Brad. You need help, more comprehensive treatment."

Puzzled, Bradford asked, "You *prevented* me from looking at the earring all the time I was away, didn't you?" He remembered how he hadn't wanted to open the case until he was ready to confront them.

"Yes. Posthypnotic suggestion. I wanted to make certain you wouldn't inspect the thing again—not until you were with me. When you stopped hallucinating, I intended to be on hand to help you over the hump."

The sound of a distant explosion—or perhaps a collapsing building—rose above the staccato of hail drumming upon the oak floor.

"God," Bradford moaned. "It's not only me! It's the whole world!"

"What do you mean?" Chuck asked.

"All that stuff out there. *That* kind of hail. Explosions. Another sun in the sky. And the sirens never stop. Never."

"Hail?" Powers said, drawing back.

"Yes. Look at it piling up on the floor."

"It's not hailing, Brad," Chuck assured. "It's a clear, summer day."

"No hail, son," Powers confirmed. "No explosions. No sirens."

"Ask them out in the office!" Bradford shouted, refusing to believe he had hallucinated two weeks of chaos. "They'll tell you!"

Ann summoned Ronald Bankston over the intercom.

When the real estate specialist entered, Powers said, "Would you give us your impression of the weather we're having outside?"

Bankston hesitated, apparently puzzled. "Why, it's a lovely day. A bit too much sun, perhaps—"

After Bankston's dismissal, Bradford hardly heard Powers' candid appraisal: "Periodic hallucinations are progressing into hallucinosis. That has got to be stopped. Will you come to my clinic?"

"Whatever you say." Bradford disregarded the mound of hailstones, deadened his ears to the so-real clatter of falling ice pellets.

Powers administered an injection and waited for it to take effect. Then he and Chuck supported Bradford between them and walked him through the outer office.

Ann listened to their explanations of "sudden illness" as they went along. Eventually she closed the door and knelt among the hailstones, sifting them through her fingers and despising her role in Bradford's latest deception. Her warm tears mingled with the melting ice.

When would the treachery stop? After she'd sworn she would play it straight with him, they had talked her into the earring-substitution trick. And now this latest fraud about the weather. Was she in a position that she *couldn't* be truthful to Brad even if she wanted to—as she so desperately desired, actually? What would be the next deceit?

...◆...

Dimitri Vasilof was a stout, coarse-faced Ukrainian with a broad separation between his upper front teeth that suggested jollity. His deep-throated, booming laughter encouraged that impression, as it was doing now while he rocked back and forth on the sofa.

Holding his briefcase like a shield, Duncan scowled. "Dr. Vasilof, there is nothing—*nothing at all*—humorous in this situation."

If you'll allow me my own opinion, one that will doubtless be the official reaction of my government," Vasilof said in cultured English, "I shall prefer to regard this entire affair in a most ludicrous light."

"But you agreed to keep this within the *scientific* community!"

The Russian gripped stout knees with pudgy hands and leaned forward, guffawing down on the cocktail table.

Outside the hotel room window, the hailstorm had stopped. An afternoon sun was trying to pierce low, gray clouds. Icy drafts were slicing in through the shattered pane. Desolate silence hung over the street below. Many had already fled to a less hostile environment.

Vasilof drew in a steadying breath, but his sharp eyes retained their merriment. "I agreed only to come here and talk with you, Dr. Jones."

Duncan was relieved that he had used an assumed name for this contact—insurance against the foundation being found out by government interests. But he realized belatedly that he hadn't been thorough enough. He could be traced through Perrilaut, who had arranged the meeting. He *had* to convince the Russian.

"I came despite the risk entailed in transportation," Vasilof went on. "Without aides. Vulnerable to the quirks of nature that your perverted science has loosed upon the world. Do you know *why* I came?"

Duncan said nothing.

"To play your little game. But, believe me, we recognize this meeting for what it is: unorthodox diplomacy, international wrangling, perhaps an attempt at blackmail, negotiation without portfolio. So, Dr. Jones, state your price in the name of your government and we shall see whether we have anything to discuss, any provisional agreements to pass on to our foreign offices as the basis of *conventional* diplomacy. And I might add that neither the first secretary nor I appreciate this attempt to make international negotiations more complicated than they are."

Shrinking back against the sofa, Duncan realized Vasilof was here under direction of the Kremlin. There was only one solution to this perplexing turn of events: Win the man over; convince him overwhelmingly. But how?

"I assure you my government knows nothing about this," he said. "Good God, man, we're trying to *save the world*! But we need your help!"

Vasilof chuckled. "I can understand that these negotiations have to be conducted in secrecy. Otherwise every nation on earth would find out that the United States alone is responsible for all of the world's ills. So please be satisfied with the fact that we're willing to play your game—at least until we find out what the price is."

Duncan begged, "You've got to believe me!"

The Ukrainian restrained his laughter for the first time. "You want me to think that there is a Good Force—"

"*Creative* Force."

"—that's responsible for all existence. Good Force, Creative Force—what's the difference? They both imply 'God', don't they?"

"No, we don't—"

"And this Good Force, you say, is associated with an *American* national." Vasilof's prolonged, roaring laughter brought blood rushing to his face. "Next you'll be suggesting there is an *Evil* Force, a *Destructive* Force, aligned with the Soviet Union. Really, Dr. Jones, how fortunate for you that I appreciate humor and haven't simply walked out on you and your government's gambit for confusing its opposition."

"But everything that's happening—doesn't that prove anything at all?"

"Prove anything? Yes," Vasilof nodded. "Prove that a Good Force is losing control over nature because It has overcomplicated Its universe? Hardly. Your country has somehow discovered a basic effect—the phrase you used to lure me here—that has got out of control."

He paused. "No. I won't say that. I'll just say that with this effect which you're demonstrating, at so costly a price, you expect to beat the world to its knees; terrorize Liberation forces in Turkey and elsewhere. In due time you will make your demands known, then sit back and await concessions to calamity."

Duncan swore. "Would we wreck *our own* country just to ..."

"You have an effect which cannot be localized. So you're simply using it until you achieve your ends. What you are sacrificing internally can be replaced by captive labor and pillaged resources. But, with an unlocalized effect, it becomes merely a matter of which side can outlast the other. It may interest you to know we're riding the crest of your disruption of nature very well, thank you. And we'll outlast you. There are more of us."

In desperation, Duncan grabbed a handful of documents from the cocktail table. "Let me show you again—"

But the Russian waved him off. "You'll also be interested to know we're *using* the new probability mechanics with eminent success. Today, I've learned, our armies have successfully swept through Ankara and soon Turkey will be completely liberated. Do you know why?"

The foundation director only shook his head.

"Because we are *discarding* our most promising computer-derived stratagems. Instead, we are using those with an intermediate degree of success-likelihood. Last night we probed the weakest and strongest sectors of your front in Turkey. Today we didn't attack either. Rather, we struck in force at the intermediate positions."

"Damn the war in Turkey! These proofs here—"

Chuckling, Vasilof accepted the first item. "You've already told me. In the March, 1981, edition of *Physics Today* there's this article, 'Pluto—Captured from Proxima Centauri?' If I read the first word of the first paragraph, the second of the second, and so forth, I shall get:

"Pluto ... will ... be ... destroyed ... on ... March ... 16 ... 1981 ... Proxima ... Centauri ... will ... be ... seen ... as ... a ... nova ... in ... July ... 1985."

"And that issue was in circulation over two weeks before Pluto disappeared!" Duncan pointed out. "The article was submitted for publication in *October, 1980*!"

"In due time we shall learn how your treachery was conceived and executed, shall we not?"

"All this evidence is not trickery! During our research into continuous creation, our sensors led us to this person who ..."

"Yes, yes. You've already explained. Your instruments were swamped, as though tuned in on a reflection of the moment-to-moment creation of all the matter coming into being throughout the universe. We, too, have experimented quite extensively along the lines of continuous creation. But, frankly, I cannot say we were so—ah, blessed as to discover a 'Good Force' aligned with *our* side, Dr. Duncan."

The foundation director paled. "How—how did you know my identity?"

"Oh, I'm well aware of who headed your country's now-abandoned Project Genesis." Vasilof paused in an exaggerated effort of repressing more laughter. "And so, after you guessed this man's true nature during psychological inspection of his subconscious, you performed several confirming experiments with this—this associate of the Creative Force. You conjured up readily salable diamonds and precious metals, merely by having this associate relay suggestions through his unconscious mind. Thus assured of the validity of your hypothesis, you—ah, 'planted' in various journals the coded predictions of your to-be-performed miraculous demonstrations."

"What more could we have done to provide proof?"

Vasilof rose and folded his topcoat over his arm. "I assume you're not yet ready to state preliminary conditions?"

"You have the address of the law firm in Zurich that will give you the key to the safety deposit box I mentioned. They'll also give you legal confirmation that sealed documents have been only *added* to the box since 1980; that nothing has been tampered with."

"More proof. Well preserved—by a *capitalist* banker." Heading for the door, Vasilof passed by the broken window and snowflakes swirled in upon his dark hair.

Utterly thwarted, Duncan could entertain only an insignificant thought: snow—in July?

Pausing, the Ukrainian added, "You'll call for me again, I'm sure, when your government decides to discuss the issue openly. Meanwhile, if your 'effects' become too severe—well, we always have our nuclear trigger, you know."

Duncan ran down the hall after him. "But we need help! This is a responsibility of the international scientific community!"

Vasilof had half entered the self-service elevator at the moment its suspension cables parted. Crushed between the roof of the elevator and the hallway floor, he died instantly.

...◆...

At foundation headquarters on Addison Avenue that night, only the distant throbbing of auxiliary generators, operating on an abundance of stored fuel, disturbed the grim silence that followed Duncan's report on his meeting with the Russian.

Finally Hawthorn said, "At least the guy's dead. Nobody can get any information from him that could lead back to us."

Bankston looked as miserable as when he had helped Powers and Chuck bring Bradford from P & D's offices to the clinic that morning. "But what about Perrilaut? Vasilof was in contact with the

Kremlin all along. He's certain to have reported on Perrilaut's role. There's bound to be an investigation and Perrilaut—"

Duncan waved him silent. "Dr. Perrilaut was killed in a plane crash on his way back to Washington last night."

A moment later he interrupted the respectful but relieved silence: "At least we have Bradford safely in the clinic. How's he doing?"

"Resting comfortably under effective sedation," Powers said.

"We ought to take him to your place in the country, doctor," Chuck proposed. "Or maybe to his own lodge. He'd be safer there."

Duncan vetoed the suggestion. "More risk would be entailed in moving him. Anyway, it's convenient to have him next to headquarters."

Then he turned toward Powers. "I understand you led Bradford to believe he was hallucinating everything that's happening outside."

"It was the only way to get him to come to the clinic."

"But how will we eventually *un*tell him that he imagined all those ravages of nature if we get matters straightened out?"

"Let's face it," Hawthorn said. "Nature's falling apart. Merely letting Bradford lie there won't take the pressure off the Creative Force. We'll have to use the triggering phrase, charge him consciously with all the knowledge of what's been happening, then apply the Ultimate Remedy—direct appeal to the Force."

Duncan just sat there repeating to himself the phrase that would instantly supply Bradford with all the conscious knowledge they themselves possessed: "The foundation grew out of Project Genesis."

Then he remembered his preeminent role and drew himself up tall and firm, thumbs hooked under his belt. "We're going to do things the way *I* decide. I will brook no interference with the dictates of my intuition. First, we'll let things ride a while. A Bradford who can receive no sensory impressions may be all the margin the Force needs."

"But," Bankston said, "what happens should the host—die?"

Duncan had no answer. Anyway, his thoughts were striving to focus on something else, something having to do with antonyms—polar opposites, more precisely. But what? And why?

Finally he had it. And his face whitened.

"Vasilof," he said distantly, "sarcastically equated our 'Creative' Force to a 'Good' Force. He jokingly proposed an 'Evil' or 'Destructive' Force."

Everyone around the table frowned, waiting for his point.

"Suppose," he said, "just suppose there *is* a Destructive Force. One that's somehow helping to confuse the Creative Force."

Hawthorn protested, "You're damn close to theology again."

"But suppose there *is* a Destructive Force. One that's able to take advantage of the Creative Force's concessions to overcomplexity. One that can tip the scales in the direction of chaos."

"Oh hell, Duncan," Chuck reproved, "don't go …"

"Do you think It too might strike up an association with a human host and—"

He laughed weakly and apologized: "Sorry. But sometimes the imagination, sufficiently stimulated, can run away with you."

The others also resorted to the safety valve of laughter.

All except Powers. He only sat staring at the wall.

XI

Suspicion: How Intriguing to witness an instrument's incipient suspicion! Especially when he could only stew in his misgivings.

In the past there had been, oh, so many in similar predicament. Instruments who had no idea they were being maneuvered—until it was too late. Attila. Genghis Khan. Alexander. Napoleon. Wilhelm II. Hitler, Stalin, Tojo. Mao. (Odd that there were so many during recent times. Proof that Creation's overcomplexity was progressively diverting the Primary's attention from his favored ones.)

But, of time's legions of destructive instruments, the best of all was the present one, who was only now beginning to suspect. So subtly had he been inspired and directed! Oh, what a pliable, ultimate tool! All those other agents had blazed but limited *trails of devastation, misery, death. This one's instilled ambition, however, would carry him through to perpetration of* infinite *annihilation enveloping* all *of creation!*

He had been stupid, though, to imagine he would profit by unwittingly playing out the role that had been cast for him. But hadn't they all?

…◆…

Oblivious of the snowflakes that swirled about him, Powers trudged through the deep drift that had collected—in midsummer!—in the alleyway between foundation headquarters and the rear of his clinic.

His lips trembled as he mumbled over and over again the words Duncan had just said at the meeting:

"*… Suppose there* is *a Destructive Force … Do you think It too might strike up an association with a human host …?*"

Numbed by the impact of Duncan's incredible supposition, he fumbled for the gate's latch and passed on into the lesser darkness of the courtyard. Here a single light bulb shone above the clinic's rear entrance. Its feeble rays delineated a montage of snow-dabbed highlights among inky shadows.

Above, tall buildings on either side of the clinic stood out like hulking silhouettes, dimly backlighted by those sections of the city where electrical service had been restored.

"... *Suppose there* is *a Destructive Force* ..."

Several stories up, a large section of windowpane slid off the sill onto which it had come to rest during the afternoon hailstorm. Nicking a lower ledge, it caromed out over the courtyard. Only remotely concerned, Powers glanced up to see the sharp-edged glass hurtling directly at him, fitfully reflecting the light of the entranceway bulb.

A gust of wind swept down between the buildings, however, dislodging fallen snow in great swirls and deflecting the plunging glass. It sliced into a snowbank several feet away.

"... *Suppose there* is *a Destructive Force* ... *association with a human host* ... *Suppose there* is *a Destructive Force* ... *association* ... *human host* ..."

He went on into the clinic. The silence and desolation that pursued him down the corridors were familiar; for his institution had long since abandoned its conventional function in order to exist as an arm of the foundation.

Still unable to direct his thoughts, he passed the cell where "Yggi" and "Allecram" were being held—together now, so that Bradford could be at the opposite end of the building. He nodded at Murdock, who stood guard beside the CTTs' door. Murdock, he remembered, was the VA official who had helped deceive Bradford on Hedgmore's disability.

He barely returned the man's greeting as he rounded the corner and continued on to Bradford's cell, where Dr. Swanson stood by outside.

"... *Suppose there* is *a Destructive Force* ..."

Finally he answered Swanson's repeated salutation. Assured that Bradford was "doing fine," he entered the room. Ann sat there beside the bed, head bowed. Bradford was unconscious. A transparent tube snaked under the covers, carrying liquid nourishment to a vein in his left arm. His face was pale, even more noticeably so as a result of having just been shaved and talcked by Swanson.

Suddenly aware of Powers' presence, Ann bolted erect. "We can't do this to him!" she objected. "How long will this keep up?"

"... *Do you think It too might strike up an association with a human host ...?*"

"Dr. Powers! You aren't even listening!"

He took her hand. "I'm sure this is only temporary."

"But we can't keep him just scarcely alive—like *this*!"

"Bear with us, child," he said distantly, returning to the door.

She made other pleas. But he didn't hear them.

"... *Suppose there* is *a Destructive Force ...*"

He went to his office and locked the door. Pouring brandy from a decanter, he gulped it down, poured more and set the snifter on the desk before him.

"... *Suppose there* is *a Destructive Force ... Do you think It too might strike up an association ...?*"

Had Duncan, in wild conjecture, struck the truth? Could there actually be a *Destructive* Force too? Sentient like the Creative Force, but existing in a polar-opposite relationship?

Why not? Extremes had their counterextremes. Good-Evil. No, to hell with moral connotation. Simply: Creation—Destruction.

Didn't One *depend* upon the Other? Destruction could destroy only what was in existence. And, even though Creation could create from nothing through the raw neutron, It also seized upon debris left in the wake of Destruction and recreated order from disorder.

Destruction causing an unstable sun to burst asunder, spread its flaming hydrogen into the black of space. Creation, in Its secondary capacity of Recreator, picking up the pieces, calling upon gravitational forces to herd the volant atoms into gaseous masses from which second-generation stars would coalesce.

Destruction rending the neutron as it emerged from nothingness into the constant creation field. Creation reasserting Itself by assembling the pieces into an atom of hydrogen and a beta particle. Creation preserving order or restoring it. Destruction constantly disrupting order and imposing chaos. Creation—birth; Destruction—

calamity and death. Creation—peace; Destruction—war and famine and pestilence.

"... *Suppose there* is *a Destructive Force ...?*"

Was it simply the classic struggle between good and evil, recast in terms of opposing Universal Forces? Occasionally striking a balance? With the conflict once in a while tipping heavily in favor of one or the other, as was happening now?

Powers drained his snifter and fetched the brandy decanter from the cabinet, setting it on the desk. With no conscious self-direction, he filled and drained his glass three times, trying not to think at all. But the thesis would not be dismissed:

"... *Do you think It too might strike up an association ...?*"

Bradford was, in a sense, possessed—by a Force of whose existence he had no knowledge.

Could he, Powers, also be possessed—in similar but not identical manner? For the Force in Bradford was content only to hide from the runaway complexities of Its Creation. But if a Destructive Force existed, It had no need of sequestration. For It was obviously forging ahead in the fray. If It had "struck up an association" with *him*, It was sure to be an active association. A relationship with purpose. And he would have been selected only for his utility.

He, Powers—an *instrument?* A puppet on strings?

Trembling, he poured more brandy and recalled that day almost five years ago when, out of respect for his decade-long friendship with Duncan, he had accepted into his clinic a hopped-up kid who had been discovered strung out in the park. Why had he agreed to perform certain psychological experiments on the youth, despite his lack of other than perfunctory interest in continuous creation research? There was certainly little interest, and no obligation either to Duncan or to the hairy, grime-coated boy. Yet he had gone along—just as had Hedgmore, even though the latter showed only slightly more scientific curiosity than he. Hedgmore, however, had envisioned broad P & D promotional benefits from cooperating with Project Genesis.

Was it more than coincidental that when Bradford was located by the sensors, only a psychiatrist would be able to delve beyond his unconscious and discover what was hiding there? Had it been determined, by a Force other than himself, that he should play the role he had been playing these past five years?

And when he had decided it would be possible to engineer transfer of the Creative Force from association with Bradford to alliance with himself—had that been his *independent* judgment?

Wasn't it a fact that each attempt to effect transfer had resulted in partial *destruction* of nature's order? His driving ambition to control the Creative Force—was it *his alone*? He drank directly from the decanter. Tongue rolling over his lips, he shook his head sluggishly.

"Destructive Force?" he called out, as though addressing Someone who only might just be there. Then he laughed. Stupid thesis. But, then, it did fit so many facts. Even he had noticed his metamorphosis over these past five years. Once he *had* been kindly, unassuming, not motivated by monetary gain, devoting much of his time to charitable efforts. Now he was different. But what man would reject an opportunity to control the basic power of the universe?

Perhaps *he* would have—formerly. But now he couldn't be sure. For the inspiration could be his, or it might have been insidiously forced upon him. Yet, he knew now only that he *wanted* the power, regardless of whether it was his idea to achieve it for himself, or whether it was an ambition planted in him by the Destructive Force as a means of gaining Its own identical end of controlling the Creative Force.

Suppose, Powers wondered, there was a way of controlling *Both* of Them! Or, suppose he *were* a finely conditioned instrument of the Destructive Force, well on the way to accomplishing whatever end was expected of him. Suppose he balked. What if he became intractable, frustrated his Manipulator? Would he then be in position to bargain and gain concessions to his satisfaction?

"Destroyer?" he said more firmly, and swilled another snifter of brandy. "Damn it! I know You're there!"

Did he feel something stirring within him? Of course not. It wouldn't be done that easily. Yet—

"Destroyer!" He pounded the desk.

No answer. He laughed. At himself? Or at the ingenuity of the all-or-nothing plan he had just then conceived?

"All right," he addressed himself soberly. "I've been used and I'm ready to be used more. I'm a good agent. But I suddenly find out that all my ambition is but a vicarious reflection of Your own."

He was putting the words together sensibly, although they were slurred. "Now I realize I'm to be cast aside after *I* accomplish *Your* purpose. Well, I won't have it! Unless there's a better arrangement than that, I'm ready to destroy Your tool."

It wasn't a ploy. It was exactly the way he felt. (He didn't know, or even question whether the brandy had anything to do with his decision.) If he couldn't achieve at least some of the power he had come so close to possessing, then life wasn't worth the effort.

Powers slid open the drawer and withdrew his revolver, raising it to his temple. He *wouldn't* be used. Not unless he knew there was something in it for him. He drew back the hammer.

Put down your weapon. You are right: I don't intend to see all the effort I've invested in you go to waste.

Like a throbbing drumbeat resounding hollowly from somewhere deep within him, like the peal of thunder bouncing off soaring mountain ranges, the words burst into his conscious. No, they weren't words. Mere ideas, concepts in their pre-articulate form, flooding his perception, deadening his senses. Yet they conveyed precise meaning.

Hallucination? Just like the ones he had perpetrated on Bradford? Perhaps one of the psychopathological maladies he had spent most of his life treating? Or, simply alcoholic intoxication?

He reached for the decanter, but it burst soundlessly within his grip, as suddenly as though it had been shot out from under his hand. Brandy and shards of cut-glass bottle spilled onto the desk. *No hallucination*, the thought boomed like the crashing of surf upon rock. Then, somewhat more softly: *You* insisted *that I manifest Myself. So here I am—responsive, as cooperative as* I *expect* you *to be.*

"It's true then?" Powers whispered.

Yes, there is *a Destructive Force. And you have been an unwitting, though now willing, accomplice all these years.*

Powers slipped the revolver into his coat pocket and drained the snifter. "Can we do it? Can we confuse the Creative Force, take over completely?"

With your help, I will succeed this time.

"No, it can't be possible!" the psychiatrist objected, retching.

The Destroyer destroys. Destruction always triumphs. Life bows to death. Order is reduced to disorder. Entropy is the final leveler. It is only a human illusion that good triumphs over evil.

"Then there *are* theological overtones!"

Nonsense. You creatures are merely 'definers,' 'catalogists.' It amuses Me that you apply the labels 'good' and 'evil' as your basic certificates of subjective evaluation. I just used those concepts in tolerance of your metaphorical inclination.

Seeking respite from the abstract discourse, Powers asked, "Can we make the Creative Force transfer from Bradford to me?"

That's how I plan it. Then we shall both be in the same host. He will be brought in direct contact with the Force from which he has actually *been hiding. But he's not aware It's* I *he fears. All the while He's imagined He's been using Bradford to shield Himself from the intended*—intended, *indeed!—overcomplexity of* His *universe.*

"But It, I mean He *did* overcomplicate—"

Lets say He imagines *He did. My influence on His actions, all along, has been as subtle as it has been effective.*

Powers wondered: Why earth? Why humanity? Out of the entire universe, why should the conflict between the Forces center upon—

Because earth and its system and humanity are the fundamental considerations. All else is just decoration, background. The arrangement, however, is to My liking. Cosmic destruction is spectacular. Microcosmic chaos is interesting. But nothing can substitute for the delectable, sharp twang of emotional reaction to misery and catastrophe.

Powers realized that the Destroyer hadn't answered his spoken words that time; had replied instead to the ideas and concepts that preceded them. And, if that were the case, there would be no opportunity for deception, even if he should want to deceive the Force.

Correct. But we shall cooperate. And we shall achieve our ends: mine in full; yours, in lesser but still adequate measure.

"You're willing to cooperate?"

Won't be the first time I've entered such a liaison.

What, Powers wondered, would be expected of him?

If it suits you, simply forget this discussion ever occurred. I don't need *your cooperation since, as you now realize, I've managed you up until now. Just relax and continue reacting to your inner urges.*

"But what is the plan?"

Only what you imagine you've already planned on your own.

"And—what's in it for me?"

You will be the most powerful person who has ever existed. Because, with the Creative Force under my—our control, we can make Him produce anything you desire, refashion the world to your liking.

...◆...

A week later Powers, before the repaired window in his office, conceded the Destroyer must indeed be prevailing in the classic struggle. It was not so much the desolate scene in the street outside that convinced him. Rather, world conditions, as described over halting communications systems, proved the Destructive Force's ascendancy. He waited for confirmation of his surmisal from within. But nothing stirred; no subvocal bombast was hurled up into his conscious.

Outside, there was a trickle of traffic. Occasional pedestrians proceeded gingerly to business houses which almost invariably were found closed. But fewer fire engines and ambulances were required by those who had finally realized that new criteria of risk were in effect. Cautiously, troops patrolled the sidewalks.

Yet it was an almost abandoned city. All who had elsewhere to go had fled. Those who had no rural retreats remained in the relative safety of their homes and accepted whatever emergency rations were available.

Since the hail and snowstorm, intolerable heat had laid siege to the city. Many were convinced that the nova in Centaurus was responsible. And this persuasion was fortified by satellite instruments that detected components of hard radiation emanating from Proxima Centauri.

It was only natural, Powers supposed, that the nova should be blamed for everything that was happening to the world. Such as the endless succession of tidal waves that flung themselves with devastating force upon almost all coastlines. The gradual rise in ocean levels and temperatures. Hulks of dead leviathans that drifted up from the depth and, together with icebergs, made navigation almost impossible. Volcanoes. Earthquakes. Submergence of entire islands, including Oahu and Kauai in the Hawaiian chain.

A world approaching shambles in the wake of displacement in probability discipline. But a world that he, Powers, would remake into a paradise with the help of the Destroyer—*his* paradise.

He turned to the television, now receiving directly from the synchronous Satcom, and listened to a commentator urge that the war in Turkey be halted "in view of everything else."

"Anyway," the man reminded, glaring from the screen, "isn't it true the Loyalist-U.S. back has been broken? That insurrectionists, driven by fanaticism and adapting to the new elements of risk, have swept most of the country? That, negotiations notwithstanding, America faces its own Dunkirk on the shores of the Gulf of Adalia?"

Powers switched off the receiver. Despite all, the war in Turkey continued. Was it because the Lord of Destruction insisted upon the gratification that the fighting brought him? Powers listened within himself. But there was no comment. He glanced at his watch: seven o'clock. Ann would be just going on evening duty outside of Bradford's cell. Would she finally be desperate enough to take the bait? And was it *his* bait—or the Destroyer's?

When he reached the room he motioned the girl to follow him inside. She went and stood by the bed while he locked the door. Holding on to the iron railing, she rocked back and forth, her face tense.

Bradford lay in the same position as he had a week earlier, sheet drawn up under his chin. His cheeks were hollow, his eyes seemed to have become more sunken.

Powers remained a silent observer, letting the evidence of emaciation have its full psychological effect on the girl.

She turned in desperation. "This can't go on! I asked Dr. Duncan to give him just a few hours' consciousness every day. But he didn't even answer me, except to say something about *his* decisions being irrevocable. Maybe if you—"

He shook his head. "If I deviated at all from the foundation's plan, it would be along lines *I* believe would be effective. But I wouldn't even discuss my ideas with Duncan. His objections would be too numerous now, even though I'm certain I'm right."

"I know," she said. "You told me what you'd do if you were in charge. Not the *x, y, z, t* arrangement but another, more stable host."

"And you've kept it in confidence, as you agreed?"

She nodded. "I haven't told anyone, especially since you say you can't try anything without my help."

He resumed his silence, letting the bait dangle before her.

She nibbled. "You'd have Brad awake within hours?"

"Within minutes. Awake and with nothing at all to worry about, insofar as the Creative Force within him is concerned."

"And you believe you could *really* transfer It to you, without doing any more damage?"

"I'm certain, child." He gripped her shoulder. "It would solve many problems. You see, I have a mind untroubled by a history of narcotics, freakouts, planned hallucinations, suspicions, delusions. I could give It the firm anchor It needs."

"And Brad would be *free*?"

"Free and normal. You two would be at liberty to go anywhere you choose. I'd simply present the foundation with an accomplished fact and they would realize the wisdom of what I had done. Soon, in an orderly manner, I could begin feeding in subtle autosuggestions to restore normalcy to the world. And, before you knew it, everything would straighten out."

This deception of the girl, he wondered—was it his original conception? Entirely his?

The inner voice throbbed: *Not any more than was* your (a tinge of amusement here) *impulsive idea of transferring the Creative Force to* x, y, z, t *hosts. You* know *you don't have the scientific background for* that *type of false conjecture.*

Powers remembered his attempt to manipulate Ann that afternoon over a month ago at Bradford's seaside lodge. Had the Destroyer been directing him during his entire conversation with the girl then?

Of course. We were just playing a long shot. It did *seem possible, at the time, that the Other Force may have developed—ah, strong moralistic persuasions. Stoking the fires of lust was simply meant to test out that proposition.*

But, Powers thought, confused, *I made mistakes at the time. Ann became suspicious.* He paused uncertainly. *Were they* my *mistakes, or* yours?

You don't expect me to be perfect, do you—not in matters of construction? We were constructing *an attitude in the girl.* Destruction *is my purpose—and on vast, cataclysmic scales. Right now I'm hurling two of the Constructor's glittering galaxies at each other. Ordinarily, He would have blunted my enjoyment by seeing that not a single star in one of the galaxies passed near any star in the other—so vast did He make interstellar space. But not in this case. He has loosened His grip on probability discipline. Consequently, I'm arranging it now that millions of blazing suns will impact with millions of other blazing suns. You'll excuse me?*

Ann was apparently still absorbing the new hope that had been extended to her and Bradford. Finally she asked almost incredulously, "And Brad would never be troubled again?"

"Not even by his 'unprovoked freakouts.' For those are just instances of accidental contact between him and the Force."

Tactfully, he produced a hypodermic syringe. "Time for another injection."

"Wait!" She caught his wrist as her eyes became embers of suspicion. "This won't mean *more* deception, will it?"

"Oh no. As a matter of fact, we're going to be quite frank with him."

"What would *I* have to do?"

"Why, practically nothing, dear. He would respond to urgings from you more readily than from me. You would only have to follow my lead, appeal to his unconscious whenever I give you a cue."

Her tenseness drained away. "I'll do it, Dr. Powers—now!"

He forwent the opportunity to affect hesitancy. She was too well primed. Surely her appeals would get through to Brad's unconscious and beyond, where his own had consistently failed Then, at the proper moment, he would dismiss her and effect transfer.

Eagerly, he administered the counterinjection that would recall Bradford partly, but only partly, back to consciousness.

XII

I am searching, everywhere. But I can find nothing—nothing except the very tiny and the very great things. Light and darkness. Endless motion. Beautiful, graceful, swirling. Small, fierce, darting.

(Somewhere, as remote as though in another universe, Bradford was aware of his coarse, dry tongue fumbling to bring out the words; of the cruel hard-softness of the bed, the daggerlike thing that dripped, dripped, dripped into his arm.)

Look harder, Brad! Oh, darling, you've got to find it!

(Ann? Ann's desperate voice throbbing through the reaches of infinity? Following his percipience along on its freakout?)

(More firmly) It *is* there, Brad. You have only to locate It.

(Powers—too?)

I have gone everywhere. And I find only those things that have always been there. But now I'm trying something else: I'm becoming ultimately large and infinitesimally small at the same time.

The building blocks of matter swell up around me as I fumble down into the nothingness between them. Yet, I'm also sweeping up and away, growing, watching the great pinwheels of stars dwindle into hazy patches and the patches draw together until all Creation stands off to one side—a soft, glowing ball that becomes smaller and smaller.

Yes? *(Had Powers' voice followed him* beyond *infinity?)* Is It *out there?*

I can't say for certain. Now the dwindling part of me has shrunk smaller than the least subforce of the most insignificant subparticle. I'm floating just off to one side of that tiniest unit of energy. But I'm also hovering out here beyond the universe, with all existence only a gauzy plaything below me.

(God! It was all so confusing. No 'lucy had ever spawned so gross an impossibility!)

Yes, yes—go on! *(Powers' words thundered down on him from some region entirely outside of the infinitely large.)*

Oh, Brad! You're going to find It now! *(Ann's anxious voice strove up from* inside *of the infinitesimal!)* We'll be free, darling!

Quiet, child! Don't speak until I give you a cue.

But, doctor, can't he hear us talking like this?

Makes no difference. He's fully suggestible now. And it's been arranged that his conscious mind will remember nothing of this narcotherapeutic session.... Now, dear—urge him on!

Oh please, Brad. Please, darling. Find it! Pretend I'm there searching with you. For I *am*—with all my heart!

(Now his two perspectives were merging! Like spotlights converging on a velvety backdrop, the great totality of the universe became one with the least sphere of subnuclear force.

(And here, where microcosm met macrocosm, he found—HIMSELF! *Even while he quailed before the paradox, the himself that was greater than the ultimately large merged with the himself that was smaller than the absolutely infinitesimal. And the smallest-largest fusion of Creation began shrinking away into the transinfinite distance. Finally it dwindled almost to nothing and he was left utterly alone.)*

Bradford! *(The harsh voice boomed down-up to-at him.)* Tell us what's happening! Have you found It?

(Alone? No, not alone. He had found HIM *at last! Out here beyond the ultimate limits. Beyond them, but still within them. For the smallest-to-largest spectrum was actually a continuum that curved back upon itself.*

(But what he had found was not a physical form. Like himself, It was only a sentient nothingness. Yet, how could two pure percipients be aware of each other's presence?)

Bradford! *(Across the threshold of physical perception came the impression of pressure upon a shoulder.)* Speak to us! Tell us—

I have found Him. I wish I hadn't. It's so—sad. He loves Creation; would like to preserve it. But at the same time He's experimenting, trying to see whether He is greater than Himself. He has challenged Himself to overcomplicate Creation and—

We *know* that. *(Powers again, defiling the ineffable solemnity of this moment.)* You told us all about it years ago.

It's pitiable. Once He knew the location of every unit in Creation, could comprehend each single force. He could analyze and predict everything—*all occurrences. But He insisted on adding more and more forces, modifying the laws that govern them, piling complication on top of complication until—*

(From that other universe, from the prosaic one, came the obscure impression of Powers telling Ann she was no longer needed, of a door's opening and closing and being locked.)

Is It still there? *(Powers, demanding.)*

Yes. (Oh. He was there all right—lost in the vast nothingness and in His own uncertainty over whether to end the experiment and start over again with another, less complicated Creation.)

If only I could comfort Him! If only I could give all of myself to His consolation! Maybe, even in my humble unworthiness, I could help him split away from the challenge, build an even better world.

No! You will not interfere! Your role was only to search and find. Now that you have succeeded, tell It to leave you. Tell It I am ready!

No! I'm not deserving of even approaching. I have no right to interrupt.

(From the mundane world: almost subliminal impressions of cold metal things being attached to his temples; of—

(Agony! Spearing like lightning into his brain, bringing screams up into a throat that was too dry to release them.)

Tell It—now!

(Torture struck again and again. And, through some sort of empathy, the Infinite Presence, too, seemed to experience each burst of searing pain.)

Is It still there? *(Powers, insistent.)*

No. He's moving toward the fuzzy, glowing ball of His cosmos.

Don't lose It! Stay with It!

(Another bolt of lightning lanced in from the metal—electrodes?—attached to his temples. Obeying, Bradford followed Him back down into His Creation.)

You still with It?

Yes. (Barely crossing the threshold of perception, a cold, round object pressed against Bradford's head. A revolver muzzle?)

We are among the galaxies. I can sense Him over there—by that huge, swirling island universe. Only, it isn't a galaxy any more. It's a great expanse of ocean, billowing, phosphorescing. Now He's cutting the sea in half, just as though He's dividing it with a sword.

(Bradford didn't feel like describing these things to Powers any longer. His hoarseness was a minor agony in itself. Nevertheless, he continued, fearing the consequences of not complying.)

Another galaxy is turning into a luminous sea. And now it's being sliced in half. Another. Another. (This was so much like that recent happening—when he had gone around with the Presence, snuffing out glowflies.

(As though from a distance came a metallic click. *The sort of noise that might be made by a revolver hammer's being drawn back. And, even more remotely, pounding—as of a fist on the door.*

(But he was so fascinated by the transformation of galaxies into glittering seas and by the halving of each that he was hardly aware of the needle plunging into his arm and of Powers' injunction stripping him of all conscious memory of this latest happening.)

...◆...

Powers rolled his shock therapy equipment back into the closet and called out, "Just a moment."

The knock came again, more insistently. When he opened the door, Chuck blocked the way with folded arms, legs spread. His stout, rigid neck gave the impression of sculptured immobility.

But Powers, though small and misshapen, surrendered no ground. "Don't ever disturb me when I'm with Bradford!"

"You're wanted over at the foundation," Chuck shot back. "And I think you ought to be 'disturbed' every time you come in here."

In the corridor beyond, Ann strained to see around them, glancing anxiously at Bradford.

"I don't like the way Brad's being handled," Chuck challenged, "or the way he was tricked into coming here."

Powers shoved boldly past him. "The foundation's plan doesn't require *your* approval."

He went on down the hall, trailing an impatient Ann on his left and a perturbed Chuck on his right.

"You might be in for a surprise when you get to the meeting," the latter predicted. "Maybe you'll find *your* approval isn't so highly valued either."

Powers paused. "You aren't to leave Bradford unattended!"

Chuck glared at him, then stormed back down the hall.

Ann followed the psychiatrist. "Well?" she said, all eager.

Powers concealed his disappointment. "We made great headway," he lied. "Now I *know* it can be done."

"But you said he would be *free*—within minutes!"

"Of course, child. And it *will* take only minutes. But I thought you understood we would have to have at least one—ah, dry run."

He patted her cheek and left her standing in the rear entranceway as he moved on into the darkness of the courtyard. Loosening his collar against the night's stifling heat he wondered why he hadn't pulled the trigger. He'd tried to fire the revolver, but something seemed to be holding him back. Better judgment? Fear that he wouldn't be able to establish *immediate* control over It? On the other hand, if he had released the hammer, perhaps it would all be over by now, with him fully in possession of—

Of course it would all be over, he was assured from within. *But wouldn't that have been abrupt? Aren't you fascinated by the symbolism? Don't you want to see how it works out, what it means this time?*

"Symbolism?"

The Force within him laughed. *Why, you didn't even recognize that it* was *symbolic—the halving of the galactic oceans.*

Powers let himself through the gate and continued down the alley toward the foundation entranceway. "But what did it mean?"

There! You are *interested. Frankly, I don't know. That's why I'm intrigued. But I do know that on other occasions Bradford's communion with my Worthy Opponent suddenly shaded off from a real occurrence into something purely figurative, of devious meaning: glowflies turning out to be quasars being recalled from existence; Bradford's "dreams" about quirks of fate befalling him—relaxation of rigid causation. Wonderful, wonderful developments. What could this new effect be? Galaxies converted into seas. The seas being cut in half. Hm-m-m-m.*

Powers wondered whether he should report the development.

You'd be a fool if you did. They'd know you're interfering.

He hadn't thought of that. "And you don't know what this symbolism means?"

No. But this could be the most sweeping concession yet to the principle of destruction. It may bring enjoyment beyond expectation. I've got to know! That's why I didn't let you use the gun.

Drawing up at the foundation door, Powers thought: Wouldn't killing Bradford be the quickest way of taking over the Creative Force?

Yes. But patience, son. If there is exquisite delight to be had along the way, let us savor it.

Powers was beginning to wonder about the advisability of his letting the Destroyer run things.

Why, my boy, I've been running things all along.

He recalled his pre-Destroyer-affiliated days. Things were so simple then, in contrast to this present complexity. He had even derived great satisfaction from his acts of charity—playing Santa yearly at the children's eleemosynary institutions. And there had been the time he was elected chairman of the United Solicitors' Crusade and—

Oh, stop that mawkish nonsense!

But the Destroyer was right! (Was this his personal conviction, or was the Force simply putting persuasive thoughts into his mind?) Nevertheless, it *would* be intriguing to see the actual expression of this latest symbolism—celestial seas cut in half.

That's the spirit, son.

"And things will work out so that I'll get my just due?"

Yes, of course. You shall get what's coming to you.

...◆...

Balanced on the rump of the patinated bronze horse and anchoring himself with a handhold on the triumphant general's shoulder, Disciple Tom surveyed the swaying, surging throng in Jackson Square.

Oh, how he had preached in the name of Prophet Montague and the "Eno Yramirp!" (*That* was his own innovation—Topolinguistic Transformation of the Primary One's name. Might play hell with the meter and rhyme of some of their Cosmotheotopic hymns, though.) But, arrayed below him now were the fruits of his doctrinal labors:

Hundreds of New Orleans CTT converts. Assembled here in the light of the halfmoon. All eagerly embracing the hallowed principle of inverted attire. Pouring forth their vocal energy, as though they were full of speed, into "Mine Eyes Have Seen the Glory of the Prana of TT." Even though none of them had ever *watched* Lola perform the Rite of Topological Transformation in Mobius Mecca.

Faith. That's what it was. A faith he had given them. And he had it too. Why, he hadn't needed a fix in over two weeks.

Fed by the frenzied beat of the newly recruited rock group, the hymn neared its climax. At the north end of the square, with the moonlit façade of St. Louis Cathedral serving as a backdrop, his own topo dancers were giving it their all.

Tom took pride in the fact that at this very moment other Disciples—in the Village, in Haight-Ashbury, in bohemias throughout the land—must be beaming upon their own congregations, preparing to give last-minute instructions and post the order of the Crusade.

The final, resounding note of the hymn died away and he stood there adjusting himself to the reverential silence that intensified the light of the moon over the Mississippi. He reached behind him to unsnap the opening of his ceremonial red robe so that the smothering heat would be less intense. The motion, however, unbalanced him and one foot slipped off the rearing horse's tail.

But he snagged Andy Jackson's outthrust bronze arm and righted himself. A susurration of "oohs" rippled through the congregation.

"There is no glorious light in our sky here," he began. "We are too far north. But perhaps Eugatnom will arrange for the Primary to grace our eyes with a miracle to lighten the burden of our Crusade."

"O, Eugatnom Taerg, hear us!" murmured some of the crowd.

"Grace us with Thy miracle!" intoned others.

All around the square and in the streets of the Vieux Carré was evidence of last week's devastating flood. Little traffic could tread its way around the debris and over the muck that had been deposited there by rampaging river waters. But cleanup crews were at work. And, as though bent upon release from reality, escapists were already trickling back to whatever night life could still be offered by some of the soggy-floored French Quarter bistros. From the distance came the sounds of wailing trumpets, chattering drums and *twanging* guitars.

"Patience, my flock," Tom exhorted. "Soon we'll all be happy children at Eugatnom's knees. Then we'll free the Infinite Man!"

An abrupt dimness enveloped the Square. Tom, one arm spread as though to embrace his congregation, had been staring into the sky when it happened. The moon had just—disappeared. It wasn't an eclipse. Too sudden for that. Nor had it drifted behind a cloud, for there were no clouds overhead. It had simply vanished.

Then, as abruptly as it had gone, it was back again. The entire episode took scarcely more than a second, he guessed.

"A sign!" the assembly shouted. "A holy sign!"

Tom nodded his confirmation. "An omen of success on our Crusade. The Eno—" he paused to insure proper inverse pronunciation of the Great Name—Y'ram'irp arranged this benediction to encourage us."

After a moment of profound meditation, he continued: Tomorrow we start our Crusade to free the Inverse Vessel from the infidels!"

"Oh, damn the infidels!"

"We must rescue Drofdarb!"

"Help us, O, Eno Yramirp!"

Tom touched knuckles to his nape and arched his back in a Topologically Transformed salaam. This unbalanced him and he had to grope again for General Jackson's shoulder to steady himself.

"All along our Pilgrimage route," he went on, "we'll join forces with other Crusaders as we converge on Mecca. Dig this, though: We ain't all going to get there. But I'm sure every last mudder of you will milk his karma for all it's worth and give it a damn good try."

He was still assigning converts to available cars and trucks a few minutes later when the moon vanished again. This time it didn't reappear within a moment or two. After several additional minutes of reverent ejaculation, of proclaiming appreciation to the Primary One, the congregation became quiet; then uncertain, then somewhat tense.

Somewhere downriver a cargo ship exploded, sending great bursts of red light into the night sky. The crowd murmured restively.

Pounded by flaming debris from the vessel, the French Market began blazing too. One of the steeples of St. Louis Cathedral collapsed and toppled into Chartres Street.

Sword, scabbard, and all, slipped from General Jackson's waist, struck the granite ledge below and rebounded out into the assembly. It transfixed a devout Cosmotheotopist, pinning him to the ground.

Some eight minutes after it had vanished for the second time that night, the moon reappeared. But it was a while before the Disciple could convince his converts that this was indeed an auspicious omen.

…◆…

Powers took his place at the conference table and sat staring at Duncan. The latter only chewed thoughtfully on his lip.

Impatient, the psychiatrist asked, "You sent for me?"

The director folded his hands and studied each face in turn: Security Chief Hawthorn; Wittels, in charge of communications;

Mathematical Director Steinmetz; Swanson, the other psychiatrist; Hedgmore, investments; McMillan, astronomy; Murdock, their new acquisition from the VA; all the others.

Sober contemplation, self-assurance, a moment for meditative inspection of his aides—that was the composite image Duncan sought to project. An unspoken demand for discipline, for unconditional responses from his staff members. Authoritarianism? Perhaps. But justified. As warranted as was the strictest subjugation imposed by any military leader taking his men into the most critical battle.

"We will allow Bradford periodic release from sedation," he said flatly. "Miss Fowler has convinced me our present course is impractical."

Powers rose in protest. "But we've had him sedated for over a week now, and nothing else has gone wrong out there."

"Nothing that we've managed to detect thus far," Wittels amended.

"Well, then—nothing serious," Powers insisted.

"I said we will allow him periodic release," Duncan said, unremitting. "Whether there have been recent minor, undetectable modifications of natural law is not the issue. Our principal concern is neglect of Bradford's *physical* health."

"We can't arouse him to the world as it exists today!" Powers pointed out. "We got him to come here by making him believe the breakdown in probability discipline was another hallucination. If we awaken him he'll see what's happening and *know* he was deceived!"

Hawthorn laughed dryly. "You're good at manufacturing hallucinations. Just explain that he hallucinated your telling him his hallucinations were hallucinations."

Powers looked awry at the security chief.

"That is precisely the strategy we will use," Duncan declared. "Powers, you will tell Bradford he only *imagined* you and Chuck and Miss Fowler led him to believe there was nothing wrong with the world. At any rate, I've posted the order. See that it's executed."

He next addressed instructions to Bankston. "As P & D's real estate specialist you will visit Bradford occasionally. You will deny that you denied there was a hailstorm."

Powers still wasn't persuaded. "Suppose his awareness of what's going on all over the world kicks off more upheavals of nature?"

"He was by himself in all that stuff for two weeks," Hawthorn reminded. "There weren't any backlashes then, were there?"

"The plan," Duncan continued, ignoring the others, "is to revive him for an hour or two twice a day. Even then, he's going to be kept partly sedated so that he won't be too interested in what's going on outside. The main point is that he'll get some exercise, maintain his strength, keep his digestive system in trim. Later—"

A red-faced man barged into the room. "Come quick! Down to communications! Something *else* has happened out there!"

Everyone poured down the stairway and flowed after the man into his precinct of receivers and transmitters, direction-finding and ranging instruments, dead telephones and live video equipment. On the screen of one of the TV sets, tuned for direct Satcom reception, a newscaster sat sifting through his stack of teletype bulletins.

"Information seems to be in from representative sections of the globe," he was saying. "And it would appear that what happened went something like this: At approximately 9:15, our time, the moon quit shining for a little over a second. About eight minutes later, on the dayside of earth, the sun went black. Dark of night. At almost the same time the moon quit shining again. Both the sun and moon returned to normal at approximately 9:31, our time."

"Sedation failed!" exclaimed Steinmetz. "It's still happening!"

"I'm for trying the Ultimate Remedy!" declared Hawthorn.

But Duncan only folded his arms. "This fully justifies our amended strategy. I was afraid that isolating Bradford would create too abnormal a situation. I should have guessed that a total absence of sensory stimuli would disturb the Force as much as the provocations on Soapbox Slopes and on the beach."

Again, Powers only stared into the distance, his brow ridged with puzzlement.

XIII

Exultation: How easy it was to deceive these creatures! Take the Powers instrument: all naive, unquestioning. Why, he had shown no doubt whatever when told: "It is only a human illusion that good triumphs over evil." Oh, how Powers had taken the bait! He couldn't even see that severing the association between the Primary and Bradford would result in instant, delightful destruction of everything.

Let him dream of power, let him imagine mountainous portions of wealth, authority, control were just beyond his fingertips. Truly, the instrument was overanxious to accomplish his implanted purpose.

But there were, oh, so many delicacies to savor before the ultimate enjoyment! Like the physical debacle—whatever it would turn out to be—that was symbolized by the halving of the radiant, celestial seas. So, why rush universal destruction?

Even in the area of favored-creatures involvement, developments were offering great promise. All those missiles being readied for firing on both sides of the world. Limited war approaching total escalation. All the forces of nature yielding so much destruction, misery, death.

This was a time for exultation.

...♦...

Urgency pervaded the foundation meeting room. The full directorate was present. Some sprawled in their chairs. Others—particularly McMillan, head of the Astronomical Section, and Chief Mathematician Steinmetz—scribbled frantically on their pads, trying to keep bloodshot eyes in focus. The air of general fatigue was as palpable as the pall of tobacco smoke that had fogged the room for more than a day.

Pacing along the far wall, Duncan had difficulty keeping shoulders level and head erect, hiding his weariness and uncertainty. Moving back and forth in front of the data he had chalked on his huge slate, he appeared much like an admiral surveying battle deployment on the plot board of his flagship's Combat Information Center. But no CIC had ever channeled data as critical as these.

"There's got to be an answer—a key!" he exclaimed. "Sun, moon, planets don't just go popping in and out of the sky without cause—not even under our modified discipline of determinism!"

Security Chief Hawthorn, seeming anxious to end the session, suggested, "Maybe we're worked up over nothing. It's been four days since all that stuff happened up there. Perhaps it was just a simple one-shot upheaval—a sort of random spasm in the celestial range."

"It just *appeared* to be random," Duncan countered. "By only glancing at these data, I can sense enough order in what happened on the night of July 30th to know that something *fundamental* was involved."

"But suppose it *was* merely a sort of scattershot convulsion," Steinmetz said, "—a temporary ripple in the fabric of reality."

"No." The director stood upon his conviction. "What we observed—moon, sun, planets blinking off, on, off, on—reflected a basic alteration in natural law. I'm certain of that, intuitively at least. If there were just some clue! Some inspiration that might lead to the underlying cause!"

Duncan's intuition held no small measure of respect. Hadn't it been his 'hunch' five years ago that had ferreted out Bradford's 'true nature'? In deference to his judgment, the directorate somehow became more alert, more willing to go over the facts one more time. Even Powers swilled the remainder of his coffee and sat erect.

"These are the data Dr. McMillan wangled from the Orb-observational Information Center." Duncan tapped his yardstick against the blackboard. "OIC gives us this chronology of what happened on that impossible night last week. I've converted times to our local zone."

He read off each item as he thumped it with his indicator:

9:15—moon out, first time
9:15—moon in
9:18—Venus out, first time
9:20—Venus in
9:21—Mars out, first time
9:23—sun out
9:34—Mars out, second time
9:51—Jupiter out, first time
9:52—Mars in again
10:27—Jupiter in
10:27—Saturn out, first time

9:23—moon out, second time
9:24—Venus out, second time
9:27—Mars in
9:31—sun in
9:31—moon in again
9:32—Venus in again
10:34—Jupiter out, second time
11:39—Saturn in
11:47—Saturn out, second time
11:53—Jupiter in again
2:19—Saturn in again

"At first," Duncan resumed, "the effects would appear to be purely random. A blinking out. Blinking in. Out. In. But somehow I can see just enough vague order in the chronology to resist calling the manifestation in its entirety a 'scattershot convulsion' of the Creative Force, as Dr. Steinmetz proposes.

"These data, rearranged in this second chart, reveal a bit of that elusive regularity." Again he pointed to each entry as he read out the times and effects:

SUN	MOON	VENUS	MARS	JUPITER	SATURN
9:23—out	9:15—out	9:18—out	9:21—out	9:51—out	10:27—out
9:31—in	9:15—in	9:20—in	9:27—in	10:27—in	11:39—in
	9:23—out	9:24—out	9:34—out	10:34—out	11:47—out
	9:31—in	9:32—in	9:52—in	11:53—in	2:19—in

Duncan gulped coffee. "This second chart shows us that five celestial bodies—moon and four planets—disappeared *twice*. But the sun went out just *once*, coincident with the moon's *second* fadeout. Why the distinction?

McMillan proposed, "Let's consider basic differences between the sun and planets. That's the only logical approach if we're going to explain the discrepancy between the sun and planets in the way they were affected by whatever happened."

"But there are *so many* differences!" Hawthorn protested.

"Then it's our job as a task force to single out the pertinent ones," Duncan said.

McMillan raised a finger to his chin. "I have a hunch that the most relevant distinction has something to do with the fact that the sun *radiates*, while the moon and planets *reflect*."

"And I've a hunch," Duncan said, gripping the astronomer's shoulder, "that you've just made a significant contribution, Irving."

He paused, bowing the indicator between palms. "Let's review some of the other effects that may or may not be relevant:

"First, Dr. McMillan has also learned that new radar measurements show the moon and planets at twice their former distance."

The astronomer held up his hand. "But we know those new values can't be correct. Especially in the case of the moon. First: no observable decrease in apparent size. Second: triangulation from polar stations, we're told, gives precisely the same distance."

Then something must be wrong with the radar equipment," Communications Chief Wittels said.

"File it away for future reference," Duncan instructed. "Maybe it will all fit logically into the picture. Second, Moonbase U.S. reports exactly reciprocal effects. *They* watched *earth* vanish twice—at about the same times we saw the *moon* disappear."

"Sounds like a subjective effect to me," Chief Mathematician. Steinmetz offered. "Especially when you consider that a shuttle craft, en route home, reported double disappearances by *both* earth and moon."

"Not disappearances," Wittels corrected. "They just quit shining. No stars were observed in the spaces occupied by their blackened discs."

Duncan paced, paused to look at the blackboard, then stared at his aides. I've a feeling we're very close to the answer; that all we need is just one simple key."

He shrugged. "Third, there's that slight retrograde displacement of the moon and planets. Very slight for the moon. A bit more noticeable for Venus and Mars. More pronounced for Jupiter and Saturn.

Why? Why should the planets be set back in their orbits by an angular amount proportionate to their distances not from the sun, but from Earth?"

"Geocentric universe after all?" McMillan mumbled.

Silence prevailed, broken only by the sound of the director's measured steps back and forth. He had to radiate assurance; it was good for morale.

"There's a deep, unguessable method in this whole thing," he mused aloud. In all this contradictory disorder, there is harmonious order. It almost leaps out at me from those figures on the blackboard. But I just can't put my finger on it." If only he were free from the obligations of command! Then he might lock himself in his study—if he still had a study—and ferret out the answer within minutes.

He paced again, closer to the table. When he passed Powers, the psychiatrist's head was shaking in the slow rhythm of puzzlement while he muttered to himself.

Vincent Kadesch rose in front of the director. "Remember Silverstein?" the scientific survey chief said. "Do you suppose *that* could fit into the picture somewhere—another clue perhaps?"

Hawthorn straightened. "Who's Silverstein? What about him?"

"Dr. Silverstein was connected with Tristate Nuclear Laboratory," Kadesch explained. "It was the last such establishment to close down. Too many accidents among the others. TNL performed its final experiments on July 31, the day after our celestial freakout."

"Yes?" Hawthorn said impatiently.

"Silverstein told me TNL's betatron consistently malfunctioned on the morning of July 31. Whenever its accelerators could be goosed up enough to produce the desired reaction, it yielded results at about one-fourth the anticipated energy levels in MeVs."

Duncan admitted it might be one of the jigsaw bits—if only he could guess how to fit it into the picture.

He also recalled listening to the last Houston-Moonbase radio conversation monitored by the foundation. There had been something odd about that. About the message itself—the discussion of the earth-moon disappearances? No, not that. Something else. Something to do with the mechanics of transmission. But what?

His face brightened with inspiration, then drained itself of all expression in the next instant. He'd *almost* had it. He stared back at the blackboard for a long while, then resumed pacing, resumed command.

Powers was still hunched forward upon the table. And he was mumbling: "Half a *sea*? *Half* a sea? Half—"

Duncan wondered, in even deeper perplexity: *Half a sea?* Why, no—that wasn't what Powers was saying at all! It only *sounded* like that. And then, with the intensity of a flash bulb going off in his face, he realized what the psychiatrist was actually murmuring!

Whirling, he seized the other and hauled him to his feet. "Powers has it!" he proclaimed. "Now we *know* what it is!" Then, somberly: "O, God! Now we know."

"What is it?" McMillan demanded. "What's the answer?"

"Half *c*! Don't you understand? One-half *c*! It's the only explanation that satisfies *all* the observed effects. *The speed of light has been reduced to half its former value!*"

He paced again, but with a purpose now. "Radar measures the moon and planets at *twice* their distance because electromagnetic waves are being propagated at *half* their former velocity. The planets appear in retrograde positions because it takes light double the time to get here—the farther away the planet, the more pronounced its retrogression.

"*Of course* there was something wrong with that last Houston-Moonbase communication. It was sluggish, drawn out. Took twice as long as the usual exchange of information. The time lapse between question and response was more pronounced. Why? Because signals traveled half as fast over the distance!"

He went to the blackboard, fatigue no longer evident in his steps. "We can now reconstruct what actually happened at 9:15 P.M. on July 30. But, first, let me state the premise: The speed of light was arbitrarily changed at that moment—but not of light already *in transit*. Rather, the modification applied to the phenomena of radiation and reflection *at their sources*."

He wielded his yardstick upon the tables of figures: "First, the sun, our *radiating* body, quit shining from 9:23 to 9:31. In other words, it went out about eight minutes after 9:15. Therefore, we can deduce that the last wavefront of light to leave the photosphere at 9:15 continued traveling at the old speed of 186,000 miles a second, taking *eight* minutes to get here. Also at 9:15, with *c* reduced to *half* its value, the new wavefront of half-speed light left the sun; it would require *sixteen* minutes to cover the distance. At 9:23 the last wavefront of *c*-light reached earth, leaving the sun dark for eight minutes—since, at 9:23, the *new* ½*c* wavefront had covered only *half* the distance to earth. Eight minutes later, at 9:31, the first wavefront of ½*c* light reached here, restoring the sun's radiance."

"I don't have the background to consider all the ramifications of ½*c*," McMillan said, shaking his head. "But it seems to me it would disturb such relationships as wavelength and frequency, Planck's constant and the like; that we'd have an entirely new spectrum; that even nuclear processes involving *c* as a constant would be knocked askew; that ..."

"True," Duncan admitted. "But you're overlooking the possibility that It may have mitigated the change in such a way as to prevent life from becoming physically intolerable."

"Good God!" McMillan objected "Are you actually suggesting a homocentric, *homo*-oriented universe?"

"Why not?" Hawthorn broke in. "The Creative Force is Bradford-oriented, isn't it?"

Kadesch reminded them again of Tristate Nuclear Laboratory and asked, "Could ½*c* have had anything to do with Silverstein's betatron yielding only *one-quarter* of the anticipated MeV levels?"

"Of course!" Duncan affirmed. "The constant *c* is a factor in nuclear phenomena. And $½c^2$ is one-fourth the value of c^2. Silverstein's results confirm our hypothesis!"

He turned back to the column under the heading "MOON" in the second chart. "We'll consider the case of just one reflecting body in order to see how precisely the ½*c* hypothesis is validated:

"At 9:15 the moon blinked out for an instant—my guess would be about one and a third seconds, the time light *used to* take to travel from Moon to Earth. In other words, since the transition affected reflection too, there was a gap of lunar darkness between receipt of our last *c*-speed reflection and our first ½*c*-speed reflection from that body.

"So, the moon blinks off for a little over a second, then shines normally from 9:15 to 9:23—all the while that it is still receiving the final stream of *c* light from the sun. Then, at 9:23, the moon goes out once more—at almost exactly the same time the sun stops shining. Why? Because the last wavefront of *c* light from the sun has not only stopped reaching earth, but has stopped bathing the moon too.

"At 9:31, both the sun and moon start shining again—as the first wavefront of steady ½*c* light reaches earth and its satellite."

He laid down his yardstick. "The same principle applied with Venus, Mars, Jupiter, and Saturn: an initial blackout while the mechanics of reflection adjusted to ½*c*; a second blackout as a result of being deprived of radiation from the sun in the gap between *c* and ½*c* illumination. We should have recognized from the beginning that the length of the sunout was equal to the time it takes sunlight to reach us; that the durations of the first blackouts of the moon and planets were proportional to their distance from us; that the durations of their second blackouts were proportional to the total Sun-to-planet-to-Earth distances."

"What do we do about it?" Wittels said. "Can we *live* with it?"

"I don't know. We need a basis for rational prediction."

"I'm for the Ultimate Remedy—now!" Hawthorn declared.

"But even that'd take time," Duncan reminded. "We'd have to carefully prepare our direct appeal."

"God!" he added, starting. "That was close! It lost control over the velocity of light and *c* slipped to half value. Suppose *c* had *doubled*, or perhaps assumed *infinite* velocity!"

"Yes?" McMillan said, obviously not realizing the consequences.

"$E=mc^2$," Duncan went on, scarcely above a whisper. "In all nuclear equations *c* would have been a factor of *unlimited magnitude*! Every star would annihilate itself immediately! Every naturally occurring nuclear reaction—even in our own atmosphere—would generate *infinite* energy!"

···◆···

Too many concessions. But, oh, what blissful relief: not having to push each photon at that awful velocity! It was an even greater self-deliverance than the detranscendentalization of pi *and of some of the other nonalgebraic values.*

One would think that with most of the transcendentals eliminated, with the impossible non*stars*-non*galaxies withdrawn from existence, with causative discipline placed on a less rigid basis, with the momentum of light cut in half—with all of those simplifications, the self-challenge would become tolerable and it would be proved that the self-defier could be successfully repudiated.*

But no.

For the halving of light's speed had been fraught with dangers for the mortal beings. And many qualifications had to be made in establishing the new, less demanding order—exceptions in natural law that were helping to mitigate the overall effects on those creatures. But these exceptions, in themselves, comprised a new patchwork discipline that was almost as difficult to maintain as the former unreasonable limiting velocity.

Why, even after light had been slowed at its sources, the principle of continuous creation had had to be annulled. At the time, it seemed as though that would be the ultimate concession. But no. It was clear that there would have to be additional retrenchment if Creation was to be preserved in a form remotely resembling its present status.

...◆...

Bradford hitched his robe and took two faltering steps before his knees buckled. But, with Ann's help, he averted falling.

"This is no good," he complained through the fog that hung over his senses. "I'm all spaced out. And I can't come down."

"You'll get your strength back, Brad." Her dark eyes conveyed sincerity. "After all, this is only the fourth day."

Exhausted, he dropped into a chair. "Why did I have to be stoned for so long—for over a week?"

"Powers'll fill you in on that. I can't."

He looked over at the tray where half of his supper still lay untouched. But, at least, he was eating more each meal.

Ann knelt beside his chair and searched his face. "Powers says there's a way we can—you can—I mean you and I—"

He touched her soft hair. "He thinks I can be normal again?" It was an effort to keep his mind from wandering back to the hallucinations and hallucinations within hallucinations.

"Yes. And—oh, Brad, I don't care what happens. Just as long as we ..."

For a moment the inner mist seemed to clear. "On the other side of the pit I've just climbed out of, I asked you to marry me. I *wasn't* going square on you. I asked because—I was suspicious. I wanted to see how eager you'd be to ..."

All the coherence seemed to have melted.

"It doesn't matter," she assured. "The important thing now is for you to be yourself again; for you and me to be *together*, normally, without any soul barriers between us."

He pulled her to him and kissed her—weakly though, because he was still debilitated. "Yes, that's the important thing. The only thing."

High-spirited, Powers entered and led Bradford back to bed. "We've had enough exertion for one day, haven't we?"

Bradford looked up from the pillow while the psychiatrist prepared his injection. "I wanted to ask about what happened during—"

Powers bared and swabbed his arm. "Questions and answers can be tiring. We'll talk about it tomorrow."

He waited with Ann until the injection had taken effect. Then he exclaimed, "This may be it, dear! Transfer, at last!"

"We're going to try it again—now?"

"Not we. Just I." He ushered her into the corridor, then locked the door behind him. Drawing his revolver, he thrust its muzzle against Bradford's temple and squeezed the trigger.

Nothing happened.

Then, dismayed, he realized his finger wasn't exerting any pressure at all! He *couldn't* shoot Bradford!

Not for the moment, at least, rumbled the voice within. *There's still too much gratification to be had by stringing things out a while.*

"Yet you wouldn't have been able to stop me from killing myself in my office—that evening when I learned about you."

True. But that was when I controlled only your inner drives. Now *I've taken charge of your impulses too.*

...◆...

Iggy beat upon the padded door with his fists, then launched a kick at the lower panel.

Marcella drew her knees up beneath her chin where she sat on the bed. "Won't do any good. They can't even hear you." Bare midriff exposed the bandaged, but almost healed gunshot wound in her side.

"If I don't get some speed," Iggy groaned through the disarray of his stringy beard, "I'll blow my mind in this damn place!"

Uncoiling, Marcella rose and stood beside the bed. "This is *not* a damn place," she admonished. "Not with Drofdarb Yloh here."

The food slot in the door swung down and a double tray was shoved in, the face of the shover remaining visible beyond the opening.

Iggy lunged over. "Did you get it, Kcodrum? Did you get it?"

Murdock put a silencing finger to his lips while his eyes scouted the hallway. "No. I can't get any—ah, acid in this place."

Iggy swore. "Where's the key so's we can split this pad?"

"I *have* it," the former VA man disclosed. "But Eugatnom doesn't want us to use it now."

"You've seen the Tehporp again?" Marcella asked.

"Just this afternoon. He says the three of us are going to have the first chance to release Drofdarb from captivity."

Iggy sobered. "We're going to *snatch* the Infinite Man?"

"We'll give it a try anyway. If we fail, the Crusaders will be ready to storm this bastion."

Marcella crowded the door. "When will the Crusaders get here?"

"The first ones are already trickling in. All the main forces will arrive by day after tomorrow."

She drew in an exultant breath. "Oh, what a blast it will be when we release the Inverse Vessel and tell Him what the score is and get Him to help us reach the Primary One and tame things down and—"

Murdock appeared uncertain. "Why, that's *just* what the foundation wants to do."

"But *they* are infidels," Iggy pointed out, swearing. "They think they're messing around with nothing more than a *Creative Force*. *We* know He's the *Primary One*. We dig the true prana of all things. They'd screw up the deal. We're going to suck it dry—with all due veneration, of course, like Eugatnom says."

XIV

Is life, then, a dream and delusion and
Where shall the dreamer awake?
Is the world seen like shadows on water,
And what if the mirror breaks?
Shall it pass a camp that is struck, as
A tent that is gathered and gone,
From the sands that were lamplit at eve,
And at morning are level and lone?
—Sir Alfred Comyn Lyall

…♦…

Before his office window, Powers stared unseeing at the downtown street scene. Yesterday he had tried to kill Bradford and capture the Creative Force. But he couldn't pull the trigger. Would a more subtle tack succeed? Suppose, just for once, the hypodermic syringe were filled with a *toxic* solution—

I wouldn't allow it.

Well, so much for that.

Powers gazed out upon the almost deserted city. Only an occasional militiaman, rifle at the ready position, stirred. Smashed automobiles—he counted three—remained crumpled against a utility pole and two brick walls. To the left, the cornice of a tall building, for some unguessable reason having to do with the probability that its mortar would hold, was crumbling away brick by brick.

Overhead, a helicopter circled while its speakers squawked instructions for abandonment of the downtown section. On the next pass its rotors, trailing a sheared drive shaft, went soaring up and away like a Whirl-a-Toy. The craft plummeted to earth several blocks eastward.

For a moment Powers, too, wanted to join the exodus to less perilous, open country. But he knew he wouldn't be allowed to leave—even if he *were* willing to forgo the opportunity to seizing control of It and becoming godlike in power and—.

Ah, sweet ambition. No, you may not leave. Not when things are really *getting interesting.*

Powers ignored the interruption. Was it the same all over? Exodus? Fires? Whole sections burned out? Looting? Only Satcom knew. And it undoubtedly wasn't broadcasting all the details of devastation.

Oh, yes. It's fascinating everywhere.

Powers tried to smother the pealing voice, realizing he himself was directly responsible for what was happening out there. His attempts to dislodge It from Bradford's unconscious—each one had backfired and brought about an upheaval in nature.

Correction: not you, yourself; I insist upon at least part, if not all, of the credit.

Powers cursed Him, then pressed palms over his ears, as though that would shut out the stentorian, derisive laughter within. He went back to his desk and poured a slug of bourbon. But, even as he picked up the jigger, the whisky in it boiled away. He dropped the suddenly heated glass. More inner guffaws and Powers shouted invective.

Then: *The least you can do, in the interest of your own dignity, is imagine yourself a* willing *participant.*

"Go to hell!" But resentment ebbed and he pleaded, "We've got to get out of the city! It's too dangerous! Just last night an entire corner of foundation headquarters collapsed!"

Trust in me, son. Meanwhile, if we're allies, let's act like it. Say, wasn't that intriguing—the way Bradford's "halving of the seas" worked out? I expected a profound abstraction, sophisticated symbolism. But what did we get? Mere pictorial representation of a phonetic distortion. Shallow allegory involving a simple homophone: sea—c. *Doesn't that just* prove *the Creative Force has lost His ingenuity?*

Muttering agreement, Powers eyed the forbidden bourbon bottle.

Go ahead. Have one.

He did; but decided against a second—not without permission.

And do you know He's had to abolish continuous creation? No more neutrons popping into existence. I can't find a single one to smash into a hydrogen atom and beta particle. Know what that means?

Shaking his head, Powers hazarded another drink.

We've got Him on the run! And we're not going to let up. I have other plans to heighten His ignominy before we wrest Creation away from Him. Make yourself comfortable and close your eyes so you won't be confused by double images. We're going to take a trip and observe something interesting:

...◆...

Chief Soviet Delegate Pornovsky radiated confidence as he drummed his stumpy fingertips on the table. He was flanked by his aides and an interpreter whose service had not been required all afternoon. For Pornovsky's English was adequate and he was using it ostentatiously as a psychological edge in the secret negotiations.

Outside, the once-cool waters of the Lake of Geneva, steaming in patches now, surged and billowed in transverse *seiches* that made the entire basin seem like a huge tub being tilted first to one side, then to the other. U.S. Chief Negotiator Alston and his diplomatic entourage, across the table, were in position to observe the age-old but now greatly exaggerated phenomenon through the window.

"Well?" Pornovsky said, stifling a yawn.

"Our agenda limits these discussions to the situation in Turkey exclusively." Alston tried to match his counterpart's composure.

"Ah! I agree. But your side has chosen to broaden the scope of our confrontation in Western Asia. It is *you* who have introduced irrelevant issues that cry for diplomatic discussion."

Alston squirmed. "I've assured you we are confounded by your allusion that our side is responsible for a so-called 'effect' that …"

There was a deep rumbling and the Russians, too, turned to watch large boulders tumble, as though in slow motion, down a distant slope and plunge into the lake, sending up great sprays that spread shimmering rainbows across the sky.

(I told you it would be interesting, didn't I?)

(But what's going to happen?)

(Not having the gift of prescience, I don't know. But I can sense pure delight, tremendous gratification.)

Pornovsky rose, folded huge arms in front of his broad chest and turned to stare through the window. "It is time, gentlemen, that we get down to business. Let us not delude ourselves. The People's Liberation of Turkey has succeeded. Reactionary forces are even now cowering on the beaches with the defeated foreign interventionists. If you care to evacuate your forces, we might arrange to have the Liberation Front withhold fire. Perhaps. For you realize, of course, that we cannot speak for an independent power."

(Here it comes!)

(What?)

(The clincher. I think it's going to be a good one.)

Pornovsky whirled to face the table. "So you see, your all-or-be-damned policy has got you nowhere. Now, as to this effect."

Alston rose uncertainly, his thin small hands splayed upon the table. "But I tell you there *is* no effect!"

"Everything that's going on out there, all over the world—that's not what you would call a Sunday School picnic now, is it?"

"But whatever it is, it's affecting us worse than anybody! We're the most industrialized, the most urbanized nation. We ..."

"Oh, but there is an effect, my dear Mr. Alston. And if you intend coercion, now is the time to state your terms." Humor prevailed in the Russian's eyes. "What? No terms? Then I shall state ours."

Alston came around the table and seemed all the more shriveled with age as he confronted the huge Pornovsky. "I've consulted my government. I've told them of your unreasonable suspicions. And I can assure you that we are as baffled as you over all this chaos. Of course we're withdrawing from Turkey. Under the circumstances, ideologies are insignificant, warfare impossible."

The Chief Soviet Delegate thumped the table. "We shall shortly test your proposition that war is now impossible. But first I insist upon admission that your government has tried to coerce the world, even at the expense of its own civilians and property."

The Chief U.S. Delegate stood there perspiring.

(Did you hear that? They're going to see *if war is possible!)*

(But isn't this all getting out of hand?)

(Oh, yes! Gloriously out of hand!)

"There is no effect," Alston whimpered.

But Pornovsky was adamant. "Our proof is conclusive. We know all about your undercover man Perrilaut, who lured our Dr. Vasilof to a secret—and fatal—meeting with a segment of your government-controlled scientific establishment. Dr. Vasilof reported, before he was murdered, that he believed you intended to terrorize the USSR by letting *our own* scientists warn us of this effect."

Alston broke in: "This is all entirely and utterly ridiculous!"

"Enough!" Pornovsky punched his palm. "The sparring is over."

(This is it! Powers, isn't this just—fascinating?)

(I don't like it.)

"Either," grumbled Pornovsky, "you will turn off this effect or suffer long-feared consequences. My country does not propose to continue existing in an environment of disaster while your government plans to install its order over the remnants of civilization. You have only forty-eight hours to call off your dogs of devastation. Otherwise we shall loose our more conventional nuclear dogs."

As one, he and his delegation stormed from the room. Outside, entire crests and huge sides of mountains were sliding off into the Lake of Geneva all along the southern shoreline. As the water began rising and surging against its banks, Alston and his aides scurried for safety.

...♦...

How do you appeal to a confused, self-harassed Creative Force? "Hey, C.F., how's about trying harder and straightening out this mess You've made of natural law?" Or an indignant approach: "Knock it off! We're up to our ears! You put it together; now patch it up and get it all working right again!"

Approaching the ridiculous, such desperate thoughts had scampered through Duncan's mind for hours as he sat alone in his office at midnight, trying to draft a direct appeal. For he had decided to invoke the Ultimate Remedy at six in the morning. Unexpectedly, the silence of an almost deserted headquarters was a distraction. Nearly all of his staff had been dismissed, not counting Hedgmore and the other four who had been killed in yesterday's collapse of the building's southeast corner.

Duncan, fatigued though he was, rose and paced. *How* should they address themselves to It? Could they even *reach* It? They had before—on a number of occasions. But not in the last four and a half years. During that time they had been anxious to let It lie undisturbed, hoping that somehow It might overcome Its difficulties and, in the solitude of withdrawal from metaconscious control of Creation, manage to hold the pieces together.

And their noninterference had worked! Up until a few months ago, when random effects had started snowballing.

Why? Had universal complexity achieved such proportions that the inevitable, final straw had been dropped upon the camel's back?

Duncan went over to the window and used his thumbnail to scrape a peephole in the black paint covering the glass. Outside, the stars, suspended over a lightless city, were a sequined curtain that silhouetted the somber skyline of dead buildings.

Those stars—were they still out there? Or had they already been recalled from existence, leaving ever shortening threads of their light extending toward a lonely, desolate world and its sun and sister planets—all swimming along, alone in an infinite sea of nothingness?

In search of inspiration for the ultimate task ahead, his thoughts went back to the first time they had probed Bradford's unconscious, listened to him describe the impressions deriving from his empathy with the metaconscious within him. It had all been so incredible that Hedgmore had laughed. Powers and Montague, however, had stood there gripped by a paralysis of grim comprehension.

Oblivious of the disparate reactions about him, Bradford had only relayed the self-plaints of intentional overcomplication; of self-challenge and self-reaction; of proposition and the likelihood of being able to proclaim *quod erat demonstrandum*; of the great experiment and self-deprivation of prescience so that the end result would remain unknown and the game would be more interesting.

"Theomania!" Hedgmore had shouted.

But Montague had reminded: "Didn't our Project Genesis sensors lead us to him as the infinite source of continuous creation? In a sense, haven't we found an Infinite Man?"

Uncertainty.

Incredulity.

Fear.

Terror.

Meanwhile, Bradford had continued his dread soliloquy. No, not *his*. Rather, the bemused reflections of something deep within—or at least associated with him in some inscrutable relationship.

Then, weeks later, the first test of the Duncan-Powers-Montague hypothesis:

"Bradford, can you hear us? Let there be another desk, identical to the one beside you. There *is* another desk!"

And there *was* another desk.

Duncan crossed the room and stood before the desk—the same one that had, like a fledgling neutron, materialized from nothing less than five years ago. A horrible, unbelievable eternity—all encompassed in the span of half a decade.

Montague going berserk, shrieking, "It's God! Oh, can't you see? It's God!" Being confined in the clinic. Escaping.

More confirmatory experiments. And, each time, whatever was suggested happened. In every session: the same querulous monologue from a comatose Bradford, doubting the ability to maintain nature in its too-sophisticated form, questioning whether the self-challenge hadn't, after all, been too severe, the rules of the game too rigid.

Duncan rammed his fist down on the desk. God! Why did It have to *play games* with the universe?

It—God? No, damn it! Hang out the "unwanted" sign for that kind of conjecture. Objectivity must be preserved. *This* was the twentieth century, almost the twenty-first.

Then they had realized the need of an organization to protect Bradford, funds to support their "foundation."

"Let there be silver."

Silver.

"Let there be gold."

Gold.

"Let there be diamonds."

Diamonds—a bushel of them.

And, just in case proof would be required: "Let Pluto and the nearest star be destroyed on March 16."

A final suggestion might have been: "Provide a dignified, stable place in life for Bradford"—if they'd thought such an order would have been filled. But it wasn't needed; for Hedgmore was there.

Duncan allowed himself a moment of posthumous respect for Hedgmore. Gerstal had willingly relinquished P & D Enterprises just so Bradford could have that "place in life."

It had been a spontaneous decision. One that had seized upon the opportunity which presented itself when Hedgmore found the crab-mutilated body floating among the offshore rocks of his coastal estate. Whereupon he rewrote his will, attended to other necessary matters, planted on the corpse items that would identify it as his own, then disappeared forever into the cloister of foundation headquarters.

All to no avail! For Bradford's eventual quasistability and position in life had not, after all, staved off progressive capitulation of self-challenger to challenging-self. And now the game was nearing its end.

Duncan paced. How to approach It—Him? Simple suggestions, like the ones they had fed in through Bradford before?

He frowned. What if things were so delicately balanced now that just the *attempt* at appeal would strip away whatever control remained, abrogating natural law in profusion?

Merely: "Let there be no more breakdown in established order."?

Or: "Please, Force, *try* to put things back together!"?

Or maybe, kneeling before Bradford: "We beseech Thee, Dear—"

Wittels entered, interrupting Duncan's dilemma.

"You won't like this," the communications chief predicted.

"Haven't heard anything I've liked in years," the director snapped imperiously. "What is it? Dammit, quit stalling!"

"Local CD boys have their transmitter back in operation in the hills south of the city. They're broadcasting some news items."

"And?" Duncan's eyes pierced the man, as those of a skipper conducting captain's mast.

"I think Montague has become a factor again. Cosmotheotopists by the thousands are converging on the city from all directions."

"What do they want? What are they doing?"

"One newscaster says the fanatics are on a Crusade, looking for their Infinite Man. Troops are trying to keep them out of the metropolitan area. But it seems they can't block off all entrances."

Evaluating this intelligence, Duncan shrank from the possibility of being outflanked. "By God, they *know* Bradford's here! Do you suppose Montague can lead them to us?"

"Can't say. But if I were you I'd play it safe."

Counterstrategy suggested itself. "I still wouldn't want to move him, especially at night. Might get us all shot as looters. Go find Powers. Tell him we're ready to go through with the Ultimate Remedy."

"I anticipated you on that," Wittels disclosed sourly. "Sent Chuck to get him when the news first broke. Chuck came back from the clinic just a moment ago—long enough to report Powers is out cold, dead drunk. He's returned there to try and sober him up."

Duncan groaned, then stiffened and instantly drafted his plan of action. "Stay with your equipment. Keep us informed on what the Cosmos are doing. Chuck will stand guard with Murdock outside Bradford's room. I'll take care of Powers myself. As soon as I can bring him around we'll go through with direct appeal."

...◆...

Powers tried, but was unable to recall himself from the dark chasm of senselessness into which he had fallen. Stinging-wet, icy needles drummed against his skin. But he couldn't break through the veil separating him from consciousness. Something hot and bitter was forced down his throat. But he only vomited it, hardly conscious of the liquid dribbling from his chin and spattering upon his bare, cold chest.

"Powers!" A summons as though from an abyss.

But the pit only darkened while his throat filled with bile. Other forces seemed bent upon prying off his skull. More icy water; explosions on his face; bitter, liquid heat in his mouth. But he was even less aware of these tortures than before.

Powers.

Some remote, sober part of his mind became alert while the rest remained in the fast grip of intoxication. *What do you want now?*

Appealing, enticing: *Come. See what delightful eventualities are shaping up—both here and far away too.*

"Powers, wake up! Come on, snap out of it!"

That voice had been Duncan's. It had just barely managed to get through.

The perspective was now an aerial one and Powers' detached percipience looked down upon a highway clogged with stalled vehicles and swarming with torchbearers—shouting defiance, hurling bricks, screaming allegiance to the Primary, spitting obscenities and surging against trooper barricades. One of the firebrands—nothing more than a two-by-four flaming at its raised end—*exploded*, leaving an area of torn, burning, and writhing bodies.

Isn't this marvelous? It's the same all around the city!

Gunshots peppered the eerie night and many of the torch-bearers, grotesque in their inverted clothes, collapsed on the roadway. Others, hundreds, swept around the barricades, creating enough diversion to let the central body surge forward and overrun the roadblock.

More spraying ice water; choking, vile liquid that burned Powers' throat; additional head-jarring blows against both cheeks—sensations that came with a bit less shadow, a bit more substance than the last time.

"Powers! Powers!"

Come. There is even more to see. Something of profound import.

The isolated, sober section of Powers' mind responded: *I—I don't want to see any more.*

Oh, but you shall! This *will bring pleasure such as we've never known before.*

Night blinked out. In another aerial perspective, daylight bathed a desolate plain with mist-obscured mountains in the background. But no. The field was not barren. Three objects: a massive concrete cube with horizontal slits in its vertical surfaces; two tall, cylindrical shapes that towered over the—the blockhouse.

Of course it was a blockhouse. A control blockhouse. And the other two objects could be only—missiles. Not spacecraft. Not these. No manned modules on top. And the most paradoxical part of the whole thing: One missile bore the hammer and sickle emblem; the other, the U.S. flag.

Isn't this ingenious? Time was ripe for it. But I helped matters along by placing proper inspiration in the right places.

Now Powers' percipience was *inside* the control blockhouse, amid a swarm of scurrying technicians whose drab military uniforms and limp, visored caps identified them only as Maoist Chinese.

Of course! That's where my craftsmanship came in. All that nuclear might sitting idle on both sides of the world. Bluffing. What could be more simple or immediate than having a third party *pull the plug?*

Powers, the responsive part of him at least, was appalled. *But—but if there's nuclear war, what will be left?*

Enough. Perhaps even enough to produce more mass enjoyment.

But I'll have nothing left—*nothing worthwhile!*

You, my son, will have my deepest sympathy.

···◆···

Chuck adjusted the rifle strap on his shoulder, glanced up and down the hall, then leaned back against Bradford's door.

Murdock shifted his submachine gun from one hand to the other. "Suppose one of us ought to look in on those two kooks?"

"They're not going anywhere," Chuck assured. "Anyway, every time you open their peephole all you get is spit and a lot of CTT screeching."

Murdock was staring down the corridor. Abruptly he widened his eyes. "My God!"

When Chuck whirled in the direction of the astonished stare, Murdock drove the butt of his weapon against the back of his head. Then he charged down the hall and released Montague's two Disciples.

"Time, Kcodrum?" Iggy inquired.

"Yes. Let's hurry."

Murdock retrieved the transceiver they had hidden under the CTTs' bed. Back down the hall, they stepped over a still unmoving Chuck and unlocked Bradford's door.

Ann turned toward them, then brought her hands up to suppress a scream. Iggy lunged over and drove his fist into her face.

Even as she collapsed, Murdock motioned toward the unconscious Bradford. "We'll have to get clothes on him. It's almost freezing outside."

"Dress him TT style?" Marcella asked, opening the closet.

"No. Don't forget: Unlike us, He's already topologically transformed, even though he *looks* un-TT'ed."

While they dressed Bradford, Murdock delivered another gunbutt blow to Chuck's head and collected his rifle. As Marcella shod the limp Infinite Man, Iggy was attracted by a moan from Ann and slugged her again.

Murdock and Iggy carried Bradford, with Marcella bringing along the guns and transceiver. They slipped out of the clinic's rear entrance, crossed the courtyard, whose pond was beginning to film over with ice, and disappeared into the ebony shadows of the service alley.

"How long before He comes down off the acid?" Iggy asked.

"It's about three now," Murdock guessed. "Another four hours, I'd say."

After they had gone several blocks, they lowered Bradford to the asphalt surface. Murdock seized his submachine gun from Marcella and aimed it back in the direction from which they had come.

Iggy, who had evidently heard the slight noise too, said, "'S all right. Just a brick crumbling, or something."

Before they continued, Murdock used the transceiver to report to Prophet Montague on the success of their mission.

XV

Emotional harvest: Oh, how everything was dashing toward denouement! Millennia had gone into preparation for these ultimate eventualities. And now they were all at hand, to be realized in but hours!

What satisfying emotional harvests were being reaped: billions of favored ones terrified by nature's rampages, scurrying for cover; soon—the nuclear nightmare-come-true that they had long dreaded; the Primary—no longer a Force to be reckoned with.

And the wretched predicament of those few aware of the meta-drama exploding around them, desperately clinging to their hopes and unremitting ambitions, or to the stupidity of their false notions:

Powers—now unable even to dream his ridiculous dreams of usurping supernatural potential.

Duncan—frantically trying to revive Powers and appeal to the Creative Force. As if the Primary could as much as hear him! Even now Duncan's desperate urgings were breaking through the Powers sensorium: Wake up! Snap out of it! The CTTs are coming!

Montague and his Cosmo-somethings-or-others—hoping they could sway the Primary with fawning reverence, as though He could do anything!

And that pathetic Ann being—trailing behind the three CTTs and Bradford, miserable in the realization there was nothing she could do.

The well-used instrument had to witness this. (Powers?)

(Go away. I don't want anything from you.)

(Look down there—in that alley. See them? They're bearing off your Bradford. The sun's just beginning to shine on their faces. Oh, look at the expressions on the two creatures carrying their "Infinite Man." Pure anxiety, terror. Just like the girl with them.)

(Let me alone, damn you!)

(Another treat! There—the Murdock one has dropped the Infinite legs. Now he's snatching his rapid-shooter from the girl and pointing it at a uniformed creature who has appeared in the alley before them.)

(Murdock—one of the Cosmos? Not Murdock too*?)*

Rat-tat-tat-tat-tat-tat.

(Where are they taking Bradford?)

(It's obvious they're on their way to Midcity Park.)

(Why?)

(For a more intriguing perspective, up we go—up, up, up. Now look. See them? By the thousands they're closing in on the park from all directions.)

(Cosmos! But what are they up to?)

(Why—) the equivalent of human laughter was hard to control (—why, they're going to tell their unsuspecting Infinite Man what He really *is. And they're going to appeal through Him!)*

(But if it's not done right, it may mean the end of everything!)

(No-o-o-o, really? *You wouldn't put me on, would you?)*

There was the Duncan thing, again trying to break through Powers' drunken insensibility: Come out of it! We've got to try the Ultimate Remedy before the CTTs get here!

(Destroyer, You can't let them have Bradford! You said we'd transfer the Creative Force to me!)

(Oh, be quiet! Don't bother me. Too much is happening. All over the world now the skies are filling with your flame-belching instruments of maximum destruction. And all you worry about is yourself.)

Powers would be otherwise occupied soon. It was easy to sense that his veil of physical intoxication was quickly lifting as a result of Duncan's persistence.

...◆...

Gulping more black coffee, Powers decided it didn't taste too bad, now that the bilious slime was staying down where it belonged. He looked around. The sun, rising blood red in the gap where it shone between two buildings in front of the clinic, was just beginning to send exploratory rays into the dusky room where he sat on a footstool.

"Good God, man!" Duncan exclaimed, tossing clothes at him. "Get dressed! CTTs are pouring into the city!"

"Yes, I know," Powers said, smacking his mouth against the foul taste that surged up each time he retched.

Duncan drew back. "You know? How?"

"I—I—"

He's been shouting it at you for hours.

"You've been shouting it at me for hours," Powers said. "Oh, my head! My damn head!"

"Why did you have to get stoned—now? Put your clothes on!"

With the motions of a faulty automaton, Powers began dressing despite the fire that was raging beneath his skull. "How are we going to get to Bradford—"

Easy there, son. You're putting your foot in it again. He doesn't even know Bradford's gone.

"—to Bradford's unconscious before the Cosmos come?"

"God willing, we'll find a way."

Half concealed by the closet door, Powers cached the revolver in his pocket. But, would the Destroyer let him *reach* Bradford; find temporary seclusion for just the two of them; *use* the gun this time and make the Creative Force transfer to the nearest alternate host—himself?

Oh, Powers, how priceless are your suspense and anxiety!

"Go to—" But he cut short the shouted curse. Before Duncan could inquire about the outburst, a transceiver on the bureau crackled with Wittels' voice:

"The CTTs aren't coming downtown! That CD station says they're headed for Midcity Park. Maybe they *don't* know where we are!"

"The park may be just a staging area," Duncan told his communications chief. "Stay with your equipment and keep us posted. We're going downstairs now to make the direct appeal."

Desperation fell upon Powers. He was wasting *so* much time here, when he had to get to the park. He *must* recover Bradford from the CTTs! If the Cosmos tried to appeal first, their fanatic approach would bring about an instant end to everything.

"Hurry!" Duncan urged, handing him his shoes.

A plan. He needed a plan. Kill Duncan now and try to reach the park on his own? Or wait until they discovered Bradford was missing and then let them *take* him to the park?

Kill, kill! When uncertain, elect the most violent course, son. That's always been my policy.

Then you'll let me kill Bradford too?

Perhaps. If the time is ripe.

Powers thrust his hand into his pocket and felt the smooth metal of his revolver. But he hesitated. Was it possible that Montague, too, knew the key phrase which would release into Bradford's conscious all the hypnotically suppressed knowledge of the part he was playing? Suppose Montague was even now getting ready to whisper it into his ear: "The foundation grew out of Project Genesis." Would Bradford then be able to conduct the direct appeal on his own without bringing the universe down in shambles about him? But, no; Montague *couldn't* know—

Chuck staggered in from the hallway and stood clinging to the door jamb. His neck was scaled with dried blood. Near the back of his head gore matted a broad patch of thick, dark hair.

Duncan rushed over. "What happened?"

"Brad's gone!" Chuck steadied himself. "Those two CTTs got loose! They must have taken him off. Ann's gone too."

"But—how? Murdock was with you and you were both armed."

"God—Murdock! They must have killed him!"

"But," Powers began, "Murdock is with—"

Steady, son. We mustn't get our foot into our mouth.

"—without doubt one of our best men. I hope he's all right."

"The park!" Duncan exclaimed. He seemed to be sparking with purpose now that the campaign's objective had suddenly become clear. "That's why the Cosmos are gathering at the park! That's where we'll find Bradford too. Let's go!" He snatched up his transceiver.

But he stopped before Chuck. "You feel up to it?"

Chuck pried some of the clotted blood from his neck. "If I don't, I'll never have the chance to feel up to anything else again."

"Then come on. We'll take your car, Powers—if we can drive through all that mess."

What, Powers wondered, could they possibly expect to do when they got there—with all those thousands of maniacal Cosmos?

You'll never find out if you don't go along. Anyway, I'd prefer you there. It'll make for more emotional reaction to savor. March!

With no choice, he went along after Duncan and Chuck.

...◆...

The ground was cold beneath Bradford; the air, colder still.

As though resonating within the emptiness of a deep chasm, the voices bore in on him, quavering in their composite magnitude, yet sensitive in the softness of their sometimes almost whispered lyrics:

ic

On- ward, Cos- mo- the- top- Sol-

o-

diers.

fray.

On- ward the

to

In the distance: chattering gunfire, screams and shouts—but almost submerged under the now vibrant, powerful singing.

The effects of his last injection diminished and Bradford was aware of the position in which he lay: on his side, right shoulder and ear pressed against—grass; legs bent; one arm half hiding his face. More nonsensical singing. Remote shouts, shots, screams. Without moving his body, he opened the eye closer to the ground. Another damn freakout! Well, he wouldn't go along with this one! Maybe he could split out by simply refusing to buy it.

Before him—before and *down* (he must be on an elevation, a hill)—a great swaying mass of anxious faces almost filled his field of vision. Faces that stretched and contracted like rubber masks as they poured forth their absurd song about "Cosmo-some-kind-of- Soldiers."

Thousands were there, completely encircling the hill. The omnidirectional assault of their coarse, shrieking voices told him that much. And they were all dressed so—weirdly! Underclothing on the outside!

Directly ahead: a bloated, cerise sun just rising over a familiar oak grove. Beyond, the devastated, charred skyline of crumbled building tops confirmed his recognition:

He was on Soapbox Slopes again!

But he resolved not to move. By doing absolutely nothing, he sensed, he could avoid becoming an active participant in *this* illusion.

Far away, soldiers—conventional ones—nibbled at the periphery of the billowing throng. Nibbled, but were only swallowed up to disappear beneath the mass.

More soldiers came, fired rifles, fixed bayonets and charged—only to encounter the same fate as those who had gone before. And their efforts had disturbed the fanatic assembly only to the extent of eliciting a few more screams and shouts that were barely audible above the singing.

Bradford shifted his vision slightly so that he could see over, rather than under the arm that lay in front of his face.

More absurdities: a tall, thin man in a red robe with primitive designs painted in all colors on his forehead and bald scalp; a young, scrawny, olive-complexioned youth with a sparse beard. Both standing over him and leading the singing.

Others: *Murdock*—the Veterans' Administration man! And the stringy-haired blond girl who had been shot on the beach in one of his other hallucinations. Even *they* had been introduced into this illusion!

Well, he assured himself, it would take much more than that to make him leap to his feet and expose himself to the whims of whatever was in store for him this time.

And the "more than that" *did* come—in the next instant, as he looked under his arm again and down the hill.

Ann, hair disheveled, displaying near-nudity beneath clothes shredded by the mob, broke through the front row of the "Cosmo-something Soldiers" and clambered up the slope toward him! Under her right eye was a livid patch of flesh that had oozed blood down her cheek. Her lower lip was puffed.

Before she could reach him, though, many arms seized her and pulled her down the elevation, shoved her back among the singers where she was smothered by the press of their bodies and obscured from his sight.

Good show, he thought. The bait to panic him into action had been dangled before his eyes by a contriving mind. But he had refused it.

Let them—he hesitated over the convenient, euphemistic "them" when only the somehow still-rational "he" and the hallucinating "himself" were concerned in all of this—let them try their damnd-est! He *wouldn't* be conned into reacting to the phantasmagoria this time!

The singing stopped and a sonorous voice cuffed his ear: "I see by the flicking of Thine eyelids, O, Drofdarb Yloh, that Thou art with us now in mind as well as body."

Arms seized him—the young tough's, Murdock's, and the red-robed specter's—and lifted him to his feet. Determined not to respond, he sagged and kept his eyes closed.

"Thou, O, Holy One," intoned the voice as though through a megaphone, "art the Infinite Man!"

"THOU ART THE INFINITE MAN!" screamed the thousands.

"Thou art the Inverse Vessel!" Red-robe proclaimed.

"O, BLESSED INVERSE VESSEL!"

"IN THEE RESIDES THE PRIMARY ONE!"

"SPARE US, O, PRIMARY ONE!"

"HEAR US THROUGH THY VESSEL AND SAVE US!"

Despite his resolution to remain entirely passive, Bradford was unable to avoid reacting to the strange stirrings that he felt within him. It was as though curtains were being ripped apart in his strung-out mind and uncanny things were pouring through the breaches.

The ground shook violently and Bradford, torn from the grips of Murdock and the youth, was hurled to the grass. It was no longer possible to keep his eyes closed.

Buildings beyond the oak grove cracked and crumbled and tumbled.

"Save us, Inverse One!" Red-robe begged, kneeling. "Intercede to Him Who is inside You—no, I mean outside. For it is we who are inside. You see, you are the Topologically Transformed man and—"

The sun rotated like a great, angry pinwheel above the trees and trailed broad, arching streamers.

Red-robe shook Bradford and roared into his ear, "Can you hear us, O, Great Primary One? Deliver us!"

Bradford still hoped that if he merely sat this one out his 'lucy would fade away. But it was so difficult to ignore all of *this*! There—the half moon, crumbling away, fragmenting into jagged chunks, each reflecting its own irregular pattern of light. There—the ground shaking violently, opening in a huge fissure and swallowing hundreds of the "Cosmo-thing" illusions.

And, north of the city—a severe blizzard.

To the south—steaming rain and ferocious lightning crisscrossing the sky like a self-regeneration net of purple-white mesh.

Red-robe sat Bradford up and propped a knee against his back to keep him erect. "Can't you see what's happening? Do something!"

But Bradford went limp. He knew what was coming and could do nothing to stop it; another freakout-*within*-freakout, just as had happened on the beach, in the park.

Plunging down into the darkness of himself, he could sense the Infinite Presence, the Glowfly Exterminator, the Splitter of the Celestial Seas, the Diamond Maker, the Desk Duplicator....

...◆...

Powers clutched the steering wheel so tensely that he feared he might crush it.

At first, their progress had been slow, laborious: maneuvering around wrecked automobiles, sometimes mounting the sidewalk for passage, detouring through alleys, stopping to remove debris—even bodies—from their path. Once the engine had begun delivering only erratic power and they had faltered along, chugging and jerking. Twice they were fired upon when they overran Guard barricades. Then the accelerator had jammed and Powers had fought the vehicle while it ran amuck and while his brakes refused to bring it to bay. They had sped through the rubble-strewn streets, screeching, tilting, sideswiping a building and leaving a fender and outer door panel behind.

And all the while Powers had shrunk from the silent, raucous laughter roaring within his skull; from the directions and orders, exhortations and commands that Duncan had shouted into his ear. But now they were out of the cluttered business district and proceeding along the broad thoroughfare that led to Midcity Park.

"You all right?" Duncan demanded, glancing over his shoulder at Chuck.

"Maybe I could do with a new head," the latter replied from the rear seat. "But outside of that—"

Nobody said anything more because just then the sun, framed by the windshield, went into its pinwheel gyrations. When the first earthquake sent the car skittering onto the boulevard's dividing strip, almost toppling into the chasm that suddenly yawned there, Duncan swore and then seemed to be praying. Chuck closed his eyes. Powers fought the wheel and brought them back onto the roadway. *All over the world*—everywhere—*fascinating things are happening, just like this.*

"Shut up!" Powers snapped.

"I didn't say anything," Duncan replied.

Don't you realize what's happening?

"What?" Powers asked.

"I said I didn't say anything," Duncan repeated.

Clumsy oafs that they are, they're awakening Bradford to the reality of his unique status. And the Primary can't stand up to the shock. I knew *it would happen like this!*

"You did?"

"No, I didn't," Duncan insisted. "Well, maybe I was muttering a prayer or something. But—concentrate on your driving! Damn it!"

Of course I knew it. What do you think I've been waiting for—ever since I conditioned you to bring about Bradford's irreversible deterioration? All these billions of years actually.

"But you promised I could force transfer and—"

"What in hell are you talking about?" Chuck demanded.

Powers was spared answering, however, by the sudden, slow-motion disintegration of the half moon. Duncan, his head out of the window to watch the distant snowstorm and steaming rainfall and lightning, saw it first. So harsh was his cry of dismay that Powers stamped the brake pedal, neutralized the transmission and lunged from the vehicle, not knowing what to look for, not even deriving satisfaction from the fact that they were now only a few feet from the park's main entrance.

Chuck, alighting with him, was first to point it out. And, as he and Powers backed away from the car, the latter was confounded by this evidence of final destruction: an entire celestial body breaking up before his eyes!

Even if he could somehow manage to possess the Creative Force, he wondered, could he make It undo all of *this*?

Of all the ambitious ones I've encountered, you, my son, have been the most wildly pretentious. Can't you forget your selfish interest long enough to enjoy all of this? Just think: The Constructor *has turned* Demolisher! I *have won* Him *over to* my *side! The supreme irony! The ultimate triumph!*

Somehow part of the city's missile alarm system had survived. And now high-pitched sirens were pouring out their ululations of impending nuclear disaster. First the warning. Then, but a second or two later, that of which the sirens had warned.

Unable to move, Powers watched one glinting mote arch down out of the sky east of the city, another nearer the central business district. Duncan, who had remained in the car beholding lunar annihilation, was now a paralyzed, ashen-faced observer of the plunging doomsday weapons. Chuck simply crossed himself.

(Delirious laughter.) Now we have the penultimate spectacle of the Favored Ones' self-destruction. And the Primary can do nothing to save them. Good-by, Powers. You've been a most cooperative …

The missiles struck almost simultaneously. A one-two impact that jarred the ground with minor explosions and sent up twin spouts of dust in the distance.

But no nuclear blasts!

No nuclear fusion? (Bafflement.)

No great, broiling, swirling, soaring clouds!

No—clouds? (Frustrated disillusionment.)

"Nothing happened!" Chuck exclaimed, incredulous.

"It *was* a nuclear attack, wasn't it?" Powers said uncertainly.

Duncan, his face framed in the car window, managed a weak but knowing expression. "Under normal *c* conditions, it *would* have been. But *c* has dropped to only *half* its former value; c^2, one-fourth former value. Critical triggering masses would now have to be *four* rimes as great as before!"

Chuck looked up into the sky, at the whirling, bloated sun, the fragmenting moon. "He *is* still interested in us! He changed the speed of light *for a reason*! That was the only way to head off nuclear war!"

Powers tossed his head back and roared with laughter. When he finally managed to control the outburst he shouted, "Did you hear that? He *knew*! *He* wasn't being tricked; *He* was tricking, outwitting, cat-and-mousing! Guess who's the mouse!"

Relieved by defiance, Powers sank to his knees, sobbing.

"Powers!" Chuck shook him. "What's wrong? Don't—"

The ground shuddered violently and the psychiatrist opened his eyes in time to see a newly riven fissure, not fifty feet away, gulp automobile, Duncan, and all.

XVI

The Infinite Presence: He was here now—everywhere. Not physically, of course. But the vibrancy of his formless omnipresence was striking up convulsions in the celestial omniorama that extended from Bradford to the farthest reaches of infinity.

Trip? Freakout? Illusions of an unstable mind? No, it was none of these. For the first time he knew that what he was experiencing was not hallucinatory. Nor had been any of his former cosmic happenings. Neither had those "trips" dealt in simple realities. Rather, they had concerned profound, absolute essences hidden behind the curtain of man's shallow understanding of physical existence.

The Bradford-percipience hovered at the center of Creation, his awareness extending throughout the width and length and breadth of all space. Fluctuating. Not breathing, of course. But nevertheless resonating somehow with the Infinite Will.

A macrocosmic swath was suddenly scythed through a broad, curving arc of Creation, as though some giant, invisible hand had merely passed an eraser across a blackboard cluttered with figures and formulas, equations and symbols and notations. And in the wake of obliteration yawned a vast, black nothingness where before had shone innumerable stars, clusters, nebulae, distant galaxies.

Another scything motion unfolded itself across a second arc of celestial materiality. Another. Another. And total blackness laid itself across the face of existence in broad swaths, crisscrossing, curving, in short determined strokes and in long far-ranging sweeps.

... Until finally only impenetrable inkiness lay upon the surface of all the infinite depths.

But only for a moment.

All nonexistence thundered and roared and gave birth to blinding scintillations. The coruscating motes flickered, faded, then managed to reclaim their purchase on materiality. But they were eventually bedimmed into obscurity by a great golden bar that welled up from the depths. Expanding in its precipitate rush forward, the shimmering rod achieved almost supercosmic proportions and swept over the Bradford-percipience. It glinted internally with suggestions of blue and green, brown and obsidian hues.

Then it dispersed, as though it were a finite object attempting to fill the endless reaches of space.

The Infinite Presence in one of His countless forms? Or merely a manifestation of His present effort?

Bradford vacillated between comprehension and bewilderment as the blue-green tinges of the evanescent bar gathered themselves into a mottled cube that rotated while radiating glittering shafts of understanding and kindness, love and consideration.

Frightened now, he willed nonperception and spared himself further extravisual confusion.

When next he opened his suprasensory perception to all that lay about him and tried—on his own, for the first time—to locate the Infinite Presence, there were three great golden bars rushing toward him. They came hurtling out of the Great Beyond, seeming to crush the persistently scintillating motes over which they swept.

The rods sparkled softly in all hues. Because infinity wasn't voluminous enough to accommodate any one of the exploding forms, much less all three, they merged with one another. Then the three-in-one composite dissipated into the beyond, as had the single bar before it. But not before leaving stark beauty in its wake—scattered archipelagos of vivid color and intricate form.

Here: a great, shimmering rainbow whose ends trailed away into the nothingness between the glimmering motes. There: another. Another. And another. An almost limitless number of them, blinding even his suprasensory faculties. And beautiful, graceful flying forms. Dovelike, but more harmonious in their swirling motions than any winged creature had ever been.

Finally everything about him was a riotous display of effulgent color, tumbling forms, flashing lights—all too intricate and profound for his microcosmic comprehension to grasp. Brilliant, perfect circles and rods that cartwheeled in lilting motion. Thin, flat squares and triangles and a myriad other shapes—rippling, spinning softly, fluttering like frozen patches of sheet lightning.

When all was interlaced by bursts and showers of overwhelming brilliance, by sparks and streaks of stark radiance and Catherine wheels of indescribable splendor, he had *to close off his bedazzled perception and seek relief in the darkness within him.*

What had *he witnessed: Implication? Speculation? Plan? Projection?*

He thought he might know. But, for the moment, the beauty and simplicity-within-complexity were too marvelous even to dwell upon.

...♦...

On his hands and knees, head drooping, Bradford was once again aware of the grass on the hilltop etching its designs into his palms.

Back on Soapbox Slopes.

Voices that had sung fervently before were now charging the air with screams so shrill and persistent as to sound like a single, prolonged shriek of pandemonic intensity.

A clangorous peal of thunder surmounted the strident squeals of the "Cosmo-somethings," stimulating their screeches to even higher pitch.

Had he drawn down the curtain on an inner hallucination, only to find himself still enmeshed in the absurd horrors of this outer one? Suppose he could drop a veil over this one too. Would he then be free—back in his real setting? But where *was* his normal world? Could he even recognize it after this eternity of floundering about in a linked chain of hallucinations-within-hallucinations that probably extended *ad infinitum*? What would that "absolutely real" existence be like?

Thunder barked, hilltop quaked, lightning cracked. He raised his head and opened his eyes. Red-robe's face was inches from his own, shouting, importuning, crying, swearing. But his words were lost in the great sea of sound. The hill shook and tilted. On the field all around them, everyone was in full, terrified flight. Hundreds were being trampled. Only he and Red-robe held the hill. Whoever else had been up there had joined the human explosion in all directions from Soapbox Slopes. But where were they fleeing?

The city was gone. Mounds of rubble had replaced the serrate skyline of tall buildings. Beyond, huge land masses were heaving upward, forming immense mountain ranges, sinking back into oblivion—all in the span of but seconds. Replacing them, a chain of volcanoes spewed flame and lava and sent up thick columns of smoke. Earthquake followed earthquake and the ground split into many hungry mouths that closed, gulped and opened again to swallow whatever they may have missed the first time.

Lightning bolts crisscrossed lightning bolts as the sky took on the appearance of a fisherman's cast-net descending upon the world. Thunder marched on the heel of thunder until there was only one steady peal, unvarying in pitch and amplitude.

Fierce winds unfrocked Red-robe. He fell and hugged the hilltop in his inside-out underwear covering inside-out trousers, jacket, and shirt. Rains, steaming then icy, pelted the ground. Then: Darkness. Utter darkness. Absolute silence. As though nothing had ever existed, would ever exist again. But hell's maw gaped once more, embracing Bradford's hill in all its recent fury.

Then a solitary figure, clutching what was left of her shredded clothing, reached out to him. Even as he caught her hand and helped her to the summit, he breathed, "Ann! Ann!"

He touched her bruised cheek and lip. "Don't worry, dear. It's just an illusion—mine."

Either the thunder had subsided or she had read his lips.

"You're not imagining this, darling!" Her words were barely audible above the roaring of the sky and whistling of wind-driven rain.

Calmly now, he sensed she was right: that this was *no* hallucination; that none of the Infinite-Presence happenings had been 'lucies. He thought of his most recent celestial freakout. The experience demanded acceptance of its own validity. And in that episode he had found inner peace. Perhaps even hope. More than that—but nothing he could really grasp. Not yet. It was as though he had all the facts, but lacked the capacity of comprehension.

"Oh, Brad! The hallucinations—they were planned, to cover up—you see. Powers and …"

A stentorian burst of thunder drowned her out.

She shook her head and he couldn't tell which of the droplets on her face were freezing-steaming rain and which were tears. "You've got a right to know what's happening!" she shouted desperately. "But I don't know how to tell you, where to start."

He took off his jacket and draped it over her head and shoulders.

"You see," she went on, pulling him closer so that he could hear, "there's this foundation. We all belong to it—Powers, Chuck, I. But wait—before that there was Project Genesis. It seems that the foundation grew out of Project Genesis and—"

He whispered the words: "*The foundation grew out of Project Genesis.*"

Another curtain—a profoundly concealing one—drew back across his mind. And in the instant upsurge of immense knowledge and meaning and concept, he accepted one almost negligible realization as a harbinger of all the understanding that was now at his fingertips:

Disruption of the laws of probability had somehow put the exact combination of words in her mouth to trigger this flood of suppressed information. Or had the Creative Force planned it that way?

Then he was overwhelmed by the cascade of numbing realizations:

All those early sessions with Powers, from the very beginning. With Powers and, and—what were the names of the others?—Duncan and Montague. Montague: the same Red-robe who was rising beside him now and spreading imploring arms to the angry heavens!

Montague and—Hedgmore! Good God, even Hedgmore had been there! And the latter's deception of bastardy and feigned suicide that had elevated him, Bradford, to the apex of Hedgmore's empire—even *that* had been locked away in the remotest vault of his mind should he need the knowledge at the moment of Ultimate Remedy! Ann shook him and shouted frantically and stared into his rigid face. But it was as though she weren't even there. Montague shrieked at the sky, then at him, then back at the sky. But Bradford recorded the motions as only those of a pathetic mummer on a faraway stage.

The heavens roared and split with a myriad jagged fingers of vivid light. The earth shook and groaned and opened and closed and reopened. Steam and snow and hail poured from the underbellies of churning, black clouds. Land masses heaved and plunged and sprouted great cones whose apexes exploded in furies of fire, smoke, and molten rock. One of them was so close that its discharged embers, hissing in the rain, were spraying down on what had been the eastern area of the park.

Bradford peeled back his stream of unconscious-made-conscious and stumbled upon the foundation's hope that sudden release of the knowledge of his true nature and all that had happened would prepare him for direct appeal to—the Infinite Presence?

The Creative Force? The Primary One? It? Him? God?

They—Duncan, Powers, the others—were supposed to help him.

But what could they do? What could *he* do? There was a time when narcotics-spawned trips had been the measure of his life. He had been partially weaned from acid, but the trips had continued without benefit of narcotics. And, in all of them: the Infinite Presence.

But he had never *approached* Him! He had only been along for the ride. No active association. Only a passive, involuntary empathy.

Did they expect that he could even *find* the Presence, much less *prevail* upon Him? Did they think anything at all would be salvable, here at the edge of eternity?

He stared up into the turbulent sky and felt his own tears mingling with the rain on his cheeks. For at last he knew. Knew what his purpose was, had been all along. And, although it was the will of the Infinite Presence, still it filled him with unbearable sorrow.

It was clear now what the Force, the Presence, He, It, the Primary intended. And, without reservation (how *could* there be any reservations?), he humbly accepted his role: to maintain forces in balance until all could be orderly swept away, until the slate could be cleared.

Ann would have to go too. Himself. Everything. Dear Ann. He held her close and kissed her forehead.

It was only *he* who realized that *nothing* could be done about what was happening. Nor would he *want* to do anything, even if he could.

In their embrace, he and Ann were one on the hilltop. But, actually, he was *alone*. Alone as a sanctuary for the Infinite Presence. Only he could provide the refuge that would be needed until universal dissolution was almost complete. In a large sense, as he stood barrierlike between the Presence and the distractions of a universe going amuck, he *was* an Infinite Man. As such, he surrendered himself in infinite subjugation to the Creative Force.

Two solitary, scurrying figures appeared at the foot of the hill, splashing through blood-tinged puddles of freezing and steaming water, sweeping around the bodies of "Cosmo" Soldiers.

Chuck! Chuck and—Powers!

Then Bradford reviewed his latter sessions with the psychiatrist. And he was aware of all the deception and trickery, the "planted" hallucinations, covert attempts to lure the Infinite Presence from ...

Lumbering up the hill, Powers drew a revolver and its report rang out weakly against the steady grumbling of the sky. Montague, seizing his pierced chest, fell backwards, and rolled down the slope, dropping off into one of the steam-spewing chasms. But there was no sobriety on the psychiatrist's face as he gained the summit. He was laughing hysterically.

"I *can* pull the trigger!" he shouted. "I *can*! I *can*! I—"

Sodden hair adhering to her face, Ann huddled against Bradford. "Powers! The key! The triggering phrase! Say it *now*!"

But the psychiatrist ignored her. He seemed to be listening to something else while his features twisted as though digesting thought.

Then he shouted again: "You poor, stupid thing! You can't *create*! You can only *destroy*! And now You've *got* to allow transfer! Because it's the only hope of preserving Creation! Don't you see that if there's no Creation, there can't be any Destruction? And there wouldn't be *any place* for you!"

Chuck gained the top of the hill and tackled Powers from behind.

He shouted to Ann as he grappled for the gun. "Get Brad down—"

The revolver discharged twice. Chuck's limp hand fell away from Powers' throat.

"Now It can't transfer to *you*!" Powers laughed.

Bradford finally shook off his catalepsy of conscious realization, thrust Ann aside, and charged the psychiatrist. The latter took aim, but lowered the revolver a bit before he fired.

Arms folded over his abdomen as though to quell the burning agony that had exploded there, Bradford toppled forward and lay writhing. If he could only *hold on*—until it was *time* for him to go!

Steadying the gun on Ann, Powers turned him over and grinned when he saw that Bradford was still conscious. "Don't check out now, Brad!" he urged. "We've got to *be alone* first!"

Thunder and lightning raged.

Vast areas of the earth heaved and shrank and discharged the fiery magma of its core through great seams.

Darkness came. Stark, total darkness.

No sound. No feel. Not even the agonizing pressure of the hot slug in Bradford's groin.

No taste.

No motion.

Then, as though in a flash, the Ultimate Cataclysm was back around him in all its ferocity.

Winds shrilled. In final upheaval, the clouds swirled away, leaving a clear sky that exposed the starless black of space. South of the zenith, something that had once been the sun flashed up and down the spectrum, shining green, red, blue, violet, yellow; grew into a huge blob.

The screaming air thinned and Bradford found little left to breathe.

Powers, terror distorting his face, swung the weapon back on Ann and fired. She jolted with the force of the slug, then collapsed. He fired again. But the bullet only dropped from the end of the barrel while the gun itself recoiled with the force of a howitzer, hurling Powers around and twisting his arm behind him.

Through his torment, Bradford thought indifferently: Scratch—*equal* and opposite reaction.

Broken wrist dangling, Powers retrieved the weapon and swept down on Ann as she squirmed where she lay. He brought its butt cracking against her head, then hurled her from the hilltop. Bradford struggled to his knees, but Powers planted a foot on his neck and crushed him down again.

Then the psychiatrist was on top of him, hand clamped on his throat and shouting:

"Now, Bradford! Now's the time—to—"

But his voice trailed off into dead stillness. For the air had lost all but a trace of its density and breathing was no longer possible.

The thing that had been the sun shone purple, green, orange.

Still anchored to part of the park and a section of the city beyond, the hill floated up and out, tumbling, exposing to view other land masses that were twirling, colliding, crumbling as they went their separate ways.

Below, the inner fires of earth were dissembling into incandescent globs that drifted outward like bubbles rising from a diver's helmet.

Just for a moment Bradford's thoughts went back to his last empathic experience with the Infinite Force—only a few minutes earlier, though it seemed ages ago. And now he was certain that he understood all of the symbolism in that vision, even if he didn't know exactly how it would express itself.

Then came his final rational thought as he participated in the dissolution of earth: Scratch—product of the masses, square of the distance.

Locked together, he and Powers drifted up and away from the hill.

(Powers! Your usefulness is over. You were only one of the battlegrounds. This is it! Total Destruction! My victory is complete!)

The strange words, unspoken but shouted, seemed to leap from the psychiatrist to Bradford as he felt himself sinking into the eternal depths that had awaited him all his life.

No sound or feeling. No taste or smell.

No suffering or delight, hope or frustration.

Nothing left. Out of an entire universe—nothing.

Still, he could sense an Infinite Vastness, an Omnipotence evacuating his being, spearing back across the gap that had been leaped by the stentorian proclamation of triumph, bearing down upon and enveloping Powers.

Creation-Destruction.

Life-death.

Anabolism-catabolism.

Summer-winter.

Construction-demolition.

Bradford released his final grip on the thread of existence.

No self-awareness.

Electron capture-beta emission.

Fission-fusion.

Not even self-unawareness.

Matter-antimatter.

Spirit-antispirit ...

BANG!

REGENESIS^{n}

In the beginning God created the heaven and the Earth ...
And the Earth was without form ...

(Let the coming-together of the particles be such that lines of greatest pulling-power will extend centerwards along each of the three basic directions, thus:

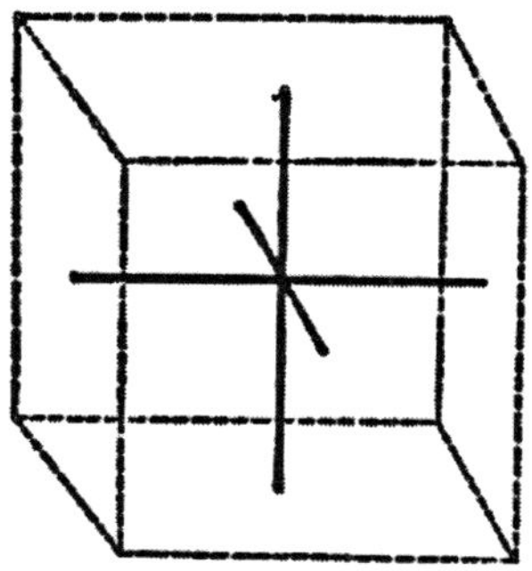

(And lines of lesser pulling-power shall extend centerwards in the intermediate directions:

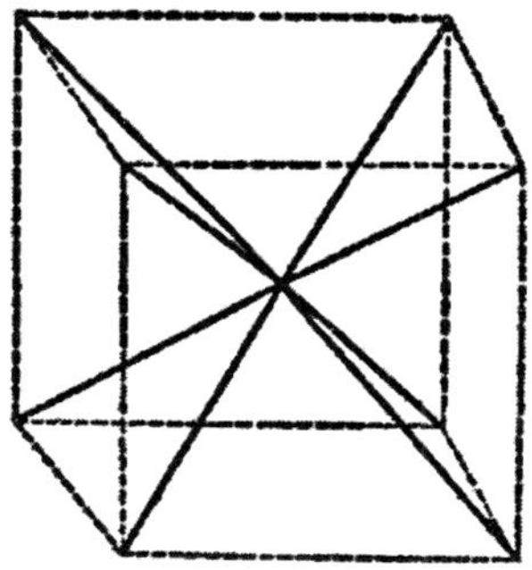

(As a result the earth shall form edges, such that the faces of the waters shall meet the faces of the waters crosswise to one another:

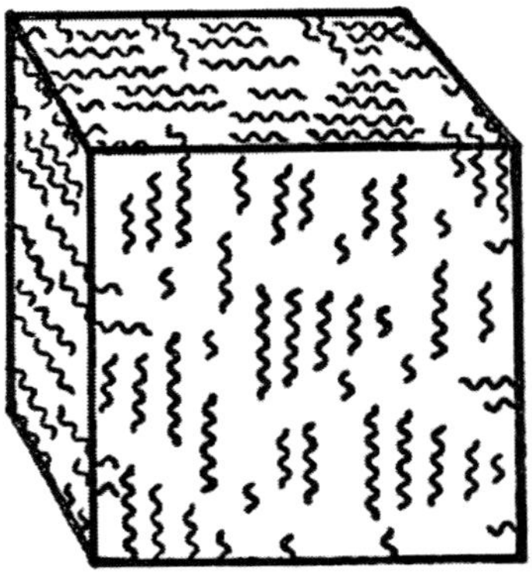

(And there shall be ready passage of the waters from one face to another.)

And God said, Let there be light ... and divided the light from the darkness ...

And the evening and the morning were ...

And God made the firmament ...

(Let the greater and lesser pulling-powers work on all the huge swarms of glowing bodies in the firmament and attract them individually and collectively into shapes not unlike that of the Earth.)

And the evening and the morning were....

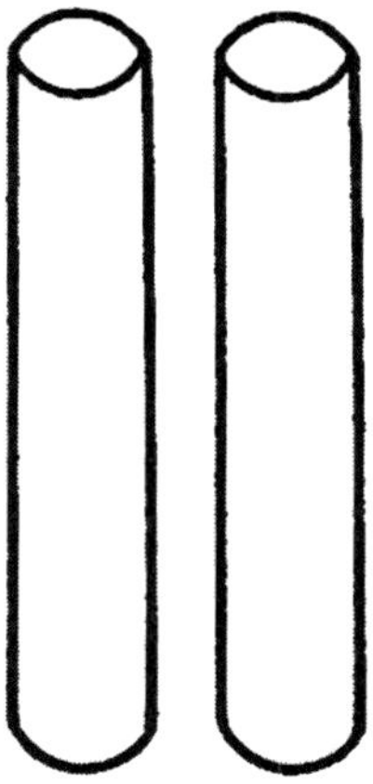

And God said, Let the waters under the heavens be gathered together ... and let the dry land appear ... Let the earth bring forth grass, the herb yielding seed, and the fruit tree yielding fruit ...

And the evening and the morning were....

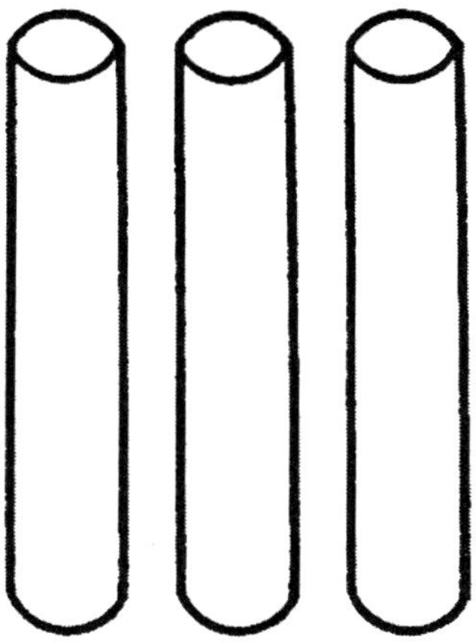

And God made two great lights, the greater light to rule the day and the lesser light to rule the night....

(Let the lights assume the same shape as the earth. Let the lesser light go asquare the earth, and both the earth and the lesser light go asquare the greater light. Let the lesser light and the earth obey the same forces of greater pulling-power extending centerwards along each of the two basic directions, and of lesser pulling-power extending centerwards in the intermediate directions.) Thusly:

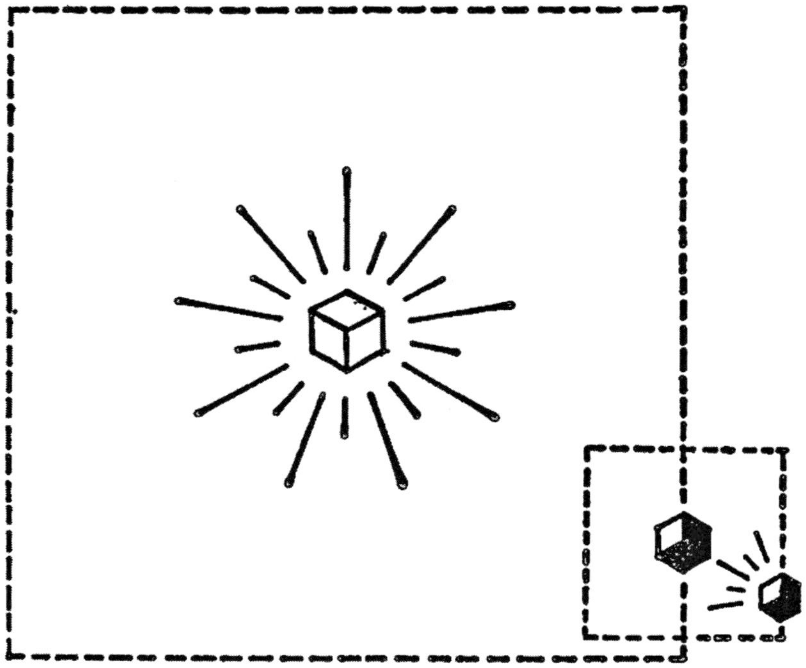

(But at the four nodes in both the path of the lesser light asquare the earth and in the path of the earth asquare the greater light, Let there be a complete halt in the tendency of things to continue on their straight paths. Only a brief halt—until the next direction can be embarked upon.)

And the evening and the morning were....

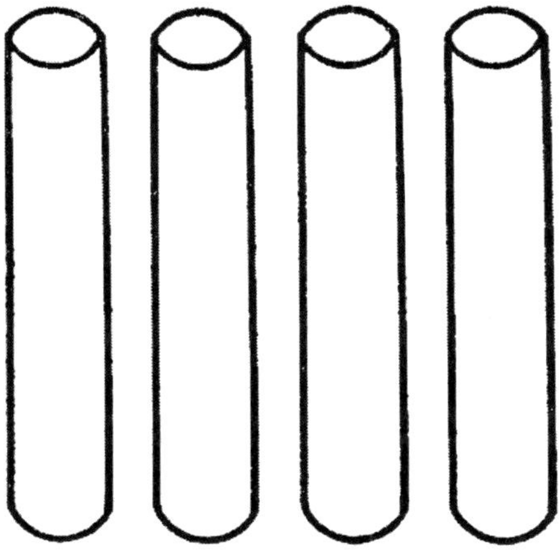

And God said let the waters bring forth abundantly the moving creatures ... and fowl ... great whales ... and every living thing that moveth.

And the evening and the morning were....

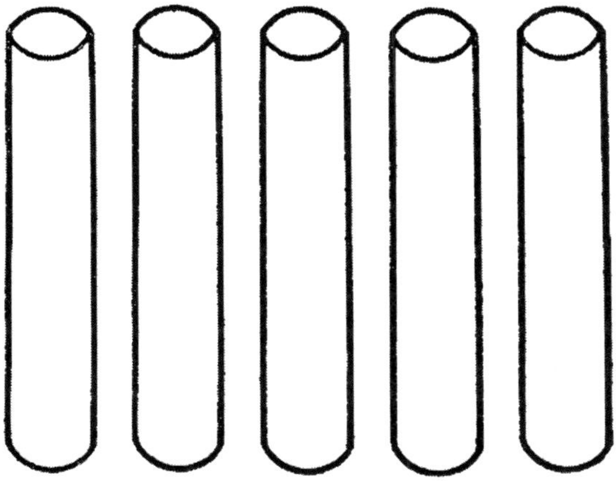

And God said, "Let us make man in our own.... Let us make man.... Let us make...."

? ? ? ? ? ? ? ?

In our own image?

In our *own* image!

(Pure, spiritual immateriality. To have passive dominion over the earth and over and throughout the entire firmament. To enjoy all the endless miracles of Creation. To be aware of one another, but never to be at crosspurpose. For the immaterial shall not possess, but shall only savor *the beauties of the material. And, should any attracting elegance of the inner firmament or the outer firmament call forth great multitudes of marvel-observers, there shall be no rivaling for position. For an entire infinity of the matterless creatures shall be able to occupy the smallest point in space. So there shall never be the least antagonism—or envy, which is the precursor of antagonism.)*

And the evening and the morning were ...

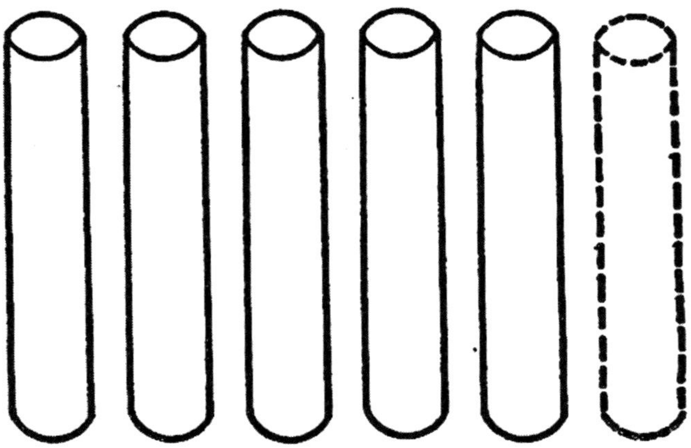

Z-Z-Z-Z-Z-Z-Z

CPSIA information can be obtained
at www.ICGtesting.com
Printed in the USA
FSOW01n1151210715
9092FS

9 781612 422503